Everyone deserves a well-earned vacation, don't they? Guess again!

Plans have been made and the bags are packed but Detective Stephanie Chalice is having about as much fun as Michael Vick at an ASPCA fundraiser.

The new story finds Chalice and Lido on the East End of Long Island, vacationing with Max, their new arrival. Things go wrong from the very start. Their vacation rental burns to the ground, bodies pile up, and just to make things interesting, Lido . . . All I'll say is that you'll never believe it.

Chalice may be out of her jurisdiction but she's never out of questions or determination and soon connects two unsolved homicides. As always, the whole is greater than the sum of its parts, and her initial findings plunge her deeper and deeper into the most extraordinary investigation of her career.

Baby Girl Doe

Stephanie Chalice Mystery #5

By

Lawrence Kelter

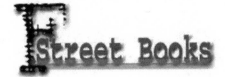

For

Dawn and Chris

Acknowledgments

The author gratefully acknowledges the following special person for her contributions to this book.

As always for my wife Isabella for nurturing each and every new book as if it were a newborn child, and for her love and support.

Baby Girl Doe

Stephanie Chalice Mystery #5

Lawrence Kelter

"Words have no power to impress the mind without the exquisite horror of their reality."

~~Edgar Allan Poe~~

BOOK ONE

Chapter One
April 18, 1985

Dr. Simon Van Zandt approached the nurse's station and picked up the telephone. Perspiration trickled from his temple while he waited for the head of obstetrics to answer his call. The phone rang eight times before transferring his call to the answering service. Van Zandt clicked the receiver without leaving a message and paged Dr. Mark Finkel.

"I don't like her color," Nurse Hastings said as she rushed to Van Zandt's side. Her BP is dropping."

"How low?" he asked.

"Sixty-two over fifty-one."

"It's down since the last time I checked it."

The elevator clanged. Van Zandt whipped his head in the direction of the elevator and waited for the doors to part.

Mark Finkel was no more than five-and-a-half-feet tall, a mere tea sandwich of a man but he bounded out of the elevator with the confidence of a giant. "You paged me?" he asked making no attempt at pleasantries as he encountered Van Zandt at the nurse's station. "What's going on?"

"Thirty-three weeks pregnant with twins," Van Zandt began. "The patient arrived with prematurely torn membranes. BP is sixty-two over fifty-one and falling. She's been in active labor since she arrived, but the pregnancy hasn't progressed.

"And the babies?"

"One heartbeat is strong, the other is slower and weak," Van Zandt said. "I'm thinking possible anaphylactoid syndrome."

"Rare," Finkel commented after a moment of thought. "But I'm glad you called me. Is she on oxygen?"

"Yes. She's showing some signs of dyspnea but I'm not sure it's abnormal."

"Labored breathing? History?"

"This is her first pregnancy."

"Is her husband in the delivery room?" Finkel asked.

"No." Nurse Hastings replied. "We've been trying to reach him, but we haven't had any luck. She got here on her own."

"Christ," Finkel swore. "All right, let's have a look." They walked briskly to the delivery room. He took one look at the patient, turned to Hastings, and whispered, "Prepare for an emergency C-section. What's the patient's name?"

"Caitlin Alden," Hastings replied.

Finkel leaned over the hospital bed and put his hand on the patient's forehead as he began to speak. "Caitlin, I'm Dr. Mark Finkel, chief of obstetrics. How are you feeling?"

"Nervous and weak," she replied. "I can't control my breathing. Are my babies all right?"

"Yes, your babies are fine," Finkel said, "But your pregnancy is not advancing as quickly as we would like, and it might be a good idea to consider a C-section. Are you all right with that?"

Caitlin thought for a moment and then nodded. "Please, Doctor. I'm worried about my babies." She began to cough and cry at the same time. "Do what you think is best," she said weakly.

"Pitocin didn't strengthen your labor, so I agree with Dr. Finkel," Van Zandt reassured her. "Cesarean is our best option."

Caitlin's coughing increased in frequency. Van Zandt turned to Finkel with a knowing look in his eyes.

"I don't think there's any point in waiting," Finkel said. "I'll scrub and assist Dr. Van Zandt." He smiled encouragingly. "Let's deliver those twins right now."

Nurse Hastings replaced Finkel at the patient's bedside. "We're going to give you a little Versed in your IV to make you more comfortable and then the anesthesiologist will administer an epidural. Do you know what that is?"

Caitlin nodded nervously and continued to cough. Everything was moving so quickly. "Do what you need to do," she said.

Van Zandt assisted the nurses in preparing Caitlin for surgery. "One of the heartbeats is strong," he said to the patient as he helped prepare her for transport to the OR. "The other is a little weak. I want to get the twins out as soon as possible."

"Did you reach my husband yet?" she asked with urgency.

"We'll keep trying, Caitlin." Hastings checked her watch. "It's almost six. I'm sure he'll be getting home from work soon. One of my nurses will keep calling your home."

"Thank you," Caitlin said gratefully. She looked up toward the ceiling and took a deep breath. She suddenly grabbed Hastings' hand and began to cry. "I'm really nervous."

A courageous smile was part of Hastings' everyday repertoire. "Your babies need you to be brave. Can you be brave, Caitlin?"

She nodded as the syringe of Versed was pushed into her IV. Her eyelids fluttered and fell. They were barely open as she was rolled to the OR.

Chapter Two

"Have we heard from her husband yet?" Finkel watched as the OR nurse cleansed Caitlin's abdominal area and covered it with a sterile dressing.

"Not yet," Van Zandt responded. He was checking the instruments on the surgical tray when he noticed a tremor in her arm. He got Finkel's attention and motioned toward her shaking arm. "Did you see that?" he whispered.

"Yeah," Finkel said unhappily. "Involuntary tremor—you made the right call. This is looking more and more like an amniotic fluid embolism." He tapped his finger on one of the monitors. "Her blood gasses are deteriorating. We'd better hurry."

Van Zandt looked at his patient's face. Her eyelids flitted for a moment and then closed. "She's practically unconscious. She shouldn't be that relaxed from the Versed alone."

"Heart rate just fell below fifty, Doc," the anesthesiologist warned.

"Push one milligram of atropine," Van Zandt ordered. He picked up a scalpel and looked at Finkel. "Ready?"

"How are the babies?" Finkel asked.

"One heartbeat is a steady 150. The other one is only at 85," the obstetrics nurse said with concern.

"Making the incision now," Van Zandt said as he cut through the flesh on Caitlin's lower abdomen just above the pubic hairline. "I'll use a transverse incision to open the uterus. Suction ready?" he asked as he glanced at the nurse from the corner of his eye.

"Ready, Doctor," she replied.

Van Zandt's hands moved deftly. "Okay, I'm in. *Suction,*" he said firmly.

Finkel reached in and removed the first child. Fluid was suctioned from the baby's mouth and the newborn began to cry immediately. "It's a girl," he said enthusiastically, hoping that Caitlin would hear him and react to the good news. "A healthy baby girl. He clipped the umbilical cord and handed the baby to the nurse. "Here comes number two." He reached in. "Scissors," he shouted. "The umbilical cord is wrapped around the baby's neck." He reached in, snipped, and unwound the cord. He lifted the baby out and handed it to a second nurse. "It's a boy," he boomed. He turned aside to the nurse, "I don't like the baby's color. Get him on oxygen right away." The tremors in Caitlin's arms became more intense and frequent as the second baby began to cry in the background. Her head twitched and then began to shake uncontrollably.

"Push another milligram of atropine, STAT!" Van Zandt barked as he removed the placenta.

"Heart rate is forty bps. She's in bradycardia," the anesthesiologist said. "The atropine isn't helping."

"One milligram of epinephrine," Finkel said quickly. "Ready the crash cart."

The anesthesiologist had his eyes glued to the heart monitor. "Heart rate is still dropping. I've lost her pulse."

"Shit! How are you doing?" Finkel asked Van Zandt. "Get her closed up." His eyes darted back and forth between the heart monitor and the incision site. "Begin CPR." He looked up at the anesthesiologist. "I need external left jugular access and a right femoral triple lumen catheter. Finkel's hands moved quickly and delicately. The catheter was readied and inserted. "I—"

"Getting worse," the anesthesiologist announced. He held his breath for a moment. "Damn! She's in V-fib."

"I've got her closed up, but she's still bleeding from the incision site," Van Zandt said.

"Charge paddles to 200 joules. Clear!" Finkel applied the paddles to Caitlin's chest.

"No change," the anesthesiologist warned.

"Charge to 300," Finkel shouted. "Come on, lady. Come on." He readied the paddles. "Clear!"

Chapter Three

Bill Alden burst through the doors into the hospital emergency room and rushed to the reception counter. "Caitlin Alden," he cried. "I got a call; my wife was admitted with pregnancy complications," he explained, panting and out of breath. "How is she?"

"Let's have a look," the receptionist said as she pecked at the computer keyboard. She picked up the telephone. "I have Bill Alden here in emergency . . . Okay. Thank you." She put down the telephone. "We're trying to locate Dr. Van Zandt. He'll come down to speak with you as soon as he can. Why don't you have a seat over there?" She pointed to a row of chairs. "I'll call you as soon as he arrives."

"Can't you tell me anything?" Alden protested. "I'm half out of my mind."

"I just came on duty, sir, and the only information I see on the system is to contact Dr. Van Zandt. I'm sorry."

Alden sighed. He looked over at the unoccupied chairs and reluctantly walked toward them. He plopped down and buried his face in his hands. He checked the wall clock and noted the time, half past eight, several hours since the first message had been left on their home phone. *Christ, I blew it this time. I really blew it. God, I hope she's okay.* His stomach growled. *What the hell did I do?*

He glanced at the clock again hoping that he could will the doctor to his side. A deep ache developed in his jaw from clenching his teeth.

How long was I out? All he could remember was awakening from a stupor to see the sun setting over the Atlantic. *I can't do this anymore, not now, not with children. I just can't.*

"Mr. Alden."

He looked up and saw that the receptionist was beckoning to him to approach the reception counter. "Yes?" he asked before reaching her.

"Dr. Van Zandt is waiting for you on the fourth floor. You can take the elevators just down the corridor," she said as she pointed out the direction. "He'll meet you at the nurse's station."

"Fourth floor. Got it. Thank you. What's the doctor's name again?"

"Van Zandt. Dr. Simon Van Zandt."

"Great. Thanks," he said as he hustled down the corridor. He squeezed into the elevator with a hospital attendant who was wheeling an empty bed, and pressed the button for the fourth floor. He smiled quaintly and received an equivalent smile in return from the man who had the word *Morgue* embroidered on his hospital jacket. His heart began to thump within his chest.

He tried to think about his babies to mask his guilt and worry. He pictured his son as a little leaguer deep in the outfield tracking down a fly ball. It helped to ease the tension. The intense ache he felt in his jaw lessened. The doors parted, and he sprang toward the nurse's station. "I'm here for Caitlin Alden. I'm her husband."

"I'll page Dr. Van Zandt," the nurse said intentionally avoiding eye contact.

"How are they?" Alden asked. "My wife and the babies?"

The nurse had her eyes glued to a clipboard, making an entry on a patient's chart. "Dr. Van Zandt will be here in a minute."

"Is something wrong?" he asked with alarm.

"I really don't know," the nurse continued. "Like I said, Dr. Van Zandt will be here in a—"

"Mr. Alden?" Bill Alden turned to see a doctor calling to him as he approached. "I'm Dr. Simon Van Zandt. I attended to your wife's delivery. Can you come with me, please?"

Alden followed as Van Zandt turned and walked through a set of swinging doors at a pace that would allow Alden to catch up with him.

"What's going on, Doctor? How's my wife?"

Van Zandt was silent for a second. "I'm afraid there were some complications with your wife's delivery, Mr. Alden." He pushed on the door that led to a consultation room. He gestured to Alden with an open hand. "After you."

A woman sitting at a circular table jumped to her feet. "Mr. Alden," she began with a pleasant expression and a controlled voice. "I'm Gladys Hirsch, head of social work services. Won't you sit down?"

"What's going on here?" Alden asked angrily, his eyes cutting back and forth between Hirsch and Van Zandt. "Where's my wife?"

"Please, Mr. Alden," Van Zandt said. "Please sit down."

Alden reluctantly took a seat. "What's going on?"

Van Zandt placed a medical chart on the table as he sat down. "As I said, there were complications with your wife's delivery. She arrived at the hospital in pain. As you know she's a full month shy of delivering full term. She was in active labor with premature rupturing of the membranes. We waited as long as we felt prudent, but her labor didn't advance. We were worried about the wellbeing of the babies, so we performed an emergency C-section."

Alden frowned. He covered his mouth and fought back tears. "Did she lose the babies?"

Van Zandt glanced at Hirsch, prompting her to interject. "Please, Mr. Alden, let Dr. Van Zandt explain."

"One of the twins is fine, Mr. Alden," he began, "but I'm afraid that your son was with limited oxygen for a very long time. I'm very sorry, we're not sure about his condition yet.

We're going to need more tests. The umbilical cord was wrapped around his neck . . . but you have a beautiful healthy daughter."

Alden began to cry. Hirsch grabbed a wad of tissues and pushed them into his hand. "How's my wife?" he sobbed. "Does she know?"

Hirsch sighed and looked at Van Zandt, her eyes showing that she didn't envy his task. "Your wife is unconscious, Mr. Alden. She developed a condition known as amniotic fluid embolism. In effect, your wife had a toxic reaction to the amniotic fluid and fetal cells that sometimes enter the mother's bloodstream prior to and during delivery."

"Oh dear God. What happened?"

"Your wife's reaction was very intense. She manifested with hypotension and bradycardia."

"English, Doctor. Plain English!" Alden demanded angrily.

"Her blood pressure dropped, and her breathing became erratic. We gave her medication to counteract her symptoms, but they continued to worsen . . . ultimately her pulse stopped and her heart went into ventricular fibrillation. We shocked her a couple of times to bring her back, but her brain was oxygen-deprived for a long time." Van Zandt's head dropped. It took a moment for him to continue. "She's in a coma, Mr. Alden. I'm afraid her prognosis is not very good."

"But people come out of comas all the time. She can wake up, can't she?" Alden asked beseechingly.

"I'm sorry to say that's doubtful," Van Zandt explained. "Because of the severe brain insult, she may never awaken. Her life expectancy is very short. If she does hang on . . . I'm afraid it will be in a vegetative state. I'm truly sorry. I wish there was more we could do."

Alden covered his eyes. "But how could this . . ."

"We're here to help you through this," Hirsch said in a motherly voice. She reached out and took Alden's hand in hers "I know it won't be easy but with time . . ."

"What's time going to do?" Alden said as he wept. "My wife is gone and my son . . ."

"I know it's terrible news, Mr. Alden but look at the positive. You have a beautiful daughter to take home and to love. Try to focus on that." Hirsch smiled bravely despite the fact that Alden's eyes were awash with tears.

"What am I going to do?" he cried.

"You'll just have to take one day at a time," Hirsch said. "*One foot in front of the other, one step at a time.* After a while it will get easier." She looked up at Van Zandt, cuing him to stand. "We'll leave you alone for a few minutes and then when you're ready I'll take you to see your wife and children."

Van Zandt put a comforting hand on Alden's shoulder. "I'm very sorry, Mr. Alden. We did everything we could." He lowered his head and walked out the door without looking back.

"I'll be right outside when you're ready," Hirsch said. "Take all the time you need." Hirsch left Alden to think about the future he would live without his wife.

BOOK TWO

Chapter Four
Present Day

"Yup, she went up just like that."

Gus and I stood next to Richard Tate, the Montauk fire chief, watching our vacation rental go up in flames. White and orange flames soared toward the sky throwing off enough heat to cook a goodly-sized Butterball turkey. I turned toward Tate and saw firelight flickering on his face. "I just can't believe it. Any idea what happened?"

"Hot as the dickens all week long and absolutely no rain—sometimes all it takes is a spark," Tate said. "We won't know for sure until the fire is out and it's safe for my men to enter. Sorry about that, my friends. You must be really bummed out." He turned his head until he could see my son's face. "Don't seem to bother the little guy none." He smiled at our son despite the fact that Max was out for the count and completely oblivious to his presence. Max was asleep with his face smooshed against my shoulder. He did, however wiggle his nose. Maxwell Francis Lido, newest of the clan, was playing it cool—the commotion of a dozen firefighters dashing about in a mad frenzy didn't seem to bother him one little bit.

"Wow, this really sucks," Gus said as we literally watched our vacation plans go up in smoke. He raked his fingers through his hair, a clear sign of frustration. "Why does this shit always happen to me? I must be the friggin' Antichrist."

I think he doth protest too much. "Yeah, you're the Antichrist all right: young, handsome, and newly married with a gorgeous baby son. Gee, I can see why your life really sucks," I said with unfiltered sarcasm. "I don't know why you don't just end it all."

Tate elbowed Gus. "God love ya, man. You certainly know how to pick 'em." He winked at me. "Don't take any shit from this big palooka, Stephanie." Turning to Gus, he added, "You should bless your lucky stars that you weren't in the cabin when it caught fire."

It wasn't the first fire I had witnessed, not by a long shot, but it was the first time that one had directly impacted my family or me. We had rented the cabin for the last couple of weeks of July, time with Max … you know, quality time alone with the adorable little guy. I was as disappointed as Gus, but I didn't want to show it. "Hey, Rich, I don't suppose you know of any places we can rent at the last minute, do you?"

"Sorry, Stephanie, you're talking to the wrong person." Tate removed his fire helmet and wiped sweat from his brow with his sleeve. "Go cool your heels while I check on my men. I've got Gus' cell number. I'll call you after we get this fire under control." His cell phone rang just as he moved off. "Tate," he answered, and then his voice disappeared behind the clamor of the firefighters.

I looked at Gus and shrugged. "Now what?" We had just spent more than three hours in the car, and the prospect of heading back to Manhattan was about as enthralling as a rampant case of head lice. "You think we'll find another place to stay?"

Gus rolled his eyes. "*Yeah,* good luck." He looked absolutely miserable. He had been so excited about the vacation and was really looking forward to spending time with his baby son. It was one whopping disappointment for a brand-new daddy to overcome.

"I told you we should have brought marshmallows."

Gus shook his head. "Not funny, Stephanie."

Montauk is a summer hot spot for city dwellers and is absolutely packed Memorial Day through Labor Day. "All right, look . . . we'll figure something out." I was doing my best to sound encouraging. "I'm sure there's another place—people cancel all the time." Max lifted his head and moved it until his sleepy little face was next to mine but never even opened his peepers. "It's too hot for him out here. I'm getting back into the truck. Coming?"

"I'll be there in a minute." He handed me the keys and then dug his hands into his pockets. He looked beaten.

"Okay, I'll give you two minutes to sulk, but then you have to get over it. Deal?"

Gus nodded.

"Good. Your son and I can't have you swallowing a 9mm over a charbroiled hovel." I walked over to our SUV which was parked safely out of harm's way about thirty yards down the road. I put Max in his car seat and cranked the engine. I couldn't remember air conditioning ever feeling as good. I silently said a prayer in memory of Colonel Carrier, the man who invented air conditioning.

I put my head back against the headrest and looked out through the window. The fire seemed surreal now that I was encapsulated within the climate-controlled womb of our SUV. I watched the flames rage from the small countryside cabin—sparks and burning embers swirled in the air as currents spun them about. I could smell the aroma of burnt wood in the air flowing through the vents. Firefighters sprayed the trees next to the house to prevent the fire from spreading.

I saw Gus taking it all in with a hapless expression on his face. "That's your daddy out there," I said to Max. "He wanted to give you a nice vacation and now he's sad." I thought about the tools in Max's repertoire of daddy-pleasing gimmicks. *Let's see, what can we do to cheer daddy up?* I couldn't come up with much—aside from being downright lovable, Max's repertoire was pretty much limited to cooing, burping, and smiling and he was definitely most proficient at the burp. "Burp for daddy when he gets back into the car; he'll like that. You know what? Don't even worry about it—I've got it covered." I mean how much pressure could I put on a sleepy little boy? *You do have a full complement of feminine wiles at your disposal, Stephanie. Time to step up your game, girl.* Like most new parents, Gus and I were not getting a ton of sleep, and our romantic connection had suffered as a result. I figured my husband could use a little impromptu carnal stimulation.

Gus trudged back to the SUV with his head down. I yanked my blouse apart the moment he pulled the door closed, spraying buttons in every direction. One of them hit him on the nose. He did his best to fight his emotions but lost the battle, bursting out in laughter.

"Very subtle, Stephanie. What's the matter, didn't you have time to slip into a peignoir?" He turned back to check on Max. "Did you see what your mother just did? No, of course you didn't. There are never any witnesses around when you need them." He kissed me full on the lips." Man, you are out of your mind. You get nuttier with every passing day."

"Most men wouldn't complain. What if you were married to a prima donna? What if my conversational range was limited to *buy me, take me, show me, bring me*?" I said imitating one of those Real Housewives television divas. "What's the worst that you can say about me . . . that I'm a smidge uninhibited?"

"Jesus, button up," he said. "There are firemen everywhere."

"Are you for real? There's an eleven-hundred-degree fire burning over there—under the circumstances, I don't think I'll draw much attention."

Gus smiled. "Baby, you certainly light up *my* life."

He leaned in for a second kiss just as an explosion went off. The SUV rocked from the force of the blast. I jumped in my seat and looked out the window to see firefighters hurrying away from the cabin. "What the—"

"I'll bet it was a propane tank. I doubt they have natural gas lines this far out in the woods."

"God, I hope no one was hurt." I checked Max. "There's no question he's your flesh and blood." Gus was capable of sleeping through a nuclear blast. "The little man didn't move a muscle."

"It's a Lido family trait." Gus put his hand on the door lever. "Stay with Max. I want to make sure everyone's okay."

"Be careful!"

"You bet." Gus smiled as he got out of the car. The disappointment he had displayed just moments ago was gone, and he was once again the strong and charismatic man I loved. He glanced back at Max and then at me. "I've got a lot to live for."

Chapter Five

Max couldn't take his little brown peepers off my sweet potato fries. He had been fed, changed, and seemed totally content to ponder the mystery of my deep-fried high-fat munchies. I wondered what was going through his mind, *Hm, doesn't look like anything I've ever eaten before. Seems easy enough to manipulate though—I think I'm up to the task. Lovely orange color—looks like a crayon but smells like heaven. I want one.* Max reached for a fry and uttered a demanding, *"Ah!"*

"Aw look, Gus, he wants my junk food. That's so sweet."

Gus rolled his eyes.

"He's a carb hound just like his mommy. I'll bet his first word will be *piz-ghetti*."

Gus looked puzzled.

"Spaghetti is tough for little ones to enunciate. Trust me, he'll be crazy for the stuff."

"Oh." Gus was in the process of devouring a man-sized burger. Beef makes him happy, and I'm happy when he's happy. The burnt vacation home had really put a damper on our evening, so if a mound of freshly ground Black Angus could make him happy, Black Angus it would be. Through a mouthful of beef, he muttered, "I think it's too soon to go down that road. He's got an entire lifetime to devour French fries."

"Not even one?"

"No."

"Really? The baby puffs again?" I groaned on behalf of my son.

Gus nodded.

"This flies in the face of my eat-whatever-you-want-mantra. I don't want my son to think all food tastes like wallboard."

"I'm not talking about a lifetime of quinoa and tempeh—let's just get him off to a good healthy start, okay?"

"I'm wolfing down fries, and you're three molars deep into a cow patty. Is it any better that he grows up thinking his parents are hypocrites?"

"I'll worry about it when he knows what the word hypocrite means. I'm only eating this because I'm stressed," Gus said defensively.

"Judging by the number of burgers I've seen you put away since I've met you, it appears you've been stressed most of your life."

Gus glared at me.

"Fine." I reached into my baby bag, which was large enough to transport a small Fiat. "You know I thought it would totally be the other way around—with you being the one trying to sneak the little buckaroo a Slim Jim." I shook a pile of banana-flavored puffs onto Max's tray. "No junk food for you," I said. "Daddy's a bore."

Max shoved a handful of puffs into his mouth, but never took his eyes off my fries.

"I still can't believe that the stupid cabin caught fire." What were the chances of *that* happening? The thought of going home and unpacking the truck was more than I could bear. I scrunched my lips, pretending to pout, and spoke in a child's voice, "I want to go on vacation."

We had made our way to the MTK Café, a place to fill our bellies and buoy our spirits while we formulated Plan B. There was no way that I was getting back on the Long Island Expressway where you can spend a lifetime just trying to get from point A to point B. "So what now?" I asked. "I really don't want to drive three hours back to the city."

Gus looked up. He had a little cow grease on the corner of his mouth. I reached across the table and wiped it away for him. "It's almost nine o'clock," he said powerlessly.

"Let's find a hotel room for the night. We can look for a new place in the morning."

"If we find one, it won't be cheap."

"Don't worry about it, Ebenezer." I scowled at him and clenched my fist. "Consider it an investment in your personal wellbeing."

Gus laughed and tried to speak with his mouth full. "That's big talk for a sex crazed—" His eyes bulged, and then he began to choke. The technique for the Heimlich maneuver raced through my mind. I was already out of my seat when the girl at the next table stood and smacked Gus squarely between the shoulder blades, dislodging the food that was stuck in his throat.

"Oh God," she said. "Are you okay?"

Gus covered his mouth.

I could see that he was no longer in distress.

He nodded. It took a moment before he was able to speak. "Thanks," he said. "That did the trick." He stood up to thank her. "I should know better than to talk with my mouth full."

"Hey, it's okay," she said. "Glad I could help."

Most cops aren't overly cordial to strangers, and generally speaking, Gus was no exception to that rule, but ... the woman had just saved his life after all. "I'm Gus." He pointed to me. "This is my wife Stephanie."

"Hi." She flashed a quick, energetic smile, a real go-getter smile, and then turned her attention to Max. "And who is this?" she said with a nurturing voice and a broad smile. "Who is this handsome little man?"

"That's Max." I think she overwhelmed him. Max's chin quivered, and he started to cry.

"Oh, I'm sorry," she said. "I didn't mean to—"

"Don't give it a second thought. It's way past his bedtime." I lifted him out of his booster seat and bounced him in my arms to quiet him down. "It's okay," I told him. "Daddy's all right now that he's not gagging on cow parts." I sensed that Max was really pooped—he nodded out in mid-cry. I had him in my arms but managed to extend my right hand so I could shake hands with my husband's savior. "Thanks for the assist."

"No problem," she said as she glanced at Gus. Her eyes lingered a moment longer than I liked before turning back to me with an expression that said, *I helped your husband, and you didn't.*

Yes, Gus is a catch and he's my catch. I narrowed my eyes at her a little, not a scathing glance just more of a step-off-beeatch sneer.

"I was closer. I'm Camryn Claymore," she said introducing herself. "What a handsome family. I'm glad I was able to help." Camryn was slightly built and professionally dressed, in slacks, a silk blouse, and loafers. She wore a lot of makeup: face powder, concealer ... the whole enchilada, much more than most young women customarily wore.

"I'm glad too," Gus said. "Thanks again, Camryn."

I'm a student of body language, and Camryn's body language indicated that our conversation had limitations and we had reached the end of ours. She had been thanked, and thanked, and thanked again. I thought our introductory exchange was over, but I was wrong. I guess I misread the signals—it was merely an awkward pause.

"Hey, I'm not a nosey body or anything, but I couldn't help overhearing your conversation."

She overheard our conversation? Jesus! The last thing Gus uttered was, "That's big talk for a sex crazed—" A little embarrassing, ya think? Anyway, at least she knew that I was taking care of business in the bedroom.

"So your cabin burned down?" she asked. "Was that Bill Alden's place?"

Gus nodded with large eyes. "Yeah. How'd you know?"

"I just got a call from my office—I'm in real estate," she said. "Montauk's really a pretty small community. The whole town will know about it before it makes the local news broadcast."

"I know," Gus said, "I'm from around here."

Camryn's eyes sparkled. "Oh really, where about?"

"Southold," Gus replied.

"Oh," she pooh-poohed. "Over on the North Fork?" She frowned for the briefest moment as if to say, *Southold, are you kidding?* Some East-enders are kind of elitist and look down their noses at anyone who doesn't specifically hail from Montauk or the Hamptons—I guess Camryn was one of them, an East End snob. The North Fork of Long Island is very different from the South Fork. It faces the Long Island Sound and not the Atlantic and has lots of farms and vineyards . . . but just because there's a big emphasis on agriculture doesn't mean that all of its residents are bumpkins.

Gus glanced at me as if to say *here's an idea.* "You're in real estate? You wouldn't happen to know if anything's available for the next couple of weeks, would you?"

"I can't believe this," Camryn said. "I was eating my dinner and thinking about how to approach you when I heard you choking. My brother and I just rehabbed a place. I didn't think it would be ready until August, but my brother really knows his way around a toolbox and he worked around the clock. He's still trimming up the exterior, but it's completely done on the inside. I was going to list it in the morning."

"That's incredible," I said happily. *It is incredible, isn't it?* I was honestly too relieved to be suspicious of our newly found serendipity. "Is it *nice?"*

"Can we afford it?" Gus asked sheepishly.

She shrugged as if to say *I don't know.* "It's completely redone. It's not like Bill's place—it has modern furniture, a new steam shower, oak floors, and a granite kitchen. Can I ask what you paid Bill?"

Gus turned to me to ask for my approval.

I nodded. I mean what was our alternative, a two week vacation back in the sweltering heat of the city pushing Max around in his stroller?

"Seventy-five hundred for the two weeks," Gus said.

Camryn gritted her teeth. "That's a little cheap. Um ..." Her head rocked back and forth while she appeared to mull over the number. "Can you do a little better? We dumped a ton of money into the place."

"It's better than having it sit empty for the next couple of weeks when you could be getting income from it," I said. "How fast do you think you can rent it anyway?"

Her expression said *oh yeah, that's right*. "Okay, but only because you'll have to put up with some noise while my brother finishes up. The view's not as good as Bill's, but it's very secluded, and like I said, the inside is brand spanking new."

It had been a very long day. I stretched and retreated to another place in my mind. I pictured a brand-new steam shower made of tumbled marble with spotless chrome body sprays. I could almost feel the hot water running down my back. "You know what, Camryn? Let's go take a look."

Chapter Six

The doorbell rang at nine a.m.

"Oh-dear-God, *who the hell* is that?" I hate to wake up grumpy, but I guess Max wasn't quite at ease in his new surroundings and had been up most of the night. I had just dozed off when the doorbell rang.

Camryn had showed us her place right after we had finished dinner at the café, and it was after midnight before we had a chance to look around and sign the rental agreement. We unpacked the Pack 'n Play and our toothbrushes and went out hard. Well at least Gus did—hard enough to sleep through the night and Max's incessant howling. I on the other hand had spent more time awake than an Eskimo vampire during the winter solstice (you know, when it's dark almost twenty-four hours straight). I rubbed my eyes and then glanced over at my men. They were both sleeping blissfully. I slipped on my shorts and top and tiptoed barefoot down the stairs to answer the door.

I yawned as I opened the door. "Yes?" I said with bleary eyes and smudged mascara.

"Hi, neighbor," a petite young woman said in an effervescent manner. She was bright-eyed and bushy-tailed as it were—ninety pounds of sunshine in a print sundress. "I saw your car as I was driving home from church and had to pull right over. I'm so excited. This place has been empty for so long."

I was so out of it—she made me feel like a proverbial barfly who had just awakened from an alcoholic stupor. "You went to church?" I said through squinty little slits. *Already? How can anyone possibly be so energetic at this ungodly hour?*

"I'm Kaley." Little Miss Sunshine was practically bouncing up and down as she offered her hand. "Did you just move in?" she asked optimistically. Kaley pointed to a chimneystack just visible through a clearing in the trees. "That's me, over there. That's my place."

"So we're neighbors."

"Yes!" she blurted exuberantly.

"But only for two weeks; we're just renters."

Kaley's smile faded, and the corners of her mouth turned downward. She looked so despondent that I wanted to buy her a pony just to see her smile again.

"I'm Stephanie. *Sorry.* You seem like someone I'd really like to have for a next door neighbor."

"Who's there?" Gus said.

I turned and saw him coming down the steps with Max in his arms. My tired I-can't-bear-the-light-of-day expression gave way to a smile when I saw my boys.

"Let's say hello." Gus said to Max.

Max was laughing and cooing. *Sure, go ahead and mock me, you lovable little shrimp—I'd be laughing my ass off too if I just slept a solid nine hours.*

I turned back to Kaley just in time to see her smile rise once again. It looked like her internal generator had just rumbled to life and was cranking a million gigawatts of electricity. "Who is *this*?" she said with unbridled enthusiasm. "Who is this adorable little guy?"

Gus came to the door. "Hi, I'm Gus," he said, "and this is Max."

"He's *gorgeous*," Kaley said. "Oh my God, he's *so* cute. Can I hold him? I love babies."

The mother in me said, "What? You want to hold *my* baby?" The cop in me wanted to check her rap sheet. But then I looked at that sweet young girl—she was almost trembling with excitement. "Do you want to come in?" I glanced at Gus for approval.

He nodded.

Kaley was so animated that I thought she might swoon.

"I wish I could offer you something, but we just got here late last night," I said. "All we have is baby food and tap water."

"Oh, I'm fine. We had refreshments at church. I just want to hold Max." Kaley floated into the living room. She was a lithe little thing who didn't seem to be encumbered by the forces of gravity . . . or a bra. Okay, she was pretty small up top, but she deserved top marks for being firm.

I saw that Gus had noticed as well. In fact, it looked as if he was guesstimating her perky little cup size.

She sat down and extended her arms. Max smiled as he settled into her delicate little lap. "Oh this is heaven." She giggled. "I'm *so* happy," she said looking positively embarrassed. "You know if you ever need someone to babysit this little guy . . ."

"That's good to know, but as I said, we're only here for a couple of weeks."

"I know," Kaley said. "I wish you could stay forever."

Aw! She's so precious—can we adopt her? I told Gus, "Kaley's our neighbor. She lives on the other side of the clearing."

"You and your family?" Gus asked.

"No. The place is mine now. My parents retired to Florida and left it to me. I'm here finishing school."

"School?" Gus asked.

"Yeah, I'm going into my last year at Stony Brook this coming fall." She stroked Max's cheek with her finger. "You don't go to school yet, do you?" she said in a baby-pleasing voice. Max gushed. "You're so lucky. Yes you are. Yes you are."

A cell phone rang. Fortunately it wasn't mine. It was taking all I had just to absorb Ms. Energetic's endless stream of enthusiasm. Gus picked up the phone and answered, "Lido."

"Gus, it's me, Rich Tate. Just checking up on you and the family."

"Hey, Buddy," Gus replied. "Thanks for the call."

"How'd you and the missus make out last night?" Tate asked. "I can't believe your luck. We were out there until two a.m. putting out that blaze."

Gus seemed surprised. "Really, a little cabin like that?"

"It's all wood, my friend. Every time we thought we had it contained, a new fire popped up somewhere else. So where are you staying?"

"We got incredibly lucky," Gus said, "We went over to MTK for a bite and bumped into a realtor who had just renovated a place. We checked it out after dinner and signed a two-week lease. I slept like a log."

I'm glad someone did.

"You're kidding," Tate said "Where? Not the Fisher place?"

"I have no idea." Gus turned to me. "Hey, Steph, did the realtor mention if this used to be the Fisher place?"

Kaley gulped so dramatically that her eyes bulged.

"Hold on a minute," Gus continued. "I think it just might be."

"What's with the Fisher place?" I asked

Kaley's eyes darted back and forth nervously. A story was coming.

I saw concern in my husband's eyes as well. "Hey, Rich, let me call you back in a bit. Yeah, looks like it might be the Fisher place."

I examined Kaley's expression and knew that she was about to say something I didn't want to hear, something that was going to send me off the deep end. Our vacation rental was perfect and so much better than the termite-infested old cabin that had burned down. *Damn it! I knew that finding this place was too good to be true.* Was someone murdered here? Was it inhabited by ghosts? Jehovah's Witnesses? I had a bad feeling about what Kaley was about to say. "What happened to poor Mr. and Mrs. Fisher?"

Kaley was playing with Max's hands. She looked up. "Oh, nothing happened to them."

Oh thank God. I had overreacted.

"It was their daughter, Sarah," she continued. "She disappeared . . . and no one has heard from her since."

Chapter Seven

"And his wife died too?"

Kaley nodded sadly. "I guess it was too much of a strain on her. She wasn't the healthiest person to begin with, and after Sarah disappeared ... well, you understand. I think she had a heart condition."

"Did you know their daughter?"

"Sarah? Yeah. Nice girl. She moved to Manhattan awhile back, right after she graduated from college. You know how it is out here: small-town USA. Everyone thinks Montauk is all glitz and glamour, but it's deader than a corpse around here after the summer comes to an end. It's kind of boring, and everyone knows your business. The winters are cold and depressing. Sarah was always independent." Her mind seemed to wander for a moment. "I envied her moving to the city like that."

Gus and I sat on the edge of the sofa as Kaley related Sarah Fisher's tale of woe. We listened to her as intently as if we were being briefed on a homicide case. "Do you know any of the details?"

"Not really. She sort of disappeared into thin air."

"People don't just disappear," Gus said. "People disappear for many reasons, but there's always a story."

"I feel terrible," Kaley said. "I'm sure you're right. I just don't know what happened. I know there was an investigation, but I don't think they found out what happened to her. I was staying at my aunt's house at the time because it was closer to campus, and I only got bits and pieces of the story. I heard they found her apartment in the city empty."

An empty apartment probably meant that Sarah had moved out intentionally, but why? It sounded as if she had just begun to enjoy the independence of living in her own apartment in one of the most exciting cities in the world. Why pick up and leave so soon? Was she in trouble? Something just didn't add up.

Gus glanced at me knowingly, and I could see that we shared the same concern.

"Anything else you remember?"

Kaley was still playing with Max. She looked up, and her eyes began to travel back and forth uncomfortably between Gus and me. Max must have sensed it as well because he became fidgety and held out his arms for me to rescue him from the clutches of Little Miss Sweetness and Light. I guess he had come to his senses and realized that he'd be more comfortable in the embrace of his amply-endowed mother than on Kaley's boney lap.

"What's wrong?" I asked her.

Kaley looked past us to the window. "A woman was murdered."

"What?" I felt my blood run cold.

"A woman was murdered," Kaley repeated. "She was pushed in front of the train at the East Hampton railroad station."

"You're sure?" I knew the statistics on railroad deaths pretty well and wasn't sure if Kaley was completely clear on the details. "Most people who are hit by trains are suicide victims. Are you sure that this was definitely a murder?"

Kaley nodded nervously. "The railroad engineer was quoted as saying that the woman had been pushed. It was in *Newsday*. I think maybe that's why I don't know much about Sarah's disappearance. Everyone was talking about the murder back then."

"Was the victim someone from around here?" Gus asked.

"No. No one knew her," Kaley said. "I think she was from upstate someplace."

"Do you remember her name?"

Kaley was silent for a moment. I could see that she was searching her memory. She shook her head. "Sorry, I can't remember . . . Oh wait. Alana. That's it. Alana something."

I was on the East End of Long Island inside a gorgeous vacation rental and away from Manhattan and the Midtown North police precinct, but I didn't feel as if I was on vacation any more. "When did all this happen?"

"At least a year ago, I guess. I remember that I was studying for my finals, so it must have been springtime."

We didn't like to talk about death and murder in front of Max. In fact, Gus and I never discussed the job when the little man was awake. It was sort of an unspoken rule.

Kaley looked at me—she almost seemed to be cowering. "I hope I didn't upset you too much," she said regretfully. "Lousy way to start a vacation, huh?"

Upset? Me? Why? Just because our vacation rental burned to the ground and now you're slamming us with tales of woe? "No. I'm okay, but I think Max needs some attention. After all, it's his vacation too. So . . ." I smiled for Kaley's sake, but my stomach was in knots. *My God, this pretty little thing is the emissary of doom. If you'd be so kind as to get the hell out of our house . . .*

"Oh sure," Kaley said as she sprang up from the sofa. "I've got a ton of stuff to do anyway." She smoothed her dress and then looked up with the same beaming smile she wore when we had first met. I guess she was one of those people with the ability to compartmentalize and was back in a serene and happy place. "Sometimes I don't know when I've worn out my welcome." She walked to the door. "It was so nice meeting you. Don't forget: call me if you need a sitter for little Max."

I took Kaley's number before she left, but definitely not for the reason it had been offered. There was no fire today, but for the second time in two consecutive days, I smelled smoke.

Chapter Eight

Gosman's Café was just what the doctor ordered. We parked our butts at an outside table with a huge red, white, and blue, umbrella—just enough sun for the adults and just enough shade for the baby. The ocean view was spectacular and helped to stabilize my emotional state while Kaley's tragic stories tore through my mind like machinegun bullets through the fuselage of a German Messerschmitt.

Max was styling in his NY Giants football garb, a baby Giants cap, and a deep-blue jersey that read *Giants Rookie*. A pair of Baby BanZ sunglasses completed the look. He appeared very chic as he smeared sliced strawberries on his face. He was just cool enough to show everyone that he wasn't the kind of guy who took himself too seriously.

I was still feeling stressed as I blew out a deep sigh. "Man, I need a drink. How about you?"

"I could use a beer," Gus replied, "but—"

"You don't mind?"

Gus shook his head. "One of us has to be the designated parent."

I grinned. "For sure. I don't want to get booked on a PWI."

"PWI?" Gus ventured.

"Isn't it obvious?"

He shrugged.

"Parenting While Intoxicated. Thank God Max is off the boob. I owe you, babe." I hailed over the closest waitress.

A gal with jet-black hair dashed over to take our order. She took one glance at Max, fist pumped, and shouted out an enthusiastic, "Go Big Blue!" She whipped out her Droid. "Can I snap his picture? My husband is a huge Giants fan. He'll laugh himself to death when he sees this."

"How can we say no to a Giants fan?" Gus asked.

"My husband's a fanatic, and me . . . I totally want to have an affair with Eli Manning," the waitress said.

Really, even after his dismal performance in 2013? I laughed. "Cool. I'm glad to see that we have exactly the same priorities."

Gus gave me the hairy-eyeball stare.

"Just having some fun, babe," I said. "Lighten up."

Max missed his mouth and just about crammed a strawberry up his nose as the waitress snapped his picture.

She checked the shot. "That's just *awesome*," she hooted and then flipped around her phone so that we could see Max's moment of genius.

"He's such a ham," I said as I looked at his picture. "He's always been very comfortable around the paparazzi."

My comment appeared to give the waitress a moment of pause. Montauk was crammed full of celebrities this time of year: actors, rock stars, and yes, even those who were just famous for being famous—I think she was trying to decide if we were part of that exclusive circle. "What can I get you?" It seemed that our moment of near-celebrity was short lived.

"How about a Bellini in a quart-size glass?"

"Tough morning?" she asked.

"Preceded by a long and sleepless night. The Giant rookie over here can be a real diva when he wants to be."

"Him?" she said compassionately. "With that face? Sounds like he's got the qualities necessary to turn pro." The waitress smiled and then turned to Gus. "And for you?"

"Iced tea," Gus replied. "I slept like a log."

Our waitress gave Gus a thumbs-up and hustled off.

"I got about three hours sleep last night. And those stories Kaley told us . . . I mean, what the hell?"

"I bet you didn't expect anything like that when you invited sweet little bible-toting Kaley into the house," Gus said.

"Ya *think*? Little Miss Sunshine really shocked me. I can't get those stories out of my head."

"Oh gee," Gus whined. "Here we go." He threw up his hands in defeat. "Yeah, I know, I'm thinking about it too . . . but I'm not going to let myself get crazed over it like you do."

I yawned and rubbed my eyes. "It was upsetting to hear about the Fisher family. That's bad karma."

"Bad karma?" Gus grimaced. He pressed his palms together and lowered his head until his fingertips touched the tip of his nose in a Buddhist greeting. "Yes, Oh Enlightened One."

"Don't be a jerk."

"A thousand pardons, my awakened spirit guide."

"Make fun if you like. I just hope the place isn't haunted."

"Of course it is," Gus said flippantly. "The first place burned to the ground, and this place is haunted. Let's leave and look for one with bedbugs and asbestos violations. Look, we see this kind of thing every day in the city. What makes you think there's any less crime out here in the sticks? As far as I know, you usually sleep like a log when we're home . . . um, except for your crazy nightmares and all."

"I know that Manhattan doesn't have a monopoly on crime. It just creeps me out to know that we're sleeping under the same roof as a family who has seen so much misfortune."

The waitress dropped off our drinks. She smiled at Max again, but the dude played it cool. He ignored her, opting instead to blow bubbles into his sippy cup—he's such a natural-born heartbreaker. She moved on to the next table.

"You can't tell me Kaley's story didn't bother you."

"Here's to us," Gus toasted, trying desperately to change the subject. "Try to remember we're on vacation. What do you say we rent jet skis after lunch?"

My stomach was empty. I took a large swig of my Bellini and sat back, hoping to feel an immediate buzz. I put my feet up on the railing and cast my gaze at the sea. For a brief moment, I relaxed and all appeared to be right with the world.

The sun was bright.

The water was green.

I took a second slug, still hopeful that a buzz would kick in. *Come on now. I'm ready. Come and get me. Anytime now.* "Jet skis, you say?"

Max made a contented baby face.

"Look at him," Gus said. "We made one beautiful baby boy."

"I know. Look at that handsome little puss."

"I don't want to brag," Gus began, "but what were the chances we'd have anything less than a stunning little stud baby?"

"I don't know. I guess we both look pretty good on the outside, but everyone's got a ton of genes banging around inside them. It could've been one of those *fugly* genes that hopped aboard the Michael Phelps sperm, swimming a record one-hundred-meter freestyle up my hooha."

Gus sneered at me with a comical face. "I've got news for you, babe. If I thought there was any chance you were going to give birth to a bouncing baby troglodyte, I would have dumped your ass in two seconds."

Yeah, right! "I guess it's a good thing you didn't meet me before I had all the surgery."

"What in the world are you talking about now?" he asked disbelievingly.

"Sure. I had a hundred thousand dollars worth of cosmetic surgery before we met. I did the nose, the cheeks, the chin, the boobs, and the butt. Before I went under the knife, I looked exactly like Marilyn Manson."

Gus snickered. "Are you trying to tell me that I could've had a son who looked like an anorexic Goth ghost?"

"It's all just a roll of the dice, babe, but I guess we got lucky." I tickled Max's chin, and he smiled. "I guess we hit the jackpot, didn't we?"

"Oh there you are." Our real estate agent/vacation rescuer, Camryn, waved to us as she stepped up onto the café deck, carrying an envelope in her hand. She wore a shady, big-brimmed hat and enormous dark glasses. If I didn't know any better, I'd guess she was trying to outsmart the paparazzi.

"Geez, talk about Marilyn Manson, look who's coming our way," I warned.

"That's cruel," Gus said.

"I don't know," I whispered. "You mean she doesn't creep you out just a little?"

Gus shot me a scathing glance and a demanding, *"Shhh!"*

"It looks like *these* folks are having fun," Camryn said as she approached us. "Thanks for meeting me here—my office is just down the street." She handed Gus the envelope. "That's your copy of the signed rental agreement." She pulled up a chair and sat down.

Max saw her and flared his nostrils.

"*So?* How was your first night in Shangri-La?" she asked. "Isn't the house beautiful?"

"We love it," Gus said. "I slept great."

"We met one of the neighbors this morning," I said. "Everyone is just *so* friendly."

"A neighbor?" Camryn asked with a leery, raised eyebrow. "Who?"

"Kaley. What a sweet girl. She stopped by on her way home from church."

"Oh." Her smile returned. "I love her. She's a doll," Camryn extolled enthusiastically. "She volunteers everywhere: at church, Long Island Cares, and homeless shelters. She's a real blessing for the community."

"That's good to hear—she offered to babysit for us."

"She's completely reliable and trustworthy." Camryn said. "I wouldn't hesitate for minute to use her."

"Yeah. I got that feeling from talking to her." I looked at her pointedly. "She also told us about Sarah Fisher and her family."

Camryn's happy expression shrank. "I wondered if that might come up," she said reluctantly. "Not a real happy story is it? I didn't know the Fishers personally. I bought the house from the bank after they foreclosed on it." She turned to Gus and then me. "It's not a deal breaker, is it? I'm happy to return your check if you want out. Last night will be on me."

"No way," Gus said in an assertive tone. "We're good." He glanced at me. "*Aren't we*, Stephanie?"

I had just drained the last of my Bellini. The last wave of alcohol finally did the trick. I could feel my mind drift ever so slightly. "Oh yeah . . . I'm good."

"Great," Camryn said. "I feel so much better knowing that's out of the way." She pushed back her chair and stood. "You'll have a great time out here. Rest and relax."

We watched as she walked off. "I'd hate to have to tell the Fisher story every time someone wants to rent the house," Gus said.

"Yeah. Me too."

Gus quickly glanced at the menu. "Hey, do you mind ordering the seafood Cobb for me? I want to check on the jet-ski rentals."

"Eager to get the party started, are we?"

Gus nodded excitedly.

"Go get 'em, tiger."

Gus bolted out of his chair.

I turned to Max, whose face was now mostly smeared with strawberries. I reached into my bag and pulled out the baby wipes just as Richard Tate approached the table.

"That's better," he said. "You and Gus get the 411 on the Fishers?"

"Yeah. That was one hell of a buzzkill."

"Not the best way to start a vacation, but what can you do?"

My head rocked from side to side. "I guess we'll just have to take it in stride."

"Terrific. Although you may have a hard time getting your deposit back from Bill Alden for the old cabin."

I shrugged. "How come?"

"We found a body lying in a recliner when we went through the debris. I'll bet you dollars to donuts the old timer bought the farm."

Chapter Nine

"I can't sleep."

Gus moaned in his sleep. I watched him for a moment to see if his eyes would open. They didn't.

"Hey, I said, I *can't* sleep." Those words are usually enough to wake him out of the deepest trance. *Can't sleep* being a euphemism for *hey, big fella, I need it bad*. I nudged his shoulder. "Did you hear me, sexy, I said I can't sleep," I repeated in my most seductive voice.

He finally stirred. "Steph, I'm so tired." Gus had been out on jet skis for hours and had really gotten his brains rocked by the East End waves. I could see why he'd be exhausted. "Can we do it tomorrow?" he pleaded. I could tell that he was starting to drift off again.

"Come on," I said, "wake up."

He looked over at the Pack 'n Play. "Is it okay with Max next to us, or do you want to go into another room?"

"I don't want to have sex."

"You *don't*?" He sounded both weary and disappointed.

"No. I need to talk."

"Talk?" he said in an incredulous voice. "You woke me up to talk?"

"Yeah, talk. I'm really strung out about what's happened to the family that lived in this house."

"For real? We're on vacation, hon—isn't sleeping part of the equation?"

"How can you sleep with everything we heard today? A murder on the railroad tracks, a girl gone missing, and a fire at

the cottage we were supposed to rent—my shit-storm detector
is going a mile a minute."

"I think you're making too much out of it."

"Is that how you really feel, or are you just giving me lip
service so that I'll let you go back to sleep?"

Gus stretched. I could hear his spine popping. He pushed
himself up against the headboard and jammed a pillow behind
his head. "You're so creeped out about all this that you can't
sleep? What can we do about it?"

Cops are usually pretty good at staying uninvolved because
crime is part of our everyday lives. It goes on everywhere and
everyplace. We're always getting asked to help out on matters in
which we should have no involvement. "I know, I know, I can't
solve everyone's problems. It's just—"

"This one's calling out to you?"

"Yeah, my antennae are up."

"So the vacation be damned? You're gonna stick your nose
where it doesn't belong?

"You know I've got a sixth—"

"Sense?"

"Uh-huh."

Gus gave me that look—it said, *I don't want to agree with
you but I have to.*

"I just want to do some checking around. I was ready to let it
go until I heard that Bill Alden probably burned to death in his
cabin."

Gus shook his head in an *I-give-up* sort of way. "Maybe it
was a grease fire."

"Tate said that he was going back to the cabin in the
morning. Do you mind if I go with him to have a look around? I'll
be home by noon, and we can jump back into vacation mode the
minute I get back."

"Sure, I'll hang with Max. I can teach him important man
stuff, like cat calling and crotch scratching."

"Seriously?"

"Actually, I brought my pole—maybe I'll stick Max in the papoose and walk over to the bay for a little bottom pounding."

My eyes grew wide. *That sounds erotic.* "Pole? Bottom pounding? I guess you figure it's never too soon to teach your son the facts of life."

Gus snickered. "I'm talking about fluke fishing."

"Oh. I thought you and Max were going to have 'the talk.'" If called upon to testify, I could certainly attest to Gus' prowess as a pounder, bottom, top, and every which way. If he could fish as well as he could . . . well, then I might have to change my name to Mrs. Gorton. "Make sure you teach him about safe bottom pounding—a young man can never be too careful these days."

He glanced over at Max. Our son was a vision of purity and innocence, an angelic smile plastered across a sleepy little face.

"I take it there'll be no bottom pounding tonight." Gus didn't wait for an answer. He fluffed his pillow and assumed the position—the fetal position, that is. He was out again in a flash.

Chapter Ten

It had rained during the night, and the ground was still wet as I walked from my SUV to Bill Alden's old burnt cabin. The humidity was high and the air was thick with the aroma of burnt wood, which covered the exterior of the house. The frame and outer shell of the house were pretty much intact, although the handsome orange cedar planks were burnt and blackened. Tate's fire chief truck was parked in front of the house alongside a gold Chevy Impala. I wondered who was in there with him.

Access was not a problem as the front door was lying on the ground outside the cabin. I stood at the entranceway and looked in. The floor was soaked with water. I heard voices inside. "Hey, Rich?" I called. "It's me, Stephanie."

I heard the crunch of footsteps on debris. Tate wore a broad smile as he approached. He held up his hand. "Wait right there," he said. "You need a safety helmet." He walked up to me. "What's the matter, you couldn't help yourself?"

I shrugged. "You know how it is; once a cop always a cop."

"Follow me. I've got safety gear in my truck."

I got a blast of Old Spice as Tate opened the rear hatch. Several empty bottles had been haphazardly discarded within. One of them rolled off the tailgate and clattered to the ground.

"That's quite a collection of cologne bottles you've got there. You get a deposit back when you return the empties or something?"

"No," he chuckled. "I use the Old Spice to mask the fire smells; otherwise, I stink of smoke all the time."

"No problem. My dad used Old Spice. It reminds me of him. Still you ought to think about recycling." I glanced at him accusatorily. "Every gallon of oil we waste..."

Tate shoved a helmet and jacket at me. "Here, recycle *this*," he said jovially. "I've got gloves for you too."

"No need." I reached into the pocket of my jeans and pulled out a pair of blue latex gloves.

"I suppose that's essential vacation gear."

"You never know when you'll come across a fresh crime scene... they also come in handy for changing diapers."

"So you're not over the Fisher story yet, are you?"

"No." *That's half the reason I'm here. I was up most of the night thinking about Sarah Fisher and the girl who was killed by the train.* "Stuff like that doesn't just roll off my back."

Tate chuckled. "Gus must be thrilled about you coming out here and snooping around like this."

"It's part of our wedding vows: 'I promise to love you unconditionally, to support you in your goals, to honor and respect you, and indulge your every delusional whim.' He knows what he signed up for."

Tate laughed heartily while I slipped on my firefighter's jacket and helmet. "The poor bastard. I guess that Gus doesn't mind you wearing the pants in the family." He wasn't expecting an answer. He put his arm on my shoulder and directed me back toward the cabin. "Ever investigate a fire before?"

"No."

"Safety first, got it, kid? Shit falls down, floors collapse. It's heads-up at all times."

"Will do. Who else is inside?"

"Jay Charnoff. He's my fire investigator. Knows his stuff inside and out."

"Any thoughts about how it started?"

"Oh yeah," Tate said confidently. "Jay's just about all done inside. Come on in, and I'll introduce you to him. I'll have you out of here in two shakes so you can go back to being a mother and wife."

I followed Tate's example as he moved cautiously past the debris on the floor. I stepped where he stepped and followed him into the large den, which I had seen in an online snapshot when we were looking for vacation rentals weeks earlier. The dimensions of the room were as I had expected them to be, about twelve by fifteen with sliding glass doors that led out back. As I remembered, it was easily the biggest room in the house. I could see the Atlantic through gaps in the tall pine trees behind the house. The cabin was set near the top of a bluff, no more than a quarter mile from the water.

I saw a young, average-size guy making notations on a clipboard. He stood next to the remains of a recliner, which had been cordoned off from the rest of the room. I guessed this was the recliner Tate had mentioned, the one Alden's body had been found on. Even without lights and electricity, it was not an issue to see clearly, as a huge section of the roof had burned away and provided beaucoup illumination.

"Jay Charnoff, say hello to Stephanie Chalice," Tate said.

"Are you with the insurance company?" Charnoff asked.

"Me? No. I'm just a busybody."

Charnoff turned to Tate with an expression that read, *is she for real?*

Tate's hearty laugh returned. He slapped Charnoff on the back. "Stephanie and her husband are friends of mine. They rented this place and would be in it right now if it hadn't burned down. They're both on the job in The Big Apple."

"Oh." Charnoff's expression brightened. "Hi, Stephanie. Always happy to meet one of New York's Finest. Where do you work?"

"Homicide, out of Midtown North."

"Homicide, really? That's no lightweight job."

"Neither is fire investigation."

"Before I came out here, I used to work at NYFD headquarters," Charnoff said. "Downtown Brooklyn, where you can still get a good corned beef sandwich and Dr. Brown's soda for under twenty bucks."

"Love Dr. Brown's. Cream soda or Cel-Ray tonic?"

"Cream, of course."

"Atta boy," I said approvingly. Charnoff looked pretty young. If I had to guess, I'd say that he was in his late twenties.

"What's your interest in this fire?" Charnoff asked.

"Just satisfying my curiosity. A few hours difference, and I might've been the one sitting in that chair instead of Bill Alden. I need some closure."

"The body is with the Suffolk County ME's office, Steph," Tate said. "No positive ID yet."

"What about your dollars to donuts theory?"

Tate shrugged. "Who else could it be? It's Bill's house and the old guy smoked like a chimney." He turned to Charnoff. "Jay can give you the blow by blow."

"I'm all ears," I said.

Charnoff grabbed his pen and poked the charred armrest of the chair. "The chair is the origin of the fire. The roof is burnt away above it because this is where the fire burned longest and hottest. Sniff the burned fabric."

I did as instructed. I wrinkled my nose and recoiled. "Smells awful. What is that?"

"Acrid?" Charnoff asked.

I nodded.

"It's probably acrylic," Charnoff continued. "Burns like a son of a gun and gives off all kinds of toxins."

"Smells like roasted nuts, and I don't mean honey roasted pralines."

"The house looks pretty dated," Charnoff continued. "My guess is that this chair was manufactured way before the industry observed meaningful FR standards."

"Flame retardancy?"

Charnoff nodded, turned on a pocket flashlight, and directed the beam of light under the recliner. "The floor under the chair isn't badly burned. The ash from the burnt fabric may have smothered the fire on the floor. He waited while I looked for myself and then stepped around me and walked to the doorway. He signaled for me to join him. He used his flashlight again—this time to illuminate a section of the doorframe. "You see how the inside of the frame is completely burnt but the outside not so much?"

I nodded again.

"That's a char pattern. It shows that the fire started in here and then spread out into the hallway."

"Okay, so the fire started in here, and you think the chair was the origin. Nothing suspicious?"

"Nothing, my bloodhound friend," Tate said. "There's nothing that points to the use of accelerants. It's pretty cut and dry. The body was found in the recliner, feet up. Alden probably fell asleep with a cigarette in his hand and set the chair on fire."

"Why didn't he try to save himself when he realized the recliner was on fire?"

"I don't know," Charnoff said. "That's a question for the ME. The smoke could've overcome him. Rich said he was an older guy and not in the best of health—maybe his ticker gave out first and then the cigarette fell out of his hand and started the fire. I've seen a lot of that over the years."

"So we sit and wait."

"That's right," Tate said. "It's out of our hands for the moment." He glanced at his watch. "See? I told you I'd get you in and out fast. Tell Gus he owes me."

"You don't mind if I take a look around on my own, do you?"

"What?" Tate said. "You're not convinced?"

"I'm convinced. I'm just not satisfied, and I know you'd be disappointed if I was."

Chapter Eleven

"Oh no," I said when Gus walked through the kitchen door holding his son and a cooler. "No way!" I warned. "Keep those putrid things away from me."

Gus sat Max down in his booster seat and strapped him in.

"There's no way that I'm cleaning all that smelly fish."

Gus opened the cooler and set it down on the table. He beamed proudly as he displayed the day's catch, two mammoth dead fishies floating in ice water.

Max reached into the cooler and splashed stinky fish water everywhere.

"They're monsters," Gus boasted.

I took a good look at the two dead creatures and noticed that they both had two eyes on the same side of their heads. "Oh, Christ, they're mutants!"

"No they're not."

"Then why are four eyes staring up at me instead of two?"

"Haven't you ever heard of evolution, Mrs. Darwin?" he asked sarcastically. "They lie in the mud and don't need eyes on the side that faces the bottom."

I reached over and nudged the cooler lid closed. "Adorable. I'm going online to order a fluke-print scarf for myself. Nothing shouts confidence like a woman attired in fish."

"They're both over two feet."

"I. Don't. Care."

"How can you not care?" Gus said. "Your son and husband went out and caught dinner. What's manlier than that? We didn't go to the supermarket. We went out to sea with our rods and reels and came back with the ocean's bounty. Those monsters put up a hell of a fight."

"First of all, *Ahab*, you didn't reel in Moby Dick. You went out into the tranquil little bay in a putt-putt boat, so tone down the bravado." I snickered. "You bench press three hundred pounds in the gym. I had no doubt you'd emerge victorious in a tug of war with two oversized guppies."

"I don't see how you cannot be excited!"

"Are they self-cleaning fish?"

"No."

"Well then I'm not excited."

"Wait until you taste them. There's nothing like a fresh catch—some olive oil and breadcrumbs. You'll think you've died and gone to heaven."

Gus had some mad cooking skills, but he rarely got a chance to show them off at home. Between Ma's never-ending stream of dinner invitations and having the corner pizzeria on speed dial . . .

"That's sounds great. I'll give Max a bath, and you can call us when lunch is on the table." I picked up my son. "Come on, sweetie, mommy will hose all the stink off of you."

"Hey," Gus protested. "I could use a good hosing off myself."

"I'll bet you could. Don't worry. I'm woman enough for both of my men." I shot Gus a wicked little grin. "Right after the little man goes night-night." I bounced Max in my arms and got a good whiff of fish smell when he nuzzled my neck. "He smells like fish poop—you didn't let him play with the bait, did you?"

"Are you kidding?"

Gus pulled his fish knife out of the sheath and began to slice the fluke with the dexterity of a hibachi chef. Fish parts flew everywhere—bones and guts into the trash and clean fillets into a skillet.

"Come on, little one. Let's see if we can make you smell like a baby again. Want to play with Rubber Ducky?"

Max liked Rubber Ducky. His eyes gleamed excitedly.

Gus watched us as we climbed the staircase.

"That fish better be good," I said, cautioning him playfully. "Bathing children makes me powerful hungry."

~~~

"This is incredible," I said as I savored the sautéed goodness of Gus' fresh catch. "Maybe you should go fishing again tomorrow."

Gus eyed me warily, "Why? I sense an ulterior motive."

"The entire bay is full of these tasty crazy-eyed buggers after all, and you seem to like it so much. I thought I'd give you another opportunity to commune with nature."

"Come on, Stephanie, spill it. What's going on?"

"Nothing." I shrugged. "I thought maybe I'd do a little more poking around."

"For what? You said the fire appeared to be accidental."

"It did, but—"

"Yeah?"

"I don't know. I don't understand what Alden was doing in the cabin. I mean, he mailed us the keys with the signed rental agreement. There was really no reason for him to be there."

Gus had his eyes on his plate while he spoke. It was clear that he was more interested in his meal than Bill Alden's death. "Maybe he wanted to greet us in person and show us around. Is it a crime to be neighborly?"

"Yeah, I know. I won't harp on it until we hear back from the ME's office."

"Okay, but what's so important that you want to get your son and husband out of your hair again tomorrow morning?"

"You know me. Nervous energy."

Gus looked at me suspiciously.

"I thought I'd go talk to the engineer who—"

"Who saw that woman get pushed in front of the train? Stephanie really? What kind of vacation is this turning into?

There'll be a stack of case folders waiting on our desks when we return. I don't need to keep in practice."

"It'll just take a couple of hours. I'll take Max with me and you can bottom pound to your heart's desire. Today worked out okay, didn't it? You fished, I investigated, and we're eating your delicious fish for lunch. We've got the rest of the day to do anything we like."

"I'll take, Max," Gus insisted. "He doesn't need to be exposed to a conversation about a young woman's murder or meet a train engineer who is probably struggling with post-traumatic stress disorder."

Gus' comment was on the money. I was trying to make it easier on him, but I wasn't seeing the big picture. "You're right. I don't know what I was thinking." My head slumped a little. I guess it was the guilt.

Gus put down his fork, and came around the table to give me a hug. "It bugs me too, but I can turn it off. I'm a cop a good ninety percent of the time, but when I'm on vacation, I'm on vacation." He tapped me on the head. "But I know you just can't shut it down. That crazy mind of yours is always working."

"Thanks, hon, you won't be sorry. I'll make it up to you with lots of intensely hot sex."

"Is that your answer for everything?"

I nodded enthusiastically.

"Good by me," he chuckled. "Just remember, I'm keeping score." He sat down and was about to put his fork to his mouth when the house shook. "What the hell was that?"

Max started to cry.

The house shook again and again with what sounded like hammer blows. I grabbed Max, and we ran outside to see what was going on. A workman was atop a ladder nailing aluminum trip onto the fascia board just below the roof. "Shhh," I said to Max as I tickled his chin. "It's okay."

"Hi," Gus called to the workman. "Can I help you?"

He stopped hammering and gazed down at us. "You're the renters, I guess."

"That's right," Gus said. "We're the renters. I suppose you're Camryn's brother."

"Yup," he replied. "I'm her brother."

The sun filtering through the tree caused me to squint. I shielded my eyes as I called to him. You got a name?"

"Ray."

"You gave us quite a scare, Ray."

He turned his focus back to the fascia board and continued to hammer the trim into place. We seemed to be an afterthought as he readied another nail. "I'm sure Camryn told you there'd be some noise."

"Some noise, yes. Sudden deafening hammer blows? *No.* We've got a baby with us. Do you think you can give us a heads-up next time?" My son was just beginning to settle down.

"I'll try," Ray said in a noncommittal tone.

Okay, he was way up in the air and the sun was in my eyes, but Ray didn't look like a big fellow to me. He looked like someone Gus could break in two. My husband was built like a commando. I guess Ray hadn't noticed or didn't care.

"*Hey*, can you come down here for a minute?" Gus asked.

"Come down? I'm in the middle of a job," Ray replied. "I'll be down when I'm finished."

A huge crease formed across Gus' forehead. I'd seen it before. He was silently stating, *why, you son of a bitch . . .* He was ready to get crazy and throw down.

"Not in front of Max," I whispered.

Gus shook his head. "We'll be waiting inside. Make sure that you stop by before you go," Gus said unhappily. He walked back into the house without waiting for Ray's response.

The hammering stopped a while later. I went out to check on Ray's progress, but he had already gone.

Chapter Twelve

"You just never forget something like that. Never!"
Charlie Rydell, the retired locomotive engineer, paused,
extending a shaky hand to reluctantly accept medication from
his aide. He tossed back a handful of tablets with a cup of water
then rubbed his eyes. "I just hate taking all those damn pills," he
said. He had bright-red hair and a long face with protruding
cheekbones. I wasn't quite sure of his age but had the feeling
that he looked old beyond his years. "It feels lousy to be
dependent on so much medication, but that's what happens
after you have a stroke. Take my advice—don't get old."

It wasn't the first time I had visited an assisted care
facility—this one actually seemed pretty nice. It was modern
and didn't smell of soiled laundry and neglect. Believe me, I've
been to plenty of places like that. I call them dormitories of
despair, and they're just filled with lonely old people counting
days and wishing for the end to come quickly. Sometimes I'd
interview a senior in one of those places, and I'd feel like crying
afterward. I couldn't say this place was cheerful, but at least it
was clean, and Rydell's aide seemed caring and attentive. "All
those because you had a stroke?" I asked.

"And osteoarthritis and high blood pressure . . . you name it
and I've got it. You'll have to forgive me, my memory's not as
good as it was before I went lights-out; I forget what all the pills
are for." He reached into a box of donuts and selected a Boston
cream. I had asked him over the phone if there was anything I
could bring him, and the word 'donuts' popped right out of his

mouth. "I've got lots of problems," he muttered. "Too many to keep track of or worry about."

"Oh stop it. You look fine," I said, but he didn't. He looked like a man who was going down fast. Thank God he sounded better than he looked.

"Fortunately high blood sugar ain't one of my problems. Thanks for bringing the donuts."

"It's my pleasure, Charlie. Don't mention it."

"Don't just sit there," he bellowed in a feisty tone. "Eat one!"

Charlie didn't have a problem with blood sugar, but both of my parents did or had. My father died from complications of diabetes. My mom is nowhere as bad as he was, but she takes medication and definitely has to watch what she eats. "I'm gonna take a pass on the donuts, Charlie. I'd love one, but I'll be at the beach all week and there's just no place to hide a French cruller in my bikini."

Charlie laughed. "I'd make a pain in the ass out of myself and insist that you eat a damn donut, but there's no arguing with results like that. Missy, you're built like a brick shithouse."

Why look beneath the surface? Flattery is flattery.

"Why, Mr. Charlie," his aide said. She was a petite Caribbean woman with an accent and addressed everyone by prefacing their first name with their titles; Rydell was Mr. Charlie, I was Ms. Stephanie, and the doctor who had just left the room was Dr. William. She shook her finger at Charlie, admonishing him playfully. "You watch your manners now. Don't be talking no crude language in front of the lady."

He tore off a chunk of the Boston cream donut and spoke while he chewed. "That's about the only benefit of getting sickly—I can get away with saying all kinds of shit." He glared at his helper. "That'll be all, *Precious*," he said teasing her with her own name. His cheekbones rose so high they looked as if they'd pop through his eye sockets. "The good detective and I have business to discuss."

"You're a bad boy, Mr. Charlie," she said chiding him in a friendly manner. She scooped up his empty cups, a powdered donut, and walked off.

"You shouldn't do that. She's only trying to take good care of you."

"Forget it, Detective," Charlie said in between bites. "You start your life wearing diapers. If you finish wearing Depends, you've lived way too long. I'd rather live my remaining days on my own terms." He chewed another hunk of donut. "This is delicious. You know, I wouldn't mind if you paid me a visit every once in a while. I mean you're not exactly tough on the eyes, so if you happen to be in the area . . ."

"Sure. I'll put it on my calendar," I said satirically. "So you were saying . . ."

"Oh that's right. Where was I? Oh yeah, like I said, you just never get over something like that. Poor Alana Moore. I can still remember the look on her face just before . . ." Charlie closed his eyes. His lips were pressed shut while he shook his head back and forth.

I patted the back of his hand. "Just take it nice and slow. I know this is difficult."

He continued to shake his head after he opened his eyes. "Haven't had to talk about this in a while."

"Just take a deep breath and tell me what you remember."

"Sure." He sighed. "It was a Sunday night, and I was making the westbound run from Montauk into Penn Station. I'd been making that run a long time and could do it with my eyes closed. It was early spring; the railroad cars are mostly empty that time of year. The trains are mobbed after Memorial Day but before . . . Anyway, I wasn't surprised to see that no one was waiting for the train. I was coming up on the platform—" He closed his eyes once again, and I could see from the anguish on his face that it was painful for him to relive that moment. "It's only a few minutes from Amagansett to East Hampton. The train barely has time to build up speed before it has to slow down again. I remember pulling into the station. It looked completely deserted. I had just hit the platform when I saw this young woman stumbling backward out of the shadow and toward the track. She was trying to regain her balance but her momentum ... I saw her face for a split second just as we hit. It all happened so fast—I heard the impact before I was able to push the emergency brake." His eyes closed again as he tried to squeeze the vision out of his mind. "It was terrifying, just terrifying—she literally came from out of nowhere. I tried to go back to work, but I couldn't pass that station again without thinking about what happened. They put me on another line to see if that would help, but I just couldn't work anymore. Then I got the stroke and ..."

"I'm so sorry. Did you go to therapy?"

"Did I go? Honey, I'm still going. Thank God for the union; it pays for this place and all my treatments. I used to envision hitting my own kid with the train. My daughter was about the same age as that pretty little girl. I used to—" He began to mist up. "I still have that nightmare; that pretty little girl's face as she tumbled backward in front of the train. My God, it was the most terrible thing that ever happened to me."

I gave him a moment to compose himself. "Charlie, I know you've answered this question many times before but are you certain she was pushed? You know that three quarters of the time, these train strikes are premeditated suicide attempts."

"Don't you think I know that?" he said flatly. "I know the difference between a murder and a suicide."

He sounded very confident. I didn't doubt him, but I needed to understand his rationale. "Don't take offense at this, but how could be so sure?"

"Because, damn it. Just because." He looked me in the eye, hoping I'd back down, but I didn't. I couldn't. He sighed heavily. "It—" He took a sip of water to moisten his dry throat. "It wasn't the first time I hit someone," he said sadly. "The first time ... now that was a suicide."

Oh Jesus. Really? This poor guy hit two people? No wonder he's such a basket case. "I know I shouldn't push you like this, but could you please explain so that I can understand why you're so certain that Alana Moore was murdered?"

"It was early in my career, Penn Station, evening rush hour. He was waiting behind a support column, wearing a suit like all the other businessmen. He looked like any other guy waiting for the train to go home to his family. I saw him watching the train out of the corner of his eye just as it approached. I knew something was wrong, so I blasted the horn and hit the emergency brake, but a multi-ton train just doesn't stop on a dime, now does it? He was looking right at me as he stepped in front of the train. Alana Moore was different, completely different. She was trying to catch her balance. She was trying to stop her fall, but she couldn't. Someone had pushed her—no one will ever tell me differently. Sometimes when I think about it, I can almost visualize two hands extending out of the shadow, the hands of the person who pushed her in front of my train. No question in my mind she was murdered. The poor thing ... by the time they were able to get her out from under the train, the only things that weren't mutilated were her purse and one of her pink shoes."

Chapter Thirteen

Thump. I really hate speed bumps. Thump. Thump. *Jesus, what a pain in the ass.* Thump. The parking lot at the police station had speed bumps up the wazoo. They ought to shoot the person who thought of those cursed things. They're about as pleasant as a pair of wet socks. I think it would be a great platform for a political candidate to run on. Forget about lowering taxes and creating more jobs—eliminate and abolish every goddamn speed bump on the planet. I'd get behind a candidate like that.

My next appointment was with Steve Pulaski, the Suffolk County police detective who had investigated the death of Alana Moore. Detective Pulaski set me up in an interview room and brought me a cup of coffee, which was no better than the swill we drank back at Midtown North. It was lightened with that powdered gunk which is every bit as palatable as worm-ridden sawdust. I took one sip, grimaced, and pushed the cup aside.

"I'm guessing it's not too good," Pulaski said.

Is he kidding? It ought to be listed on the EPA's list of banned pesticides. Bite your tongue, Steph. Candy-coat it. "It's a coffee drinker's worst nightmare." *Ugh! That wasn't much better. I hope he doesn't take offense.*

He held up his bottle of Poland Spring. "Yeah, it's usually pretty bad. That's why I'm drinking the ever-popular H^2O."

"Thanks for taking the time to see me," I said. I had no jurisdiction in the Alana Moore matter, and I wasn't a member of her family. Pulaski was extending professional courtesy by seeing me: nothing more. I needed to be on my best behavior and not do anything that might cause him to pull the plug on our conversation.

Pulaski plopped into his chair. "So, Detective Chalice, you're out here on vacation?"

"Yup, two weeks of rest and relaxation. We needed a break from city life. Oh, and please call me Stephanie."

"You know most cops don't go looking into cold murder investigations on their time off. Wouldn't you rather be out at the beach or something?"

"Absolutely," I said, which wasn't exactly the truth. I guess I'm hopelessly addicted to the intrigue of a homicide investigation.

"So what's the deal?" he asked.

"My husband and I are renting a house out in Montauk. One of the neighbors came by to say hello and told us about a couple of local tragedies; the disappearance of Sarah Fisher and the death of Alana Moore."

"I don't know anything about the Fisher disappearance. I mean, I knew about it, but I wasn't assigned to the case."

"I know. I'm taking one step at a time. As you pointed out, I'm here on vacation. It's just my professional curiosity. I'd like to know more about Alana Moore's death. Besides, my husband's a big-time fisherman. I've got to do something to pass the time while he's out victimizing helpless fishies."

"Fishing's great fun."

So I hear.

"It's *very* relaxing."

"Yeah, he loves it. He's out teaching my son how to fish. Of course, he should probably wait until the lad is toilet trained."

Pulaski laughed. "I guess a man is never too young to learn. Your husband should try his hand at deep-sea fishing while he's out here—the tuna are running like crazy."

"Probably not a good idea to strap an infant into a fighting chair. He can barely hold on to his sippy cup."

"Ha! Man, you should go into standup."

Let me see if I've got this straight; Gus should go deep-sea fishing, and I should go into standup comedy. My but he's just full of great suggestions. I hope he's as good at police work as he is at giving advice.

"So what would you like to know about Alana Moore?"

"Whatever you can tell me. I'd like to take a look at the evidence file and her personal effects if you'll permit me."

"I'll requisition the evidence out of storage." Pulaski opened a case file and turned it around so that I could take a look at the deceased's photograph.

Alana Moore was a pretty blonde with soft, topaz-colored eyes. "What a shame." She looked like a happy person. "So young and pretty." I looked up at Pulaski. "So what happened to her? I just chatted with Charlie Rydell, and he's one-hundred-percent positive that she was pushed in front of his train."

"You met with Rydell? He's a strange bird all right."

"Strange? I didn't think he was so strange ... a little eccentric maybe." *I mean, it's not as if he sits backward on the toilet eating a bowl of Cocoa Puffs while singing "The Star Spangled Banner"—now that's what I would call strange. Most of the people I know are kind of strange. A person would have to do something really off the wall to make me sit up and take notice.* "Why do you say that? You don't think his account of the incident was reliable?"

"I'm not saying he's wrong, but there were no witnesses and no security cameras on the platform at that time. There was nothing to go on. The MO didn't match anything on file. She was from upstate—from an area I know next to nothing about—but here's the interesting part." Pulaski riffled through the case file and pulled out a missing persons report from Rensselaer County. "She'd been missing for months before she died."

Another missing woman? "What were the circumstances of her disappearance?"

"My partner and I drove up to Rensselaer County to interview her parents. They live on a farm upstate in Hoosick

Falls. It's about forty miles east of Saratoga. It's God's country, if you know what I mean—I think we passed Michael Landon on the way up."

I didn't get his reference. "Michael Landon?"

"*Little House on the Prairie*? Nothing?"

I shrugged.

"Horse-drawn wagons. Women in bonnets? Still nothing?"

"You can try to coax the answer out of me all day long, but it's not going to help." This was one of those rare occasions when I was completely clueless.

Wrinkles formed on Pulaski's forehead. "My God, you're a kid. How old are you anyway?"

"Under thirty."

"You're pretty young to have made NYPD homicide; I'm impressed."

"Even though I don't know who this Michael Landon character is?"

He waved his hand dismissively. "Google him when you have the time. Anyway, Hoosick Falls is a real hole-in-the-wall—very rural. I mean you could set off a *nuc-u-lar* bomb and not injure anyone."

Yes, he said, "*nuc-u-lar*," just like our beloved forty-third president, George W. Bush. Despite this, he sounded relatively intelligent.

"I think they've got more cows than people up there. Now get this. They have this farm stand, and when they're off doing *whatever*, they leave a basket out front so that their customers can help themselves to the merchandise and leave cash in the unattended basket. The honor system, for crying out loud—I couldn't believe it. I bought a piece of crumb cake and left two dollars in the basket under a rock."

"Under a rock. At least they're not worried about the money flying away."

"Oh no," he quipped. "It's all very leading edge. I think they pirated the technology from NASA."

I smiled. "Good one."

"We went up there on a rainy day, and I have to tell you, that place was *bleak*."

"Folks from a small town like that . . . I'm sure her parents were a mess."

"Oh they were destroyed. You could just look into their eyes and see their hearts had been ripped out. She was twenty years old when she disappeared. Went to school one day and never came back."

"That's so tragic. Where did she attend?"

"She was taking classes at Bennington College. Commuted back and forth from home. She called her parents and told them she was going out for a bite with a friend. That was the last time they heard from her.

"Her car was never found?"

"The car washed up in the Hoosick River, but she wasn't in it. She was either abducted or took off on her own. The police department up there is small, but they followed protocol to the letter and did everything they were supposed to. Every appropriate agency was informed, but Alana never turned up."

"Until she was hit by the train."

Pulaski nodded with a sad expression on his face. "That's one next-of-kin notification I'm glad I didn't have to make."

"What kind of girl was she?"

"Her parents described her as a happy kid, pretty easygoing. I checked her out: good grades, no criminal record. She was taking classes in performance arts. Her parents said she wanted to act and dreamed about getting to Broadway one day."

"That's a pretty common dream. I wonder what derailed her career." *Did I just say derailed? I don't believe it. Talk about a faux pas. He's not reacting. I think it went over his head. Thank God.* My gut was that something terrible happened to Alana Moore way before the train hit her. "What else can you tell me, Tom? How was she dressed? Was there a local address? Cell phone records? Anything?"

"No local address, and she hadn't made any calls from her cell phone or used her credit cards since the time she had disappeared. She had some cash in her wallet at the time she was hit by the train ... her driver's license, and her school ID. Other than that, her purse contained generic stuff: makeup, a brush, a pair of shoes, a tin of Altoids, etc."

"Condoms?"

"No condoms."

"Did you ask her parents if she had been seeing anyone? Were any of her old boyfriends bad news?"

"Good questions, not-helpful answers—she wasn't seeing anyone at the time she disappeared, and she only had a couple of significant relationships prior to the time she disappeared. Everyone was checked out—they were all devastated to hear that she had died and all had verifiable alibis."

"Identification of the body?"

"Visual identification was impossible. Her head was crushed—dental records were useless; no fingerprint records on file."

"DNA?"

"We didn't check for DNA."

"Really, no DNA testing? Why?"

Her parents were too distraught—they didn't want to be tested for a DNA match. All they wanted to do was bury their daughter and be left in peace so that they could grieve privately. I can't say that I blame them. I mean try to put yourself in their place. I don't know how people go on living after something like that happens to their child."

"So basically you found a body and a driver's license."

Pulaski hemmed and hawed. "Yeah ... pretty much," he said with a sheepish expression on his face. "We investigated for quite a while but nothing panned out."

"Theories?"

"Upstate police figured she'd been abducted, but that theory was dismissed when she died. She was all dressed up and didn't look like someone who was being held against her will. We all concluded that she'd run away on her own and moved downstate to be closer to the theatrical world. Who shoved her in front of the train? I'm embarrassed to say that we don't know any more now than we did the day she died. There were simply no viable leads."

My blood was boiling, and I felt my eye begin to twitch. I think Pulaski saw that I was losing it.

"Let me see how long it will take to get the evidence out of storage," he said. Pulaski stood taking advantage of the opportunity to leave the room.

I was so upset that I absentmindedly gulped a mouthful of the dreadful coffee and almost gagged. I didn't know if it was from the coffee or the insufficient manner in which Alana Moore's murder investigation had been handled.

Chapter Fourteen

"Ma? What are you doing here?"

"I missed you," she said pretending to mist up. She stepped away from the kitchen counter and threw her arms around me.

I gave her a big smooch on the cheek. "You missed us so much? We've only been gone a few days."

"It's not the time, pudd'n'head, it's the distance."

"You could've called if you missed us so much. You know, reach out and touch someone?"

She shrugged. "I wanted to give you your privacy."

So you unexpectedly show up at our front door? My mother has a strange understanding of the word 'privacy.'

"Well it's a lovely surprise." I looked around. "Hey, where are my two men?"

"I sent them to the store for groceries. Tomorrow's Gus' birthday, you know."

"Of course I know. I'm planning on giving Max a heavy dose of baby Benadryl and sexing up Gus until his brain explodes."

Ma looked disappointed. "Don't you think he'd rather have a nice home-cooked meal?"

I can't believe this woman. "No! I figured we'd drink a bottle of wine and then I'd drag him to bed and practice world-class gymnastics."

"Stephanie," she blushed, "You're embarrassing your mother." She pointed at the stovetop. "Look, I'm making fresh sauce."

I fanned the aroma toward my face. "It smells terrific, but do you really think Gus would rather eat spaghetti and meatballs than make love to his wife?"

"I don't know," she said with a sly wink. "My sauce is pretty damn good." She hugged me again. "Forget about it . . . fill your bellies. I'll turn in early, and you can still screw your brains out."

"Are you kidding? With you in the next room?"

"Don't worry. I'll take the Benadryl too." We laughed as we walked to the kitchen table. Ma had brought a liter bottle of wine and had already poured a glass for herself. She poured one for me. "*Salute*," she said with the Italian twist at the end of the word. We clinked glasses. "Here's to vacations and pain-in-the-ass mothers," she said with a wink.

It was a bargain-priced bottle of wine, but it was pretty tasty nonetheless. My stomach was empty, and I felt the alcohol hit me right away. "I can't believe this. How did you get here?"

"I caught a ride with Ginny Menucci's daughter, Dina."

I almost choked on the wine. "You rode out here with Dina Menucci? You're kidding, right?"

"No."

"Did you pick up any sailors on the ride out?"

She made that hand gesture that only Italians make, with all five fingertips touching. "Stephanie, what the hell are you talking about?"

I smirked.

"Why? What's with that look on your face? What's wrong with the Menuccis?"

"There's nothing wrong with the Menuccis, but you know how Dina earns a living, don't you?"

"She works evenings selling restaurant supplies. Are you crazy or something?"

"Ma, listen to yourself. Who sells restaurant supplies at night? She's a call girl. My God, how gullible can a person be?"

"*Madonna mia*, sweet little Dina? Are you sure? She said Vesuvius is her biggest customer."

"Vesuvius, the Italian restaurant on 49th Street?"

Ma nodded.

"Yeah, I'm sure there's an eruption there every time she walks through the door."

"How can that be? You know Mickey V, the owner; he's a family man."

"First of all he's not Italian, even though he professes to be. He's Greek. That's why he never uses his full last name."

"For real?"

"Yes for real. His last name is Vloganitis, or Vaginitis, or something you'd need antibiotics to clear up, and he's the biggest sleazeball on two feet. Believe me when Dina visits him in the restaurant, his soufflé isn't the only thing that rises."

"So Mickey is Greek?"

I nodded with conviction. "Mickey is short for Mikolas. He got into a jam over unpaid traffic tickets several months back and asked me to help him out. That's why I know his real name."

"Were you able to help him?"

"I made a call over to my friend Tay at the DA's office. She pulled some strings. They let him pay the fines, and he was able to avoid criminal charges."

"And he's Greek."

"Like baklava, Mama."

"Oh my? Does that mean . . ."

"That's right, Ma, Dina's probably multi-portal."

She cringed. "Stephanie, that's disgusting."

"You brought it up. Do you prefer I use the term *backdoor specialist*?"

"*Madonna,* too much information." Ma pretended to retch.

"Ma, you're such a prude. You've never heard of ass play?"

"What play?"

"Ass play."

"Isn't that the group that sings about clocks?"

"Oh my God." *What am I going to do with this woman?* "No, Ma, that's *Cold*play."

"Stephanie, I'm confused."

Evidently. "Ma, ass play ... anal sex. Stop being such a Girl Scout."

She shrugged. "You mean like for a gay man."

"It's not just for gay men, Ma. Straight couples do it too."

"But why?" Ma was completely out of her comfort zone. Fine droplets of sweat broke out across her lip.

How can I put this delicately? "Sometimes a man prefers to squeeze his car into the garage instead of just leaving it to hang out in the nice wide driveway."

"You're losing me. What does this have to do with cars?"

Sometimes there's just no beating around the bush. Yikes. I can't believe I just said that. "Because, Ma, after a woman shoots two or three linebackers out of her vagina, it isn't exactly a snug fit anymore."

Ma smiled with revelation. "Ah. So you're talking about a man's pleasure."

"Correct."

"What about the woman?"

I flashed my palm like a stop sign. "I'm not going there, Ma." I wasn't saying I don't go there, but I wasn't going there with my mother.

"I still don't believe it. Dina told me flat out that she sells macaroni."

I giggled. "A hooker whose cover story is that she sells macaroni? Does that make her a *pasta-tute*?"

Ma was aghast. "This is too much." She looked pensive for a moment. "Come to think of it, she does drive a big fancy convertible."

"Believe me, the top's not the only thing in that car that goes down."

Ma put her hand to her forehead. "I must be losing my mind. She talked three hours straight about how difficult it is for women to get ahead in a man's world."

"I don't think getting head is an issue for her or any of her dates."

"I said, 'ahead ahead,' not getting head. She's a very bright girl."

"I'm pretty sure she's a lot faster on the intake than the uptake."

"Stephanie, are you drunk already? Is the wine getting to you?"

I closed my eyes and sank back in my chair. "Sorry, Ma, just unwinding. It's been a busy morning."

"What kind of busy morning? Isn't the idea of a vacation to relax?"

"I—"

"I nothing. Gus told me what you were doing. Stephanie, are you a glutton for punishment? Can't you just leave well enough alone for once? You're on vacation for God's sake."

"Just satisfying my curiosity is all."

"God love you. You're just like your father ... but while you're on vacation with your husband and your son? Give it a rest, Stephanie. Don't you know when to stop?"

"Trust me, I'd like to stop, but I can't. In the few days we've been out here, I've heard about a young woman who went missing and the young woman who used to live in this house has disappeared too. Oh, and our vacation rental burned to the ground with the owner presumably inside."

"I told you to go to the Finger Lakes but does anyone listen to me? No. You had to go to someplace dark and disturbing like Montauk, didn't you?"

"Ma," I said impatiently, "Dark and disturbing? It's Montauk, not Casablanca. We came here to have a good time and we are. I just have trouble sleeping at night knowing that bodies are piling up and women have gone missing."

Ma waved her hand dismissively. "Oh, come on, Stephanie. Admit it. You can't help yourself—you seek out all these crazies and it makes you happier than a pig in shit." She glanced toward heaven and then shook her head in exasperation. "It's inappropriate. Do you want Max to grow up thinking this kind of thing is normal?"

Ma had a point; a good one. Neither Gus nor I would oppose Max if he chose a career in law enforcement, but he would have to understand that there were other alternatives and that not everyone was a paranoid, law-enforcement nut case like his mother. "Okay. You're right. I'll dial it back."

"So I'm right?" she said with a gloating smile.

Aren't you always? I picked up my cell phone.

"Who are you calling?" Ma asked.

"Gus. I'll ask him to pick up a gallon of *adult* Benadryl and maybe some Sominex too."

Ma snickered.

I had so much aggression built up inside me. If I couldn't pursue bad guys, I'd have to channel all of my energy into a more enjoyable pursuit. God knows, putting all of my police instincts on hold was going to take a Herculean effort, and I was counting on Gus to tire me out so exhaustively that I just wouldn't care.

Chapter Fifteen

"My name is Josh, and I'm a drug addict."

My name is Ray, and I'm going to take your life. Ray zoned out right after Josh had introduced himself to the group. He had heard stories exactly like his many times before, the twelve steps and blah, blah, blah … Josh's iteration sounded generic and boring. He didn't even have any juicy admissions. The woman who spoke just before Josh had confessed to the group about getting loaded up on meth and ecstasy, becoming paralyzed behind the wheel of her father's new Benz and T-boning a minivan. Compared to her story, Josh's was barely worth staying awake for.

Despite the fact that Josh was a poor entertainer, he was just right for Ray. Josh was from out of town, a wandering soul who moved aimlessly through life. He was an unremarkable transient doing odd jobs as he found them to survive and buy drugs. For some reason, God had put them both in the same place at the same time, and as the lesson from high school physics clearly pointed out: two objects cannot occupy the same space at the same time. One of them had to go.

It was the third time that Ray had encountered the young man at the Narcotics Anonymous group. The actual details of Josh's life blurred in his memory, but he was able to retain the pertinent information. They were about the same age. Josh had no ties to his immediate family and never stayed in one place very long. He was all that Ray could hope for—a loner with a history of substance abuse, someone that nobody in town knew or would miss.

Ray had spoken with him at the last meeting, just for a couple of minutes, a strategic introduction with the sole purpose of facilitating a subsequent conversation.

Tonight after the meeting, Ray stood at the refreshments table filling a cup with apple juice when Josh grabbed a handful of Oreos from the snack tray in front of him. "Hungry?" Ray asked with a chuckle.

"I've got the munchies," Josh replied. "I was so nervous about getting up in front of the group that I had to go out to the car and take a quick drag on my one-hitter just to settle my nerves, yo."

"Yeah, I've done that," Ray said in a friendly voice. "Definitely takes the edge off." He picked up an Oreo, twisted it apart, and scraped the icing off with his teeth. "Now that's how it's done."

Josh popped two cookies in his mouth and crunched down on them. "I need a faster delivery system," he said while he chewed. "Hey, do you believe that girl who mixed crystal and X? What a moron."

Do you believe I'm really interested in anything you have to say? "Of course I believe it. I've heard much worse than that."

"Really? Like what?"

"Some jerk got messed up on speedballs, drove through an old lady's living room, and turned her into a street pizza. Another speedballer fell off a six-story scaffold at a construction site and lost a leg. I've been coming here for a long time. Stories like that scare the shit out of me and keep me clean." He shrugged. "I guess that's why I keep on coming."

"I guess my story was nothing special. I'm just lost, yo. You know what I mean?"

That's right. You're a boring little twit. "Then you're better off than the others. Some of these people have experienced real tragedy. There's still time for you to straighten out and fly right." *Well, not really.* "That's what I'd do if I were you." *And I will be you. Don't worry. I'll do you proud.*

"I'm trying, but I'm weak, yo. I quit a couple of times but I go right back to it as soon as the road gets bumpy."

"What's *it* for you?" Ray asked.

"H."

"That's tough shit to quit. So you've been clean for two months?"

"I-I . . ."

"What are you hemming and hawing about? Why are you here? Are you clean or what?" Ray asked impatiently.

Josh dipped his head shamefully. "No, man."

Man, I'm good. He thinks I actually give a rat's ass. "You're wasting everyone's time. Didn't you just stand up there and tell everyone that you were off dope?"

Josh nodded.

The meeting room had pretty much cleared out. Ray looked around. "Man, you're a disgrace. Look, I'm about to do you the favor of a lifetime. Would you like me to be your sponsor?"

"Really? You'd do that?"

"Yeah, I'll do it, but I'm telling you right now . . . when you sign up with me, you sign up for a good ass kicking. You're only fooling yourself by lying to the group, and if you continue along this path, you'll end up in the Suffolk County morgue. Is that what you want?"

"No, man, I want to pull out of this tailspin, yo. I haven't had a real home in years. I've just been running around from one place to another and not planting any roots."

Ray put his hand on Josh's shoulder. "Good. You've taken a big step. Getting clean is one thing. Staying clean is another."

Josh smiled hopefully. "I really want to stay clean, yo."

"Good. So listen, can you meet me tonight?"

"Tonight?"

"Yes, tonight. I want to give you the ground rules. I'll meet you for coffee."

"Coffee? Can't we—"

"No. No beer. No booze and especially no weed. The door only has to open a hair before you get sucked back through. You don't want a relapse do you?"

Josh didn't answer immediately. "Sure. I'll meet you."

"Great. I'll turn you into a new man." Ray grinned. *Me.*

Chapter Sixteen

"Oh . . . Oh God . . . Ooo. Oh God . . . Oh . . . Oh . . . Oh . . . Oh God . . . Oh yeah, right there. Oh! Oh . . . Yes. Yes. Yes. Yes. Yes. Yes . . . Oh . . . Oh . . . Yes. Yes. Yes . . . Oh . . . Yes. Yes. Yes. Yes. Yes. Yes . . . Oh . . . Oh . . . Oh . . . Oh God. Oh . . . Oh."

"That's' about enough of that." I found the TV remote, which was half covered by the quilt, and pushed the power button. The screen went black.

"Hey, what the hell?" Gus complained. "I love *When Harry Met Sally*. Why'd you—"

I rolled over on top of him. "Quiet, knucklehead. Ma and Max are three sheets to the wind, and I'm ready to tango."

"But that was the best part. You turned it off just as the woman at the other table was about to say—"

I pressed my finger to his lips. "Choose your next words carefully or they may well be your last." Our vacation was long overdue and sorely needed. I was looking forward to our time together with Max and also getting some desperately needed one-on-one time with my husband. I had scored some fancy frilly things at Victoria's Secret before coming out east and gone through the agony of getting waxed. I'm no wimp, but there's absolutely nothing less enjoyable than having some chick from the third world pour molten lava on your lady parts, then rip away the cloth strip along with your first five layers of skin. I swear, if alopecia were contagious, I'd keep a balding lover on the side and have him rub his noggin around down there whenever subterranean grooming was required. Being a woman is a lot of work. I mean the makeup, the hair, and the clothes—all a man has to do is shower and throw on a clean shirt.

I couldn't get the image of the bald guy out of my head. My lips curled upward.

Gus caught me smiling. "What's so funny?" he asked.

"I can't tell you. It would totally kill the mood."

"What mood?"

"Exactly." I kissed him long and hard.

He glanced over at the bedroom door. "Is it—"

"Yes, it's locked. Now pucker up and make me feel like a woman." It was after midnight. "It's your birthday, damn it. Now are you gonna put out or what?"

"You're not going to scream, are you?"

Only if you don't make a damn move! We had gone so long that I read that tawdry novel in the hope of introducing some sorely needed spice back into our love life—not *Fifty Shades of Gray* but the new one, the one about the alcoholic and the ingénue, *Fifty Shades of Grey Goose.*

"My God, what's happened to us? We used to do it in the basement laundry room."

Gus chuckled. "I know. You had the Whirlpool emblem imprinted on your butt for a week."

"That's not the point. We used to go at it like rabbits."

"Sorry. It's just that everything has changed."

"Any regrets?"

"Of course not. It's just that by the time we get to bed at the end of the day we're both exhausted."

I kissed him again. "Don't worry," I whispered. "I'll be quiet. I don't want anyone to hear us either. Can you imagine how embarrassing it would be if Ma heard us doing it?"

"I know. That's why . . . I mean you're usually pretty loud."

"You never complained about it before."

"And I'm not complaining about it now. It's just that . . . well, it's just that I'd never be able to look your mother in the face again."

I heard Max crying. "Oh dear God," I said, expressing disbelief and exasperation. "What are the chances?"

"That's the mother-son connection," Gus explained. "Now that he's christened your hooha, he doesn't want daddy going anywhere near it."

"Are you talking about our son's delivery?" I cackled.

Gus shrugged and made a comical face.

"Ha! That is absolutely the dumbest thing I've ever heard."

"It's a joke."

"Of course it is." Gus put his hands behind his head, and I noticed that his elbows were a little dry. "All that *The Old Man and the Sea* stuff has made your elbows a bit leathery, mate."

"Fishing? Really?" He lifted his arm to check out his elbows, rubbed them, and wrinkled his nose. "Gross."

"There's a bottle of Aveeno in the drawer next to you."

"Aveeno?" He formed a quizzical expression. "Isn't that for women?"

"Honestly?" I mean, Gus was once single. Show me one single guy who doesn't have a bottle of lotion in his bedside drawer. If they put out a lotion named Amber or Tiffany, moisturizer stock would go through the roof. "It's all right, macho man, I promise it won't deplete your level of testosterone. The next time you need to polish the rocket, just take a little extra lotion and hit your elbows. It'll work wonders."

"Wait, are you saying—"

I didn't know how often Gus did a load by hand, but I can't imagine that he found the concept completely foreign. "Really, you don't?"

"I'll have you know that—"

"Quiet."

I held up my hand to silence him because I heard movement in the room next door followed by Ma's voice saying, "Shhh. What's the matter, sweetie?"

We stayed perfectly still for a few moments hoping that silence would return, but Max continued to cry. Ma began to sing a nursery rhyme. I rolled my eyes and dismounted my husband. "Brings new meaning to the expression 'cluster fuck.'"

"Maybe he'll go right back to sleep."

"I don't know. I think he's hungry." I sat up in bed. "So while we're waiting for the gods to smile down upon us, why don't you ask me about my day?"

"You mean your unofficial investigation?"

I nodded.

"And you're not afraid of killing the mood with a conversation like that?"

I rubbed his thigh. "I'm not worried about getting you back in the mood when I'm ready. You're kind of a pushover."

Gus sighed and sat up. "Okay. Shoot."

"I interviewed the engineer who drove the train that hit Alana Moore and the Suffolk County detective who was assigned to the investigation."

"I thought you were more interested in Sarah Fisher, the girl who used to live here."

"I am but the detective who worked her case couldn't see me today. You didn't want me to sit around twiddling my thumbs, did you?"

"Oh, God forbid. So what did you find out?"

"I questioned the engineer. He's had a stroke, but his mind still seems sharp, and he's damn sure of what he saw. He maintains that Alana Moore was pushed in front of his train."

"What do you think?"

"I think he knows what he saw. Unfortunately there were no surveillance cameras, witnesses, or suspects."

"The crime scene unit and forensics didn't come up with anything either?"

"No. I asked the detective to pull the evidence for me to examine only—" I held my hand up suddenly. "I shouldn't be doing this. I had a long talk with Ma while you and Max were out getting groceries, and she convinced me to stop poking my nose where it doesn't belong." I forced a smile. "I'm all yours tomorrow. What do you want to do?" Max's cry became less pervasive. "See? I made Max happy."

Gus frowned at me. "Do you think you could've discussed this with me before you made your decision?"

"Why? I figured you'd be thrilled."

"I'm not thrilled. I'm disappointed."

"I don't get it. You told me—"

"I know what I told you, and I knew you wouldn't listen. Look, I know who you are and what makes you tick, and there's no way I'd ever stop you from doing what you love to do. I know you don't want to turn your back on these cases, so don't."

"But I feel so guilty. I mean I left you and Max the past two days."

"Don't worry about me and my son. This is really the first time I've had him all to myself, and I'm diggin' it. We fished. We played. I chill when he naps. I'm in heaven. In ten days, I'll be back on the job. Who knows when I'll have an opportunity like this again?"

"You're telling me I'm not wanted." I pouted.

"Baby, believe me, you are sorely wanted." He smiled one of his lady-killer smiles. "Right now I want you so badly I could burst. Take a few days. Get it out of your system. Just don't get carried away."

"Jesus, you're a damn good man." I threw my arms around him. "Max, please go back to sleep, please go back to sleep." Max's cry built to a quasi-tantrum level. "Shit. I'd better go—"

Ma knocked on the door. "I'm taking Max down to the kitchen for a bottle," she said in a deliberate tone. "We'll be at least twenty minutes. Wink. Wink. That should be long enough, shouldn't it, Gus? Stomp on the floor if you need more time."

Gus and I roared.

"You're welcome."

I jumped on Gus the moment I heard Ma's footsteps on the stairs.

Chapter Seventeen

Josh stood next to the mailbox at the end of driveway smoking a cigarette while he waited for Ray to arrive. The front of the tired colonial behind him was half-painted fresh cornflower blue from the second story up, and peeling white paint below. A tall, aluminum ladder lay on the ground in front of the house. His cigarette was down to the filter before he heard the sound of a car coming down the road. He flicked the butt away just as a moss green Subaru wagon came into view. Josh waved to Ray as he pulled up and then got into the car.

"Sorry I'm late," Ray said. He pointed to the rear area of the wagon, which was filled with tools and aluminum house trim. "I had to pick up some supplies for a job I'm working on." He was dressed in jeans, a tee shirt, and work boots; the same outfit he wore to the Narcotics Anonymous meeting that morning. "Supposed to be overcast tomorrow. Good day to get some work done."

"Yo, I didn't know you did construction."

"Really? The dirty shirt and work boots weren't a dead giveaway?"

Josh shrugged. "I guess." He pointed to the half-painted house. "I'm painting this place," he said. "I get room and board."

"No money?"

"No."

"So how do you live?"

"I paint the house in the morning and work behind the counter at the bakery in the afternoon. I've got until Labor Day to finish painting the house."

"I see. You know I've wanted to expand my business for a while. Maybe you could work with me when you're done with the house."

Josh smiled. "Wow, that would be cool, yo."

Ray pointed to the cup holder in the center console. "The front one is yours—light and sweet you told me, right?"

Josh nodded, picked up his coffee, and took a gulp. "Yo, that's really sweet."

"Yeah, I know. The guy at the deli put in two heaping spoons of sugar. Too sweet?"

"Don't worry. I'll drink it."

"Good. Fort Pond is just a couple minutes from here. Nice quiet place to talk. Good with you?"

Josh nodded.

Ray put the car into gear and slowly pulled away from the house. The car backfired as it eased down the narrow road and disappeared over the crest of a small hill.

Josh put his coffee back in the cup holder.

"Sorry about the coffee again," Ray said. "The good thing about the deli is that they do everything big: big sandwiches, big portions . . . I guess they only know one way."

"It's fine, yo" Josh insisted as he took a second sip. "I'll finish it when we get to the pond."

"Cool." They continued down the unlit road for a couple of minutes before Ray pulled off 2nd House Road. The pond was in front of them. "There's a clearing just past the tall grass. There's a little jetty we can sit on."

"Yeah, all right."

"Good," Ray said. "Grab your coffee and we'll hang out." Ray led the way, flattening the tall grass with his work boots as he strode through it. Josh followed, stepping on the flattened patches that Ray left in his wake. They were on the jetty in less than a minute. Josh kicked off his sandals and sat on the edge of the jetty with his feet in the water.

"Great idea," Ray said as he tugged on a bootlace. He pulled off his socks and sat down next to Josh with his feet also in the water. "*Ah.* That feels good. I've got blisters the size of walnuts." He picked up his coffee and sipped. "So let's talk. When did you first start using?"

"A long time ago. I was a messed up kid, yo. My folks used to fight all the time. My mom couldn't take it anymore and started dating another guy on the side. My dad found out about it and just about killed her—beat her unconscious and shit. She moved in with her boyfriend after she got out of the hospital, and it made my old man crazy. After that all he did was work and get drunk. I was on my own all the time. I stopped going to school. Life seemed really shitty. I had to steal money out of his wallet just to buy food. One day I used the cash to score some dope." He shrugged. "It's been like that ever since, yo." He picked up his coffee cup and drank.

"I'm sorry your life sucks so bad. At least you're doing the right thing now, going to your meetings and working. One foot in front of the other—you know the drill. You'll get there."

Josh yawned. He looked at the Styrofoam coffee cup. "I don't know why I'm so tired, yo. Coffee usually gets me wired."

"It's decaf. If I drink regular it keeps me up all night. Sorry, man, I got you the same thing."

"No problem."

"So you said that you gave it up a couple of times. What made you go back?"

"I was bored, yo. I was miserable. I became that kid no one wanted to know. You know what I mean? My parents were broken up, and I was high all the time, and when I wasn't, there was no money to do anything. My friends stopped hanging out with me." He yawned again and drank the rest of his coffee.

"That's the piece you're missing. You need a support system. That's what the group is for, only you can't continue to lie to us. You're using again—how long?"

"About a week, but I'm managing it. It's cool, yo, and I can stop anytime I want to." He rubbed his eyes. "Man, I need some sleep. My eyes feel really tired."

Ray examined his eyes. "Are you high right now?"

"No. No way. I swear it."

"I don't know. Your pupils look mighty big. Are you telling me the truth?"

"Totally, yo. It's just that all of a sudden I can't keep my eyes open." He pulled his feet out of the water and put his arms around his knees.

"You need caffeine. I think I've got a can of soda in the car. I'll go look for it—be right back." Ray stood.

"No, man it's okay. I just need to close my eyes for a minute."

Ray shook his head with disappointment. "Wait here." He walked off.

Ten minutes elapsed before Ray returned. Josh was on his side and sound asleep.

"Thank God," Ray said. *I couldn't take another minute of his bullshit tale of woe.* He sat down on the jetty next to Josh and placed his paraphernalia between them. "You'll like this," he said as he rolled up Josh's sleeve and tied a rubber tube around his arm. He took a lighter out his pocket and set it down next to a serving spoon. He emptied three packets of heroin into the spoon and picked up the lighter. It took only a moment for the powder to liquefy and become his chosen instrument of death.

Chapter Eighteen

I opened my eyes and stretched. *That was the best night's sleep I've had in ages.* I felt totally refreshed, like I did when I was very young and didn't have a care in the world. Ah, to be a child again and know true bliss one more time. I guess that's what Max feels like when he opens his sleepy little eyes in the morning.

A light breeze sailed through the window, fragrant with the aroma of dewy, freshly clipped grass. I rolled over on my side and noticed that Gus was still asleep. I watched him for a few minutes, happy with the memory of last night's romance. He'd given me back that feeling I'd so badly missed: the feeling of total satisfaction. We were as one last night, and I can't remember feeling as good or complete in a very long time.

The fragrant morning air was intoxicating. It was like breathing the scent of poppies, and I felt my eyelids grow heavy again. I rolled over on my side and felt my head melting into the pillow. *Max is still quiet—just a few more minutes. Thank you, God.*

I awoke to the sound of buzzing as a mosquito landed on the netting that surrounded my bed. "Where the hell did that come from?" I glanced around and saw that I was no longer in our bedroom but in a large safari tent. I heard stomping on the floor before I could fully take in my surroundings. I clutched my chest and sat up. *Huh?*

Nigel Twain was sitting on the end of the bed wearing an Indiana Jones fedora and lacing up a pair of Alden boots. A sleeve was torn off his unbuttoned safari shirt, and his exposed arm looked like a thick, muscular snake. He stood up and stomped his feet so that the cuffs of his khakis covered the tops of his boots. He turned to face me, eyes blazing, his exposed chest as magnificent as a slab of finely carved onyx.

Twain is the psychiatrist I routinely consult with on my cases. He's a gorgeous, dark, and brooding man with the psychological insights of Sigmund Freud. More than that, he's the embodiment of all that I lust for. He hasn't had as strong a hold on me since I became a mother. Gus performed like an Olympian last night—positively knocked my socks off. I thought that I had it all and needed nothing, yet here Nigel was.

"Nigel. What the hell? Where's Gus? What are you doing here?"

"You know," he said with a sly smile and a swagger in his step as he approached me. "I only come when I'm called for."

"I don't get it. I didn't call anyone."

"*Yes*, you did."

"*No. I didn't!*" I insisted.

"Maybe Stephanie Chalice the mother and wife didn't, but Stephanie Chalice the adventure-seeking suspense junky most definitely did." Twain had a musky British voice that made me quiver from the inside out. "I get it, Love. I really do. Motherhood, vacations at the shore, changing diapers, and warming baby bottles are all wonderful, but there's a part of you that yearns for thrills and mystery. You have a dark side, Stephanie, and you can't appease it with a trip to Toys R Us or knitting a baby blanket. Your lodgings were burnt to the ground. Women are missing. Homicides are going unresolved. It's clawing at you, and you can't fight it."

"I can't?"

"Of course not. That's why you sent for me."

"Oh *yeah*? What do you bring to the party?"

"A physician's mind, a warrior's body, and a penchant for tawdry wrongdoing." He grasped my hand and pulled me off the bed into his arms. "Adventure and intrigue await us."

We were face-to-face and chest-to-chest. I felt myself tingle all over. "I can't go with you. I have a family to take care of."

"They'll be fine until you get back," Twain insisted. "How long can it take to save the world, fifteen, twenty minutes tops?"

"But I'm not dressed to—" Twain snapped his fingers and a strong breeze abruptly sailed through the tent. I gasped when I caught a glance of myself in the mirror. I was wearing a see-through gauze shirt, khaki miniskirt, and knee-high leather boots. For some reason my pseudo-erotic attire didn't shock me. *Something's missing*, I thought, and just like that a bullwhip materialized in my hand. *Oh, that's more like it. I look like Wonder Woman in safari gear.*

"Nigel, you've thought of everything. Let's go. Let's go save the world."

Twain smiled and forged forward. I followed him through the opening in the tent.

A lush tropical rainforest stood before us. Water cascaded from a mountainside and crashed into the flowing river below. Banana trees and vines surrounded us, and the air was filled with the screech of macaws and monkey noises. Just an aside: I love monkeys. I have smiling monkey magnets on our fridge at home and several pairs of monkey PJs. All monkeys are good, even the flying monkeys that served the Wicked Witch of the West—they weren't really bad, just misguided.

"So, Nigel, how exactly is the world imperiled?" I asked.

Nigel snapped a branch beneath his boot. The cracking sound frightened hundreds of small birds that took to flight from the nearby trees, squawking loudly as they filled the sky. He ducked abruptly, just in time to dodge a brown globular mass that went whizzing past his head.

"What the hell was that?" I shouted.

"Monkey poop," Twain said as he broke into a run. "Move quickly."

I picked up speed just as the cute monkey noises became a frenzy of screams. A big wad of monkey dung landed near my feet. I took off running. Within a moment we were safely protected by dense brush. "Why'd they do that?"

"That's what they do."

"No." I insisted. "You must have frightened them."

"Perhaps, but they are monkeys, Stephanie, and they like to throw their shit. Perhaps not a sophisticated repellent but effective—they got rid of us fast enough, didn't they?"

"I'm a friend of the monkey. They must have been really frightened to assault us like that."

"Are you some kind of weirdo monkey advocate or something?"

"I'll have you know that I make a donation to WWF every year."

"The World Wrestling Federation?"

"No, dummy, the World Wildlife Fund. I make a notation on my check that says, 'Screw the big cats. Monkeys are adorable, and this donation is for their conservation only!' The black spider monkey is in danger of becoming an extinct species. They're in deep shit."

"Probably their own."

"Not funny!"

"My apologies. May the black spider monkey go forth and be bountiful. Let's hurry along," Twain said, "We only have about ten minutes left in which to save the world."

"That's not much time. What's the rush?"

"In ten minutes, you'll turn back into a doting wife and mother—in other words, a pumpkin. We'll be forced to scrub the mission."

"Oh. I guess we'd better get moving."

We pushed deeper into the brush. The sky darkened and thunder crackled overhead. Without warning, the sky opened up and drenched us in a soaking rain. I tried to run for cover but the spike heels on my Wonder Woman boots got stuck in the mud.

Twain grabbed my hands and pulled me free. "Careful," he warned, "you never know *whennnn*—" His voice trailed off as the ground beneath his boots gave way and he was washed away in a mudslide.

I felt the mud beneath me begin to move. Those spike heels were truly a godsend—for the moment I was anchored firmly in place. *I've got to rescue Nigel and save the world,* I fretted. I looked down the steep embankment hoping to see him, but he was gone. There was only one thing to do. I pulled my heels out of the mud and let the mudslide wash me away, hoping that God and gravity would take us both to the same place. I slid feet first at high speed, past lush vegetation and jungle critters. I came around a bend and saw a monkey standing on a rock. His arm was cocked, and he was holding a handful of you know what. "No. You wouldn't," I pleaded. It took a moment for the monkey to recognize me. He smiled. Our minds locked for a moment, and we were able to communicate, primate to primate.

"Thanks for the donation to the World Wildlife Federation, Stephanie. I went to a fine restaurant, ordered Bananas Foster, and had enough left over for a Bailey's banana colada." He extended his unencumbered hand and caressed my cheek as I slid by. "Good luck saving the psychiatrist," he said. "I think he's into you."

"Thanks, monkey. You're very intuitive."

"The name's Chet."

"Thanks, Chet," I said as I slid by. The rain intensified. Mud was rushing up my skirt. *I'm going to have to take a long hot bath to clean this stuff out of my lady parts.* I once took a mud bath at a spa—they hosed me down afterward and still couldn't get it all out.

I picked up speed and saw that I was heading for a waterfall. I tried grabbing a vine, but it snapped off in my hand. I turned forward just as I whooshed over the edge.

"*Wheeeeeeeeeee!* This is better than the Big Thunder waterslide." The water rush blasted me out like a bullet and shot me into the air; my arms and legs flailing like an old woman swatting at gnats. I hit the water feet first, which was fortuitous because the water pressure washed all the mud out of my vajayjay.

I hit the surface and wiped the water from my eyes.

Twain was waiting for me on a bluff. His clothes were drying over a fire, and he was wearing skimpy, leopard-skin briefs. He had a martini in his hand and toasted me with his cocktail. "Ready to take the plunge?"

"I just took the plunge. Oh, you mean—"

"That's right. The world is safe, and it's time for the heroes to copulate."

Wait a minute. "Don't you mean *celebrate*?" I asked, hoping to distract him from the other item on his other agenda. "Safe from what? What did we accomplish?"

"Come here and I'll tell you," he said with a sly smile.

I began to trudge out of the water. I was waist deep, and my flimsy shirt was clinging to me like a second skin. *What am I doing? Stay here in the water where you're safe from him.* My intentions were honorable, but my boots were meant for walking. I continued to stride out of the water and closer to . . .

THUD! THUD! THUD! THUD!

I jumped up in bed, drenched in sweat and my heart pounding in my chest.

Gus jumped up as well.

"What the hell is that?" I yelled. I heard Max crying hysterically in the next room.

"Son of a bitch." Gus jumped out of bed and ran to the window. I followed hot on his heels.

Ray was level with our window, high atop a ladder. He was on the top rung with a hammer in one hand and a tree limb to steady himself in the other.

"You've got to be kidding." Gus rushed to throw on some clothes while I ran into the next room to quiet Max. I was mad as hell, but I chuckled despite my anger. Hanging onto the tree branch like that, Ray looked exactly like a monkey.

Chapter Nineteen

"Hi, it's Camryn. How can I help you?"

"Camryn, it's Stephanie Chalice."

"Who?"

"Stephanie Chalice. I'm renting the Fisher house." *Ring a bell, dingbat? I left you three messages. Remember me? You accosted my husband in the restaurant last week. You wanted to kick me to the curb and run off with my family. Still nothing?*

"Oh. Um. Hi, Stephanie. Can you hold a minute?"

Can I hold a minute? "Actually—"

I heard her click off the line. *What a pain in the ass.* I was cruising down Montauk Highway on my way back to the police station and waiting for Camryn's shrill voice to crackle over the speaker. Some jerk cut me off in one of those eyesore G-Class Mercedes SUVs, the ones that only *gazillionaires* can afford and look like the vehicle driven by Field Marshall Rommel while he crossed North Africa during WWII. I was still stewing over Ray's morning wakeup call and the frustration of Camryn's inaccessibility. My road rage had built to a crescendo. *"Asshole!"* I shouted within the safe confines of my truck. How's that for passive-aggressive?

Just then Camryn's voice spewed over the speaker. *"Excuse me."*

"No, not you." *A different asshole.* "Someone just cut me off and I was—"

"Can we make this quick?" she interrupted impatiently. "I'm trying to schedule the closing on a waterfront property. It's worth a hundred K to me in commission, and I can't get the son-of-a-bitch seller's attorney on the phone."

Oh gee, my heart bleeds. "Listen, Camryn, we've got to talk about your brother Ray."

"Why? What's he done?"

"It's what he hasn't done—he hasn't shown us an ounce of common courtesy. I know he needs to complete the trim on the house, but he shows up unexpectedly and begins hammering without giving us a heads-up. He woke up everyone in the house this morning, and it wasn't the first time. He scared the crap out of us."

"Well, just talk to him about it."

"We tried, and he wasn't exactly receptive to compromise. The first time he dashed off, even though we asked him to stick around for a chat, and this morning, he refused to get down off his ladder. I mean, what's the deal with him?"

"Deal? There is no deal. He waited until eight o'clock, didn't he?" she said in a voice devoid of sympathy.

"Camryn, we're on vacation." *You know, rest and relaxation . . . sleeping in?* "If I had known we'd be waking up to a blitzkrieg every morning at dawn, I never would've taken the place."

"As I remember, you didn't have many alternatives. You would've had to go home."

Do you believe the attitude? Now listen, beeatch. "You're missing the point, Camryn. We'll give Ray every opportunity to do his work, but this bullshit show-up-whenever-you-please-policy is over. Am I clear?"

It took a moment for her to reply. "Okay, I'll talk to him, but you'll have to be *ultra* cooperative."

"And so will he!" I clicked off the cell phone and chucked it onto the passenger seat next to a box of Pampers. I know a lot of women who think they're all-powerful, but this babe took the cake. Speaking of which, I had stopped at the bakery and picked up fresh Danish and coffee for my morning meeting with Sullivan Smote, the detective who had investigated Sarah

Fisher's disappearance. I tore off a piece of a blueberry-cheese Danish and stuffed it into my mouth. *Ultra cooperative my ass— who the hell does she think she is anyway?* Max had been hysterical until we got some breakfast into him and I did not plan on going through that again. Gus was so mad at Ray that I thought he would rip the ladder out from under him and pound him into the ground. And Ma . . . well, let's just say she has quite a repertoire of Italian expletives at her disposal.

The desk officer had a huge red nose. He either had a sudden flare up of rosacea or his name was Rudolph. I laughed inwardly remembering his name. It was Randolph. Anyway Randolph, the red-nosed desk officer appeared to remember me from my first visit. "Chalice, right?" he said with a smile.

My breasts were kind of swollen, which meant that I was about a comma and two semicolons away from getting my period. I wasn't sure if Randolph remembered my face, the engorged boobs, or both. I considered either recollection complimentary. "Very good. You remember."

"You here for Pulaski again?"

"No, Detective Sullivan Smote this time. Is he handy?"

A well-tanned, gray-haired man walked through the door just at that moment. He was handsome, fit, and trim like an actor I'd seen playing a physician in a television pharmaceuticals ad. In the ad, the doctor explained how he cured his low testosterone problem with AndroGel and is now as virile as a stud bull. Of course, the disclaimer in that ad stated that women should avoid contact where AndroGel has been applied, and to call a doctor immediately if they grow facial hair or a penis. Not a great selling point. Thank God, Gus has all the testosterone I can handle.

The desk officer called to the slick-looking guy who had just entered the building, "Hey, Sully, your appointment is here."

Slick Sully smiled. His teeth were three shades whiter than freshly driven snow—so white I almost reached for my sunglasses. "Thanks, Randolph," he said.

Smote approached me and got really close, invading-my-personal-space-close. He looked skyward and pressed his palms together as if he were giving thanks. "Thank you, God." I flashed the back of my hand fluttering my wedding band and engagement ring in his face. He took note and then once again peered toward the heavens. "I take it back."

"Detective Smote, I'm—"

He smiled again and then backed a step away. "I know. You're Chalice. I looked you up after we spoke the other day. It's an old habit I've never been able to break. Call me Sully." He looked down at the paper bag I held. "Good to your word—Danish and coffee?"

I nodded.

"See, so it's not a total loss. Follow me."

"*You're* forward."

"Don't mind Sully," Randolph said with a grin. "He's banging out for good at the end of the day."

"You're retiring, Sully?" I asked.

He nodded.

"Congratulations. That certainly explains your forwardness."

"Not really, Chalice," Randolph said. "He's always been a big flirt."

Sully placed his hand on my shoulder and guided me past the front desk. "You're not just wearing the wedding band for effect are you?" he whispered hopefully.

"No such luck."

"Too bad. Let's grab a conference room."

Sully and I made small talk for a few minutes while we drank our coffee. Turned out he was a regular guy when he wasn't on the make. I almost gagged when he told me how much he'd be pulling down each year from his pension. I mean, it really gave me pause—Suffolk County salaries were astronomical compared to NYPD wages. *Maybe Gus and I ought to move out here.* Sully was buying a condo on the water in West Palm Beach, Florida and trading in his Audi for a white Maserati convertible. Not too shabby. I mean the guy was obviously a ladies' man. I could almost picture this silver-haired *playuh* tooling down Clematis Street, West Palm Beach, in his Maserati convertible with a silk scarf flapping in the breeze.

"A big time chick magnet like you—you'll be up to your armpits in widows and divorcées," I said.

"I certainly hope so. Although . . . I'm not exactly interested in women my own age."

Gee, really? "Just make sure they're of consenting age, Sully. I'd hate to see you brought up on statutory rape charges."

He smiled. "Don't worry about me. I'm pretty careful. So what's your interest in Sarah Fisher?" he asked.

"My husband and I are renting the house she used to live in. It creeped me out to hear about her disappearance—I'm just curious. What do you think happened?"

Sully shrugged. "I think she was a victim of foul play," he said most matter-of-factly. "I think she was a naïve East End kid who got sucked in by some city slickster. It's an ongoing investigation, but there haven't been any new developments in over six months. Her apartment in the city had been cleaned out, no forwarding address, stopped showing up for work . . ."

"She just vanished into thin air?"

"No. I think she's either dead or being held captive somewhere. She had about two thousand dollars in her checking account that was cleaned out in five separate ATM withdrawals."

"What about the security cameras at the ATMs?"

"That's the weird part. The woman in the security photos kind of looks like her."

"Like her but *not* her?"

"Even her parents couldn't tell us for sure. She was wearing large sunglasses in the security photos."

"Large sunglasses? Like Jackie O?"

"Exactly like that."

"She wore them each time she withdrew cash?"

"Yeah."

"Seems weird. I know some kids have their sunglasses permanently glued to their heads but still … Did her parents offer any insights?"

"No. They had absolutely no idea about what happened to her. That poor couple … Sarah's disappearance completely destroyed them. Sarah's mother died, and her father went off the deep end." Sully crossed himself. "God rest their souls."

"God rest *her* soul. He's not dead."

"Not that I know of, but the last time I saw him he was practically incoherent. I hope he's not suffering like that anymore."

"When was that?"

"Late last year. He was forced out when the bank took their house. I haven't heard from him since. Maybe that's why I never married and had kids of my own. I never wanted to worry about a family. You know what it's like being on the job. Cops see the world differently, as if there's a scumbag lurking around every corner. People think it's safe out here in suburbia, but let me tell you, *it's not.* Suffolk County monsters are every bit as sick as the depraved bastards you come across in the city. There are areas out here I wouldn't go into without a gun."

Sully opened a folder and showed me photographs of Sarah Fisher and her family. Sarah had a round face with green-gray eyes, shoulder-length blond hair, and a cute button nose.

"What was she like?" I asked.

"Her folks and friends described her as a happy kid. She was on her high school and college track teams. She had a few close friends out here, and no one could think of anyone who might do her harm. She'd just started meeting friends in the city, mostly from her job. Apparently she hadn't lived in the city long enough to build very many relationships. We checked out her phone records, e-mail, Facebook and Twitter accounts … nothing! No suspects. I interviewed everyone I thought might know what happened and came up empty. In all my years on the force, I never investigated a case with so little to go on."

Sarah was nestled between her parents in a photo. She looked just like her mother. You could look at her mother and fast forward to what Sarah would look like when she got older. Her father, now that was another story. He didn't look anything like Sarah. He was shorter than his wife and daughter—much, much shorter.

Smote must've seen the look of shock on my face as I stared at the photo. The differential in height was alarming. "You're surprised at how short her father is?" he asked.

"Yes."

"I don't think he's much more than four and half feet tall. He's a midget."

Whoa. Did he just use the M word? First of all four-and-a-half-feet "tall" is short, but that doesn't make someone a midget. Among little people, the word *midget* is considered a hate word and is viewed much in the same way that the African-American community despises the N word. Okay, maybe that's a little strong. I mean little people were not enslaved for hundreds of years like the Africans were, not unless you count that time they worked their fingers to the bone for Willie Wonka in that sweatshop chocolate factory of his. I thought for a moment and remembered reading that normal-size people can have little children and that little people can have normal-size kids. The cause is most often genetic, but it's not always passed from parent to child. "*Ixnay* on the *idgetmay*," I said.

"What are you talking about?"

"It's not cool to use the word *midget*. It's considered hateful."

"Sorry. I didn't know that."

"Most of us are not little-people sensitive. Keep it in mind. It may come in handy if you run across a tiny little cutie when you're down in West Palm Beach."

Sully rolled his eyes. "Fat chance. Anything else I can tell you? I have to turn over my files and get ready for my send-off party."

"Sounds like a busy day."

"Don't get wise, Chalice," he smirked. "What else?"

"Any chance of me getting a copy of your case file?"

"You'll have to fill out an official request, but I'm pretty sure I can get it approved. I'll make the copies myself."

"Thanks. That's sweet."

"Sweet am I? So tell me, where do you stand on the subject of marital fidelity?"

I scowled at him. "I'll tell ya where I stand ... right next to my husband."

Chapter Twenty

Max's headgear tipped me off as to the identity of our visitor. He was sitting in his high chair, wearing a shiny, red fire helmet. The Montauk fire chief's car was parked in the driveway, and I heard Richard Tate's booming laugh before I saw him sitting at the kitchen table with Ma and Gus. I caught the tail end of a joke. Tate's punch line mentioned something about the placement of a baked potato within a body orifice. It sounded pretty funny, and I'd make him repeat it before he left.

"Nice way to talk in front of an infant," I said, laying on the guilt trip. Everyone turned toward Max, the innocent victim. He was smiling and rocking back and forth, looking very much like a fireman bobblehead.

Ma was still laughing and clutching her stomach. "Oh Christ, I'm gonna pee myself."

That notorious jug of wine was more than half empty, and her wineglass was about half full. "I'm glad I left my son in the company of three so responsible adults."

Gus stood and kissed me hello. "I'm not drinking," he said, "and Max just ate." Telltale traces of dried baby food on Max's chin corroborated my husband's testimony.

Ma waved her hand dismissively, "*Bah.*" It was her lighthearted way of saying *piss off*. "The little man is fine and you've got a guest—stop being such an old stick in the mud." Translation: you're a pain in the ass. "Getting your period?" she whispered in front of Gus and Tate.

I mean, Jesus Christ, can she possibly embarrass me anymore?

I once read that in certain cultures women are sent to menstrual huts during their time of the month, in essence segregated from the rest of the tribe. I used to think it was a barbaric custom, but now, in light of Ma's unintentional but highly embarrassing comment, maybe it was not such a bad idea after all. *Hasta la vista, baby, I'll see you in a week.*

"Come here, Beautiful." Tate engulfed me in his huge arms. He was a good hug-giver, one of the best. I mean the guy was the size of a bear and looked like Brian Dennehy when he smiled. He planted a huge exaggerated smooch on my cheek.

I chuckled. The spell was broken, and I was once again my normal nutty self. It was as if a switch had been flipped.

Gus poured me a glass of wine. "Take a load off, Detective. Set a spell."

I narrowed my eyes at him and mouthed, "Ballbuster." Ah, there's no place like home ... or a recently remodeled vacation rental. I walked around the table and scooped my son up in my arms. "They're all jerks," I said in a babyish voice. I put my lips on his neck and gave him a big whoopee-cushion-sounding raspberry.

Max giggled.

"Yes they are. Yes they are. Why are you hanging around with such silly people? You've got to be careful of the company you keep. "

"Look at the expression on his face," Ma cooed. "There's nothing like a child's love for his mother."

Max laughed hysterically, and then his expression changed on a dime. He made the face that begs the age-old question asked by infants all over the world: "What's going on down there in my diaper?" His lips twisted, and his eyes bulged. The air became fragrant with the scent of Max's ... accomplishment.

Ma wrinkled her nose and then reached out for him.

"You don't mind?" I asked.

Ma shook her head and left the room with Max in tow.

Gus fanned the air in front of his face and crossed his eyes. He looked as if he was suffocating.

"Funny," I said. "He's like his daddy in so many ways."

"Hey!" Gus shouted in a jovial manner. "I don't crap myself."

"No, but your butt bombs are the stuff of legends. If you were around for WWII, you would've sent thousands of frightened civilians scrambling for the air raid shelters." I turned to Tate. "Some of Gus' Crack Rattler Missiles have been banned by NATO."

Tate roared. "You lucky bastard," he said sarcastically and slapped Gus on the back. He slowly settled down and pulled a file from his briefcase. "Here you go, lady cop." He slid a file across the table to me. "Coroner's report on Bill Alden."

My eyes lit up as I reached for the folder.

"Look how excited she is," Gus said. "You'd think she just jumped out of an airplane."

I scowled at Gus. "You want to go tit for tat, Bombardier Lido?"

Gus flashed his palms to signal his surrender. "I'm no martyr. I give."

I flipped open the report and jumped down to the bottom of the page.

FINAL DIAGNOSIS: *Asphyxiation due to: A. Inhalation of smoke with presence of carbon deposits in trachea and proximal left bronchi. B. Inhalation of carbon monoxide.*

Huh? I expected more. "Smoke inhalation? That's it?" I looked up at Tate before I continued to read and could see from his expression that I'd missed something. I went back to the top of the page and began reading the report line by line. The body's general description: sex, approximate height and weight, blah, blah, blah. It mentioned the condition of the body at the time the autopsy was performed. A forensic odontologist, who studied the victim's teeth and matched them to dental records, made a positive identification. *What am I looking for?* And then I saw something that made my eyes open wide. I looked up at Tate. He was grinning.

Toxicology Screen: *Positive for cyanide*

Blood Drug Screen: *Positive for cyanide*

Bill Alden had been murdered.

Chapter Twenty-One

"Not necessarily."

"What do you mean, not necessarily?" I asked in bewilderment. Tate and I were shoulder to shoulder, striding down the corridor toward the office of Dr. Perry Hodgkin, the physician who had signed Bill Alden's autopsy report.

Tate rolled his eyes. "The presence of cyanide does not mean that Bill Alden was poisoned. Smoldering materials give off hydrogen cyanide during a fire and afterward. The recliner Alden was found in was upholstered with acrylic fabric—there's your culprit. Nitrogen from the burning fabric combined with hydrogen and carbon to produce hydrogen cyanide. You said yourself that the chair smelled like roasted nuts."

Something clicked in my head, and I remembered a fact from a college level forensics class I had taken. Cyanide can smell like bitter almonds. The big issue, forensically speaking, is that half the population is unable to detect the odor. I guess I'm lucky enough to have gotten the nut-smelling gene. "Did I ever tell you about my sixth sense?"

"No but Gus did. He said you're some kind of crime-investigating witch. He says you can feel it in your bones. Funny, you don't look like a witch."

"You don't have to look like a witch to be one. Now put more stock in my theories or I'll turn you into a newt."

"Oh geez, a newt. That's disgusting. They're slimy and green. Can't you turn me into a stallion?"

"Well, that would hardly be humiliating or witchy. A stallion is a noble animal."

"Well, I'm just thinking, I'm past the age where I'd have to race. I mean, I'm not interested in running twelve furlongs while getting whipped by some child-sized jockey. I'd be more of a stud horse."

Christ, has a man been born who doesn't think with his wiener? "You'd like that, wouldn't you?"

"You know it. I'd be down in Kentucky munching on blue grass, getting groomed, and banging mares left and right."

"Guess again, Romeo. Do you know how long horse coitus lasts?"

"Nah."

"About twenty seconds."

"Really? That's it?"

"That's it, stud. Foreplay and seduction are reserved for humans exclusively. Is that a problem for you?"

"Hell, yes. I've never gone that long before."

I laughed so hard that I snorted. Someone passing us in the hallway gave me one of those stink-eye, what's-your-problem looks. "You're nuts, Tate."

"What do you expect? You just burst my bubble." His eyes brightened after a moment. It looked as if he had come up with a revelation. "Hey, how about oral? Do horses—"

"Only if they batter-coat their johnsons with oats. Where is this conversation going anyway?"

"You were about to turn me into a newt."

"Yup, newt it is—green with black spots . . . or maybe orange with brown spots. I can't make up my mind. Right after we talk to the coroner, though . . . I left my cauldron and potions in the car."

~~~

Dr. Perry Hodgkin looked up from his computer screen when we entered the morgue. I was immediately struck by the minute size of his bald cranium. I guess you don't have to have a big head to have big brains.

Tate extended his hand. "Dr. Hodgkin, I'm Richard Tate, the Montauk fire chief."

Hodgkin had a warm and engaging smile. "Right. We spoke on the phone."

"This is Detective Stephanie Chalice with the New York City Police Department," Tate continued. "She's here in an unofficial capacity. I hope you don't mind."

"Not at all," Hodgkin said. "I've been staring at pale flesh and fried gray matter all morning. I have no complaints about a visit from a beautiful young woman." Hodgkin had that doe-eyed innocent look about him.

We shook hands, and I felt as if I blushed a little bit. I guess a woman never grows tired of receiving compliments. Since Max's arrival, my life had consisted almost exclusively of mommy duty and work. I'm exhausted most of the time and haven't exactly felt pretty. "Thanks, Dr. Hodgkin. Nice of you to let me tag along for the ride. So what's this about fried gray matter?"

"Oh, would you like to see?" Hodgkin said with delight. He took me by the arm and led me toward one of the autopsy tables. Tate followed reluctantly. "I'm so glad that you're interested. This is one of the most unusual fatalities I've ever come across."

I've spent plenty of time in the morgue and don't usually get weak in the knees, but the cadaver in front of me was a whole other story. A woman's body was lying on the table and the top half of her skull had been removed. She was brainless, and I'm talking literally here. The brain cavity was completely empty, and her sectioned brain was lying on a tray next to her. The image was truly abhorrent, and I really didn't want to see or hear anymore about it, but Hodgkin was so excited ... I just didn't know how to cut him off.

"I said fried gray matter, but it's really the white matter that got fried. This woman was found on the beach after a storm." He touched the very top of his bald head. "She was struck by lightning dead center on the top of her head. The corpus callosum was fried, and the left and right hemispheres of her brain were unable to communicate with each other."

"What's the corpus callosum?" Tate asked.

"It's the bundle of neural fibers that connects the two hemispheres of the brain."

"Sounds like a godawful way for someone to die," I said. "The poor woman."

"Oh, that's not what killed her," Hodgkin said. His eyes were gleaming as he prepared to enlighten us. I guess he doesn't get a chance to talk much what with all his patients being dead and all. It looked like he had just gotten a new lease on life. "You can live with the two hemispheres separated. In fact, corpus callosotomies have been successfully performed for decades as a way of controlling brain seizures."

"Like in epilepsy?" I asked.

Hodgkin's eyes gleamed at least twice as brightly as they did before. "Very good," he said.

"So what killed her?" Tate asked making little effort to conceal the fact that he was bored to tears.

Hodgkin seemed disappointed about having to cut to the chase. It appeared as if he was prepared and happy to drone on about severed brains, half-wits, and what have you for as long as we could stand it. "This did," he said as he pointed to a ruptured blood vessel. "Cerebral aneurism."

"The lightning caused the aneurism?" I asked.

"Oh no. It was probably already there, but the lightning strike most likely caused her blood pressure to spike, and this aneurism on her anterior communicating artery blew." He snapped his fingers. "Burst like a balloon."

"Burst like a balloon," I repeated. I had to find a segue from the woman with the blown brain to Bill Alden's autopsy before our pedantic friend talked us into a coma. I took hold of his arm and looked into his eyes attentively. "That's brilliant. I'll bet you've made some incredible discoveries about Bill Alden's death as well."

Tate rolled his eyes and mouthed, *Thank you*.

The doe-eyed doctor had a deer-caught-in-the-headlights expression on his face. It took a moment for him to switch gears. "Oh yes, that's what you're here about, isn't it?"

"That's right," Tate said. Translation: *can we please get on with this already?*

Hodgkin walked over to the computer. "Let's see if he's still here." I watched him poke the keys on the keyboard. "Still waiting for pickup." He walked over to the morgue refrigerator and opened one of the compartments. I was surprised to see that the soles of Alden's feet were unburned. The requisite toe tag, known in the trade as a U.F. 95, hung from the big toe on the right foot. Hodgkin checked the tag. "This is him," he said as he slid the cadaver out of the refrigerator. Alden looked like the first pot roast I had ever attempted. That's not true—he looked far, far worse. I almost wanted to go back and look at the woman who took a lightning bolt to the head.

"Not much to talk about," Hodgkin said.

I was disappointed.

Tate looked relieved—it was pretty obvious that he wanted to be somewhere else, anywhere else. "The detective read the autopsy report and was concerned by the presence of cyanide in the blood and tissue of the victim," Tate said. "I told her that cyanide is a pretty common finding in a burn victim's autopsy."

"Yes, common," Hodgkin said, "but not conclusive."

"So could he have been murdered prior to the fire?" I asked.

"No way, José." Hodgkin seemed pleased by his ham-fisted attempt at being hip. "He died in the fire. He was breathing when he expired as evidenced by the presence of carbon in his bronchial tubes. Elevated levels of carboxyhemoglobin in the blood are consistent with hypoxia from carbon monoxide inhalation.

"Couldn't he have ingested the cyanide?"

"No." Hodgkin said flatly. "The victim was not poisoned, Detective. I found no evidence of cyanide in the stomach contents, and the stomach lining was undamaged despite the high content of corned beef and cabbage." He peaked his eyebrows in anticipation of a laugh. None was forthcoming. Okay, I chuckled a little but just so his feelings wouldn't be hurt. He continued, "If the stomach lining had been damaged from cyanide ingestion, it would have presented with a blackened, eroded surface and there would've been altered bloodstaining of the striped mucosa because of the strongly alkaline nature of the hydrolyzed sodium or potassium salts found in cyanide. There was only evidence of cyanide poisoning in the lungs. The hydrocyanic acid levels in the lungs were off the charts. The only surprise I encountered in the autopsy was that the liver was implicated as well."

"Meaning?"

Hodgkin shrugged. "I'm not sure."

"You're not sure?" It seemed inconsistent to me that a man like Hodgkin would be unsure of anything as it related to forensic medicine.

"That's right, I'm not sure. There was no evidence of cyanide in the digestive tract so the level of cyanide in the liver should have been minimal, but it wasn't."

"Kind of leaves the door open, doesn't it, Doctor? I usually have a pretty good sixth sense about these things and—"

"A premonition, Detective?" Hodgkin interrupted. "You've got a feeling in your gut?"

Talking down your nose, are we? "I've got a strong premonition, Doctor. Sometimes a gut feeling is all a detective has to go on. Mine are usually pretty good."

"I'm not doubting your sleuthing skills, Detective, but I'm a man of science," Hodgkin said. "I don't believe in hunches—the evidence speaks, and I listen. Facts, findings, data ... that's all there is."

"Chalice, you're looking for something that's not there," Tate said. "Alden burned with the house, and that's that."

I admit that the coroner's argument seemed pretty strong, but I was still not convinced. My sixth sense told me there was more to this than met Dr. Hodgkin's learned eye, and I was a long way from giving up.

Chapter Twenty-Two

"Hey, babe," my beloved's voice crackled over the car speaker. "On your way back?"

"Yeah," I said solemnly. "I just left the morgue."

"You sound chipper," he said sarcastically. "What's the matter, the ME didn't buy your murder theory?"

"He did not."

"Well then, he's a damn fool. Doesn't he know that you're absolutely infallible?"

"I told him all about it."

"And?"

"And nothing. The nerve of that man—doesn't he know *who I am*?"

"So he knows about your extraordinary talents, and yet he stands by his forensic findings? The fool! I'd have him brought up on charges."

"What charges?"

"Insubordination."

"Insubordination?" Hodgkin was perhaps a tad insecure but definitely not insubordinate. "I don't think so. Try again."

"Felonious mopery."

"There's no such thing."

"Yes, there is."

"You're right. There is. It's an oxymoron. Want to go for one last try?"

"How about aggravated infuriation. It's in the penal code right after aggravated assault."

"And right before aggravated spouse." Gus was trying to lift my spirits, and I loved him for it. "Thanks for being supportive," I said. "You'll get special sex tonight."

"Sex with you is always special."

Aw, isn't that sweet? "Stop being such a brownnoser. I need direction, not a yes-man."

"Just proceed in your usual headstrong, bull-in-a-china-shop way. It's never failed you before."

Gus laughed. I heard Ma join in. "Hey! What's going on over there?"

"I was making a joke . . . but it's *true*," Gus said in mid-blurt.

"And my mother finds this funny too? I'm glad I could be the butt of your joke." The famous rant from *Goodfellas* came to mind. "You think I'm funny?" I said as if I were Joe Pesci.

Gus and Ma were hysterical, gasping-for-air hysterical. I think maybe they had been hitting the *vino* . . . or maybe I just caught them in a silly mood.

"Yes," Gus cackled.

I continued in Joe Pesci's voice, "I'm funny how? I mean funny like I'm a clown? I amuse you? I make you laugh?"

"I can't breathe," I heard Ma say in the background. "I'm gonna wet myself."

I heard Max giggle loudly. *My son too? Great, now my humiliation is complete.* I guess laughter is contagious. "Okay, boys and girls, take a deep breath. Settle down . . ."

Gus hacked out one last guffaw. "I'm sorry, hon. Christ, I've got tears in my eyes."

"Stephanie," Ma began and then stopped. It took a moment for her to control her laughter. "Can you pick up some fresh Italian bread on your way home? I thought I'd fry up an eggplant and serve it with marinara sauce and angel hair."

"Oh my God, I'm drooling already." Ma slices eggplant paper-thin and fries it in olive oil—a little salt and it's out-of-this-world good. We had stopped at a pork store nearby that had some great-looking Italian delicacies. I was suddenly in the mood for fresh mozzarella. Fortunately the directions were still stored in my GPS, so I plotted a course.

We all know it's a mistake to food shop when you're hungry, but I'm hungry most of the time so it leaves me little choice. I walked into Vito's Pork Store and was immediately hit with the aroma of imported cheeses and cured meats. I looked at all the scrumptious food with wide eyes. My stomach began to rumble, and I knew that I was not going to get out of there cheap.

The man I presumed to be Vito was standing behind the counter talking with a customer. He smiled and waved hello as I picked up a shopping basket and headed over to the bakery section.

The man he was speaking with had roving eyes. I knew this because he had his eyes on my buns while I reached for a heavily seeded semolina bread. He whispered something to the owner. I couldn't hear exactly what he said but the words "hit that" made their way to my ears. I shot him a nasty stare, hoping to shut him up at least until I was out of the store. It was a pork store after all, and I guess there were pigs on both sides of the counter. I bet he'd be really good at sniffing out truffles.

"Hey, Vito, where's that sexy counter girl you hired? She around?" the pig asked.

"Angela? She's in the back?"

"Why's she in the back where I can't see her?"

"I don't know, Tom," Vito said as he rolled his eyes. "Maybe she likes it in the back."

Oh no, he didn't just say what I thought he said, did he?

"Yeah, that's what I heard." Tom laughed heartily. He was a definite truffle-sniffer, maybe morels too. Oink. Oink.

I saw an incredible-looking Stromboli that made my mouth water.

Anorexic Stephanie sitting on my right shoulder said, "Walk away."

Chubby Stephanie sitting on my left shoulder said, "Buy it."

Anorexic Stephanie: "Walk away."

Chubby Stephanie: "Buy it."

Anorexic Stephanie: "Walk away!"

Chubby Stephanie: "Buy it!"

It was a good thing I wasn't carrying a calorie counter.

Anorexic Stephanie: "You'll be sorry."

Chubby Stephanie: "Live a little."

Anorexic Stephanie: "Think about your figure."

Chubby Stephanie: "Think about the pleasure."

Such conflict: temptation and conscience were waging a war in my head.

Chubby Stephanie: "It'll make you feel better."

Anorexic Stephanie: "It's a gateway food."

A gateway food?

Anorexic Stephanie: "That's right; first it's Stromboli, and then it's ice cream and cheesecake. Before you know it, you're at the mall shopping for Spanx and stretch pants."

Chubby Stephanie: "You'll go up a cup size."

Anorexic Stephanie: *"Cellulite!"*

Hot damn! Cellulite? Really? That's how you want to roll? You're throwing down the C card? Why didn't you just cry out 'leprosy'?

I reluctantly walked away without the scrumptious meat and cheese concoction. Chubby Stephanie vanished in a puff of smoke. Anorexic Stephanie smiled. Then she put her finger down her throat and heaved. *She's such a manipulative little bitch and yes, a wee bit bulimic.*

The fresh mozzarella was still warm. I picked up the biggest one I could find and added it to my basket. I'd buy some thinly sliced prosciutto if it wasn't a million dollars a pound.

I was on my way to the counter when I heard Tom the Voyeur ask Vito, "Has that cute blond thing been coming by?"

"Who, Tom? You talking about Kaley again?" Vito asked.

My ears perked up. *Kaley? My Kaley? Sweet little churchgoing, feed-the-homeless Kaley?*

"I think so," Tom replied. "I'm not sure about her name, but that ass of hers is like a Picasso. It's to die for."

Did he say Picasso? Is he familiar with Picasso's art? Has he seen Guernica? *Is he even remotely familiar with cubist technique? That painting doesn't resemble any shapely butt I've ever seen. I'd give Kaley's derrière far more credit than that.*

"I haven't seen her this week," Vito said. "You heard about Bill Alden, didn't you?"

Tom nodded. "Yeah. I heard his house went up in flames."

"It's worse than that," Vito continued. "I heard he burned with the house."

Tom squirmed. "Oh that's nasty. He wasn't a well man, was he?"

"Far from it," Vito said. "He had so many issues, I couldn't keep tract."

"That's too bad," Tom said, "But how'd we go from a conversation about a piece of ass to a burnt-up, decrepit geezer?"

"She used to shop for him, stupid. That's why she was in here so much. You think that tiny little girl was wolfing down all that capicola and provolone by herself?" He rolled his eyes. "*Imbecille,*" he said in the Italian dialect. He redirected his attention toward me as I approached the counter. "Ah, *Senora,* did you find everything you were looking for? I'm surprised you put down the Stromboli. I make them myself."

"I was drooling over it, but I don't want to get fat."

"You're making a big mistake," Tom said with a huge, shit-eating grin. "Vito's Stromboli is to die for."

To die for? Oh, you mean like Kaley's ass? "It was a tough decision, but ultimately my conscience won out." I turned back to Vito. "Everything in here looks so incredible." A basket of the biggest, juiciest looking apples I had ever seen sat in front of the counter. "Are apples in season?"

"They are in Chile," Vito said. "They're Jonagold, sweet as sugar."

I had to have some of those big mothers. "Jonagold? They look more like Jonah Hill before he began to watch what he ate."

Vito laughed.

"I'll take six. How much is the prosciutto?"

"Parma or domestic?" Vito asked.

"Parma."

"You want the best. I have Prosciutto di Parma Ferrari, $29.95 a pound. Aged fifteen months." He put the five fingertips together just as my mother often did. *"Delicioso."*

He's not kidding about the Ferrari part—at that price he ought to throw in an Italian sports car. $29.95? Oh what the hell. "All right, I'll take a quarter pound."

"You'll love it," Vito said. "I'll slice it like tissue paper." He unwrapped the cured meat and placed it on the slicer. He handed me a slice that was as thin as the lace on a wedding veil, so thin it was translucent. "How's that?" he asked.

I popped it into my mouth. The flavor was so intense that my mouth began to water and my eyes rolled around in their sockets. *"Oh God,* that's *so* good."

"Perfecto," Vito said as he turned back to the slicer. "Quarter pound, right?"

The prosciutto was really good; I mean a-girl's-first-kiss kind of good. "Make it a half. So Kaley comes in here?" I asked, jumping subjects without an appropriate segue.

"You a friend of hers?" Vito asked in a guarded tone.

"You and Kaley are friends?" Tom asked excitedly, hoping, I guessed, that we were partners in a call-girl tag team."

"More of an acquaintance," I said. "Her house is right next to the one I'm renting. She stopped by to introduce herself."

Vito nodded, indicating that he was satisfied with my explanation. "Nice girl that Kaley. She used to shop for ... You heard me mention Bill Alden, no?"

I nodded.

"Tragic. Did you know him?" Vito asked.

"Yes I heard about the fire, but no, I didn't know him personally," I said as I checked out the pignoli cookies in the display case. "We were supposed to rent *his* place. We arrived while they were putting out the fire."

"You're lucky you found another place to stay," Vito said as he pushed the slicer back and forth. "This is the busiest the town has ever been. Where'd you end up staying?"

"We bumped into a realtor who just finished remodeling—"

"The Fisher's place?" Vito's eyes grew wide. "More tragedy. Your luck isn't very good. You do know about—"

"Sarah Fisher? Yeah. Kaley told us all about her. Doesn't exactly give me a warm and fuzzy feeling. I hope the place isn't haunted."

Vito chuckled. "Haunted? No it's not haunted, not unless you mean by that *fessacchione,*" he swore. There's no good English translation for that word but *asshole* pretty much sums it up. Vito turned to Tom. *"Come si chiama?"*

Tom shrugged.

"What's his name?" he implored. "Camryn's idiot brother?"

"Oh, you mean Ray?" Tom said.

Yes, Ray. Of course he meant Ray. I knew what Vito was driving at way before Tom spit it out of his slop-licking mouth. I said, "Yeah, I've met him. A real charmer he is. He's doing the trim work on the house and shows up without warning, pounding his hammer and scaring the crap out of all of us."

"Something's wrong with him, but I'll be damned if I know what it is," Tom said. "I think someone hit him on the head ... with a brick."

Okay, I didn't like Tom but I absolutely detested Ray so I laughed at his expense.

"How long had Kaley been shopping for Alden?" I asked.

"You know," Vito said, "you're starting to sound less like a friend and more like a cop."

"Can't help myself, I guess. I'm on the job in New York City. Right now, though, I'm strictly on vacation."

"You're a cop?" Tom asked as he extended his hands, pretending that he was willingly submitting to be handcuffed. "Arrest me. I'll go quietly."

"Sorry, I've got no jurisdiction out here." *Translation: God you're icky. Please go away.*

Tom pretended to pout.

I ignored him and turned back to Vito. "So how long had Kaley been picking up groceries for Bill Alden?"

"Several months," Vito replied, shrugging to inform me that he was only supplying a rough estimate. "She'd stop by every few days and pick up his groceries, his beer, and his cigarettes. The old guy smoked like a chimney, used to go through a carton of Camels every week." He wrapped up the prosciutto and put it in a plastic bag. "Anything else?"

"I'll take some of these," I said tapping the glass display case above the pignoli cookies. "Don't tell me you bake these too."

"No. I don't bake. I let the Keebler elves do it," Vito replied with a chuckle. He bagged my order and rang up the sale.

Tom said, "Come back soon." I could feel his eyes on me as I walked out of the store. It seemed that I was destined to make new friends every day. As I walked through the parking lot to my SUV, I heard the wail of sirens and saw an ambulance speed by. A volunteer fireman followed it. "Ha," I said as I got into my car. "This looks like fun."

Chapter Twenty-Three

I saw the fire chief's car streak by, lights on and siren blaring. I recognized Rich Tate's profile for a split second as he shot past me, racing east on Montauk Highway, traffic pulling to the side to let him through. He was followed by a short convoy of volunteer firefighters with flashing blue fireballs on the dashboards of their cars. I dropped in behind the convoy and followed.

The thinnest sliver of orange was just visible beyond the horizon as the sun lowered behind it. It was that time of day when the sky is split horizontally, the top half bright and the bottom half dark. As we got closer, it was not difficult to distinguish the fire burning just off to the north. I followed the convoy around a turn. An old green wagon was burning just ahead of us.

I rolled to a stop about a hundred feet behind the fire responders' vehicles. The passenger compartment was ablaze with bright, orange flames that reached skyward. Black smoke filled the sky. Just as I reached for the door handle, the ground shook. I looked up and saw that the wagon had exploded. Fragments of the car's exterior were propelled into the sky. It took a moment for the airborne debris to plummet to the ground, and then the firemen moved in, blasting the burning vehicle with water from their fire hose.

I moved in closer after the fire had been extinguished. Clouds of smoke continued to billow from the engine and passenger compartments, but the car body itself was now visible as firefighters worked to open the driver's door and free the person who apparently had been trapped behind the wheel. It dawned on me that I had seen a similar truck just recently, an old, moss-green Subaru with white last-generation New York State license plates.

Even as the firemen continuously doused it with water, the smoldering automobile continued to throw off an immense amount of heat. I heard a loud creak as the driver's door was ripped off the frame. I shut my eyes when I saw the remains of a man in the front seat. In the next instant, a fireman blocked my view as he leaned into the car to check the driver's vital signs. He turned back to Richard Tate and shook his head. They were too late.

Chapter Twenty-Four

Someone had been completely incinerated in the driver's seat, and although it was impossible to make a visual identification, I had a very strong suspicion who the fire had claimed. A Suffolk County police officer approached Tate and handed him a printout. I'd only seen a couple of cars go up the way this one had. I was sure the police officer had run the plate and identified the registered owner. Tate studied the printout and then exhaled wearily as he looked toward the sky. I walked over to him to check out my theory.

"Chalice? What in God's name are you doing here? Don't tell me you're monitoring the emergency frequencies."

"Not likely. I was pulling out of Vito's parking lot when I saw you racing by like all hell had broken loose. I figured I'd tag along."

"Still, shouldn't you be home mothering your baby and spooning with Gus? You've got a strange way of vacationing, girl."

Spooning? Did he really say spooning? Forget that. Did he just call me girl? "Who expired?"

"So you really just want to get right to it, don't you? Gus told me you eat, sleep, and drink the job, but I had no idea."

"Well, who expired? I've got a feeling it was that infuriating handyman who scared the crap out of us the morning of Gus' birthday."

"If you're asking who the car is registered to, it's registered to Camryn Claymore. Other than that the only thing that's expired is the warranty on my coffeemaker."

"Cute. Any idea what caused the fire?"

"Chalice, you pulled up right behind me—did you see me perform an investigation?

"No. You just struck me as being omnipotent."

Tate gave me a peculiar look. "Omnipotent? You mean like Odin, the Norse God?"

"Exactly right, Odin the Allfather, ruler of Asgard." *And his hunky son, Thor. I mean is Chris Hemsworth delicious or what?*

"It's usually a fuel system leak."

"How will you know if it's arson?"

"Arson?" Tate shook his head with despair. "Again you're starting with your murder theory shit?" I could see that Tate was in no mood to entertain a homicide query. "I'm busy, Chalice, now unless you're inviting me for more of Ma's fabulous cooking . . ."

"All right, all right, I'll go." I started to back away. I was going to ask him one more question, but there was no need. I already knew the answer. Vehicular arson is almost impossible to prove especially if the fire originates in the engine compartment. I glanced over at the toasted Subaru. It looked as if it had been hit with a bunker buster missile. Charnoff, Tate's investigator, was going to have to work double time if he was going to figure this one out.

Chapter Twenty-Five

I felt incredibly guilty about holding up dinner, but once I get a bug in my head . . . well you know, I just can't let it go. Perhaps it was all the smoke and soot that started the wheels turning in my head, but when I left the car fire, I found myself instinctively driving toward Bill Alden's burnt cabin. I didn't know what I'd find there, but I felt certain that I had to go. I grabbed one of those enormous Jonagold apples and began munching while I phoned Gus.

"I'm starving," he said. "I thought you'd be home already."

"Sorry, babe, a car went up in flames just off Montauk Highway and traffic ground to a halt."

Gus chuckled. "You torched a car?" It was a distinctive chuckle, one I knew well. It meant that he was still in good spirits, but if I wasn't home in the next five minutes, he'd start eating the furniture.

"No, but I certainly had motive. It was Ray's car."

"Ray the noisemaker?"

"One and the same."

"Eek. Was he burnt?"

"Like volcano chicken."

"Dead?" he asked apprehensively.

"If that's who was in the car. I recognized his vomit-green wagon, and the police ran the license plate. It was registered to Camryn Claymore, realtor to the stars. Anyway, you know how fast a car goes up. The gas tank exploded just after I arrived."

"After you arrived?"

Uh oh.

"So you didn't just get stuck in traffic; you responded to the incident."

"Well, it was kind of on the way."

"Stephanie!"

Oh shit. It sounded like he was ready to explode. "Um . . ."

"Stop fumfering."

"Fumfering? When did you become Yiddish?"

"Stop being evasive. Where are you now?"

"In the car?"

"It's just not funny anymore."

"I know. I'm sorry. Have a snack, and I'll be home very soon. I bought all kinds of goodies at the pork store."

"You'll have to do better than that," Gus demanded.

"I'll wrap my body in prosciutto, and you can peel it off with your teeth."

"Wow," he said with utter amazement in his voice. "You've really outdone yourself this time—that's quite an enticing offer. All right, you're off the hook for now, but you'd better be home in thirty minutes."

Alden's house was just up the road. If I moved fast, I'd be able to have a quick look around and get home within Gus' time frame. Fortunately the days were long, and the sky was still reasonably bright. "Will do, babe. Love ya." I nailed the accelerator and sped up the road toward the cabin.

It looked far worse than I remembered. Also, to my chagrin, the doors and windows had been boarded up, and I didn't have any protective gear with me. Still, I had come all this way, so I got out of the car and began looking around the property.

The ground was strewn with debris from the cabin: burnt wood, waterlogged sheetrock, asphalt roofing shingles, fiberglass insulation, and shattered glass. The air was still pungent with the smell of the burnt cabin. I didn't know exactly what I was looking for, but I was in a persistent mood, so I strolled all around, examining everything on the ground and hoping for something to jump out at me. *Nada.*

There was a pair of Adirondack chairs set at the top of the bluff facing the Atlantic. I imagined old Bill Alden in one of the chairs, enjoying the fresh air and gazing off at the distant ocean. It looked inviting, so I accepted, but checked my watch before taking a seat—there was still time for me to make Gus' curfew. *Five minutes to take in the view and then back in the car. No dillydallying after that.*

An old fork was lying on the other chair. It was cheap flatware, like the kind you'd expect to find in a greasy spoon with the tines bent and dried egg stuck in every crevice. I picked it up for a closer look, and true to form, it was bent in the middle, exaggerating the S-shape. I placed it on the arm of the Adirondack chair and turned to take in the Atlantic.

The view was beautiful. Actually it was hypnotic. Maybe it was the time of day and the angle of the sun, but I felt my eyelids growing heavy. I really wanted to let myself go because it was the perfect setting for a snooze. *No. You can't do this. Gus will have your head.* And I wasn't making a reference to oral sex. I forced my eyes open and jumped out of the Adirondack chair. A pack of cigarettes was lying on the ground under the chair. It was a pack of Camels, and I remembered Vito saying that they were Alden's brand. The pack was wet and yucky, but diehard Stephanie felt around in her pocket, snapped on a pair of blue gloves, and picked it up.

What are you doing? Hodgkin told you there was no evidence of foul play.

It didn't matter to me. I opened the half-empty pack, held it up to my nose, and took a whiff, despite the fact that I absolutely detest cigarettes. *Hot damn.* I recoiled from the smell. It burned my nostrils and smelled nothing like tobacco.

Chapter Twenty-Six

"I come bearing gifts." I plopped a grocery bag on the kitchen table while Gus and Ma seared me with their gazes. I imagined a laser cutting through a solid gold table and a restrained James Bond inching away as best he could while the beam approached his junk.

Bond: "Do you expect me to talk?"

Goldfinger: "No, Mr. Bond. I expect you to die."

Yeah, that's exactly how they were looking at me.

Gus abandoned a tall glass of beer and begrudgingly gave me a kiss. "Babe," he said with peaked eyebrows. *Translation: your husband is mightily displeased.*

Ma shook her head from side to side but was unable to conceal her grin. "Late to the ball again, Cinderella? What am I going to do with you?" She turned to the stove and raised the flame under one of the pots.

Max was absolutely giddy, bouncing up and down in his baby seat with his arms wide to welcome his mommy. He was animated like a puppy welcoming home its master after a long, lonely day of sleeping and gonad cleansing. I picked him up and smothered him with kisses until he giggled. "Look what mommy brought home," I said as I scooped the fresh mozzarella out of the bag with my free hand. "I brought *mozzie*, and fresh bread, and the most incredible prosciutto."

Gus wasted no time—he unwrapped the mozzie and began slicing it up.

"Gorgeous Jonagold apples and ... pignoli cookies for your nonni."

"Ou," Ma said excitedly. "I haven't had a good pignoli cookie in ages. They've become ridiculously expensive."

I handed her the box.

She untied the string and began munching. "These are very good," she boasted. "Okay, you're forgiven."

"Not so fast," Gus said with a piece of cheese in his mouth. "What do I get?"

"The prosciutto. I gave Vito my measurements, and he calculated the square inches necessary to cover me from head to toe."

"Madonna," Ma said with one of those stop-the-music expressions. "No dirty talk in front of your son."

Max started to make monkey sounds, whooping happily.

I eyed Gus. "That's the kind of reaction I should be getting from you."

Gus grinned. "Sorry, hon ... I can't wait for you to come to bed in a cold-cut nightie. I'll bring the mustard."

Ma cringed. "Too much information." She threw her hands up in the air and turned back to the stove.

I stashed Max in his child seat and reached into my pocket. "Look what else I have."

"A pack of Camels? I can't wait to hear this one," Gus said. "What's going on now?"

"Evidence, my dear Watson. I found it at Bill Alden's place."

"I can't believe you went there. What made you go back?"

"It's my sixth-sense thingy. Something pulled me back to the burnt cabin."

"She's a witch," Ma announced without turning around. "Like her aunt, Zia Francesca."

"So what's so important that you had to pick up a disgusting, waterlogged pack of cigarettes?"

"They smell funny."

"Funny?" Gus asked. "What do you mean?"

"Here, take a quick whiff." I had slipped the Camels into a clean, unused baggie I'd found in our SUV. I tossed it to him.

Gus handled it carefully, so as not to contaminate the evidence within. He put his nose to the opening, sniffed briefly, and began to blink rapidly. "It's pretty faint, but it smells acrid," he said, "I can't tell what it is though."

"We need the nose, Ma," I said. "What does this smell like to you?

Ma stuck her nose in the bag and smelled the cigarettes. "Nuts," she said as she rubbed the side of her nose.

"Almonds?"

Ma thought for a moment and then concurred. "Yes, almonds. Why?"

"I know why," Gus said with a big smile on his face. He sealed the bag and handed it back. "The bloodhound found a pack of arsenic-laced cigarettes."

"Madonna," Ma said. "And you let me stick my nose in there. You trying to kill me?"

"I doubt there's enough residue to do any harm, Ma. Don't worry." I looked at Gus and raised my eyebrows. "The medical examiner was wrong. Alden *was* being poisoned."

He kissed me on the forehead. "Sometimes you are just so on-point that it scares me. How did you ever—"

"Just dumb luck. I saw a pack of cigarettes lying under one of the Adirondack chairs out in the backyard. The rest, as they say, is history."

"Chain of evidence, babe, did you tell Rich Tate about your find yet?"

"I invited him over for dinner."

"Good," Ma said. "I like him."

"He's single, you know."

Ma threatened me with a wooden spoon. "I said I liked him. I didn't say I wanted to jump his bones, wise guy." She shook her head again. "How did I ever raise such a disrespectful child?"

"Just lucky, I guess."

"The pack is still in its plastic wrap," Gus said. "Maybe they'll be able to pull prints from it."

"Maybe," I said. I'd wait until later before telling Gus that I had a fair idea whose fingerprints we might find.

Chapter Twenty-Seven

Dick Aiello, the Suffolk County special services officer, wrapped lightly on the door. His stock thought process began to run through his head while he waited for the door to open. *Hope for the best, prepare for the worst.* His last call had been a difficult one, a car accident due to a drunk driver—an innocent child killed. He heard the doorknob turn. *Christ, how much longer can I go on doing this job?* He knew exactly how long. It was eighteen months before he could put in his retirement papers. *I'll just have to tough it out a little longer.*

"Yes?" A woman answered the door wearing a robe. "*Oh . . .* Hello," she said with uneasiness. "Is something wrong, Officer?"

Aiello presented his best brave face, the one that was cordial and nonthreatening. "Officer Aiello, ma'am, Suffolk County Police Department. Are you Camryn Claymore?"

"*Yes,*" she answered apprehensively.

"May I come in, Ms. Claymore?"

Camryn stared into Aiello's eyes and then cinched her robe.

Aiello followed her over to the couch and sat down.

She pulled a handful of Kleenex from the tissue box. "What happened?" she asked, her face mired with anxiety. "Is it Ray?" Tears began to drizzle down her cheek. She quickly blotted them with her tissues.

"There was an accident, Ms. Claymore. A car fire."

"Oh no. Where? When?"

"Just a few hours ago. The car was registered in your name, a green Subaru, I'm afraid the occupant died in the fire."

She gasped and sniffled. "Oh my God, my brother Ray?"

"We haven't been able to identify the victim, Ms. Claymore. Your brother drives that car?"

She nodded and sat silently for several moments appearing to be lost in thought. "God, who else could it be? Can I see him?"

"Not tonight. The body is being assessed by the medical examiner."

"But—" There was desperation in her voice.

"I'm sorry. It wouldn't help. The victim was burned extensively—unidentifiable."

"Oh no." She began to cry. "How did this happen?" she demanded.

"We don't know what caused the car to catch fire. It's been impounded and will be studied to determine the cause."

"His car just exploded?"

Aiello shrugged. "I'm sorry. We just don't know right now."

"But—" She interrupted herself and remained quiet.

Aiello had been in this place many times before. *Almost done*, he thought. The next of kin wanted hope or closure, but routinely he wasn't in a position to offer either. Back in his early days on the job, he would carry each notification with him for days, mourning and suffering just like the people he'd notified. His skin had thickened over the years. All he could do was wait an appropriate amount of time and provide his business card.

Camryn was still silent, weeping and looking lost in thought.

Aiello glanced at his watch and then handed her his business card. "I'm very sorry to bring you this worrisome news, Ms. Claymore. We'll be in touch to provide more information. In the meantime, please don't hesitate to call my office if you have any questions." Aiello stood. "Once again, ma'am, I'm very sorry."

Camryn remained silent as she walked Aiello to the door. She watched him stroll toward his car and then softly closed the door behind him. She lit a cigarette and inhaled a deep drag before dispelling smoke toward the ceiling. She poured two fingers of bourbon into a tall glass and walked into the bedroom, the sound of humming growing louder as she opened the door.

Kaley was naked on the bed, spread eagle with a Rabbit Habit vibrator in her hand. Her eyes were wide. She was panting and her chest was heaving. It was an effort for her to stop. She finally mustered the strength to shut her toy and looked up at Camryn, her face keen with anticipation. "Baby," Kaley said. "You look damn good in your grief."

Chapter Twenty-Eight

I propped myself up on a pillow. We were just hanging out in bed, no wild or kinky sex, or smoked meats of any variety. It just felt good to have some quiet time alone with my husband. At first Ma's unannounced visit worried me because I thought she'd never leave us alone, but it turned out to be a blessing in disguise. We moved Max's Pack 'n Play into her room, so when we closed our bedroom door at night, we were truly alone.

I studied my husband's face. He seemed at ease and content. "Penny for your thoughts."

Gus leaned over and stroked my hair. "Tate didn't seem too happy about your discovery."

"I don't know that I blame him. He had everything put to bed, and now he has to deal with a possible homicide investigation. He's a small-town fire chief. He needs interference from a wacky city detective like he needs a hole in the head."

"I hear you, but I'm sure that he wants to get to the truth as much as you do. I tell you, babe, when you put your mind to something there's no stopping you. You're one of a kind."

I wrinkled my mouth. "Do you hate me?"

"Hate you?" Gus looked taken aback. "What on earth—"

"For screwing up our vacation. Things haven't exactly turned out the way we planned. I didn't even get you a birthday cake."

"Maybe not, but that doesn't mean we're not enjoying ourselves. There will be many vacations in our future. I'm not worried about two measly weeks in Montauk. However, you *are not* getting a pass on the birthday cake."

I rested my head on his chest. "I worry sometimes."

"About cake?"

"No, silly. That I'll make you too crazy, and you'll leave me for some hot twenty-two-year-old."

"How much wine did you drink?"

"A lot. With Ma here, I'm not too concerned about drinking a little extra *vino*. But you didn't answer my question."

"You're not serious, I hope. Have I given you any reason to worry?"

"No, but it's a well-known fact that at some point in every man's life, he dreams about scoring with a hot, younger woman."

"What?"

"Come on . . . long, silky hair, slender bodies . . . and no one but no one has a tighter hooha than a college girl. Well, some college girls."

"Don't worry, Tugboat Annie, I like your hooha just fine."

"Really? You're not slipping and sliding around down there since I delivered Max?"

"No."

"Not even a little?"

"Babe, you're tighter than Melissa McCarthy's pantyhose."

"*Ha.* Good. Just checking."

"You never struck me as insecure, Steph. Everything all right?"

"What can I tell you? Eventually all women get a little loose in the labia. I just want to make sure you're a happy camper."

"*Yes*, I'm a happy camper. Why are we talking about this anyway? Can't we go back to talking about arsenic poisoning and women getting pushed in front of oncoming trains?"

I chuckled. "Sure, in a minute. Guess what? Ma and I had a conversation about anal sex."

Gus' eyes bulged. "No *you* didn't."

I nodded. "Ya-ha, we sure did. Did you know she thought ass play was a rock group?"

Gus laughed so hard I had to cover his face with a pillow. "Quiet! You'll wake Max."

"You're totally out of your mind, do you know that?"

"I can't say that I disagree."

"Where would I find a girl with a sense of humor like yours?"

I shrugged. "I guess you're right. Let's get back to police work. Tate is going to submit the tainted pack of cigarettes to the police crime lab in the morning. We should have a yay or a nay on my poisoning theory by the end of the day. I've got an appointment to review the physical evidence from Alana Moore's homicide and the case file on Sarah Fisher's disappearance in the morning."

"Sounds intense," Gus yawned. "I think we'll take Max to the petting zoo tomorrow."

"No. Not the petting zoo—*I* wanted to take Max to the zoo."

"Decisions, decisions." Gus did the balancing gesture with his two hands. "Let's see . . . solve multiple homicide cases or pet a goat." He rubbed his chin to indicate he was contemplating a deep and complicated decision. "I'll take the goat."

"Now I'm sad," I sulked. "I don't get to play with lambs and chickies." I placed Gus' hand on my breast. "Make me happy. Pleasure me until my head spins."

"All right," he acquiesced. "We'll do something else instead. We can go to the petting zoo the day after."

"That's not what I meant."

"Sorry, I guess I'm a little slow," he said with a smirk.

"Like hell you are." I pulled him on top of me. "What about now, babe? Are you feeling me?"

"Can I gag you?"

"Seriously? Gus, you're a fine specimen but let's not get carried away."

"No. I mean, can I tie something over your mouth . . . so your mother doesn't hear you."

"*Oh* . . . that's kinky."

Gus reached into the end table drawer and pulled out a bandana he had packed.

I turned away from him so that he could tie the knot behind my head.

He snuggled in behind me.

"I think I'm going to like this," I said, moving the bandana away from my mouth. *Make me feel so good that I want to scream.*

~~~

They reached a level of intimacy that had been lost to them since the arrival of their son. It was just a piece of cloth, just enough to change the familiar into the extraordinary and spark new passion into their relationship. He could hear her muted moaning and sense her heat growing until it became a flame and then he too blazed. It had not been planned, it just happened—a profound and perfect moment shared between a loving wife and her husband.

The hidden motion-sensing camera in the overhead lighting fixture betrayed their every intimacy.

Chapter Twenty-Nine

"**Your husband and your mother took your son to the petting zoo, and you're here looking at cold case evidence?**" Pulaski turned his head askew. "Are you nuts? If I ever pulled a stunt like that my wife would chop off my balls."

I shrugged. "What can I say? That's not something I have to worry about. They were going to postpone it but I told them I'd catch up with them somewhere between the ducklings and the prairie dogs."

"*No es bueno*, Chalice. Family time is precious, especially in our line of work. *Familia es todo*."

"Gee, you know a lot of Spanish for someone with a Polish name."

"Comes with the territory," he said. "Besides, I'm a big fan of Breaking Bad. Tio Salamanca conveyed some very important messages, despite being a bell-ringing, crotchety old mute."

Great, as if I didn't feel guilty enough, Pulaski had to pull time as the voice of conscience. I moved the evidence box so that it was between us, a barrier of sorts. "I guess I can't blame you for judging me."

"I'm not judging. I'm anything but a saint. Just passing along an often overlooked pearl of wisdom."

"Your pearl is duly noted."

He picked up a pair of case files and slapped them on top of the evidence box. "Copies of the two files you requested. They can leave the house; the evidence box stays."

He wasn't telling me anything I didn't know—I think he was just covering his ass. I scanned the tabs on the two files, case numbers, and case names: Sarah Fisher and Alana Moore.

"Great. Thanks. I'll go through the evidence box and take the files with me to the petting zoo. With any luck I can catch up with my family before they feed the llamas."

Pulaski winked. "That's the ticket, Chalice—time isn't exactly of the essence on these files. Catch up with your family and have a moment." Pulaski stood. "I'm heading out. Our admin's pretty friendly. She'll help you if you need anything."

I stood and shook his hand. "Thanks, Tom. I saw the copier—I'm fairly self-sufficient."

"I have no doubt." He left me alone in the interview room. I opened the evidence box like an eight-year-old girl tearing into a Christmas present looking for a Barbie doll. Crime scene evidence included Alana Moore's purse and clothing, everything the crime scene investigators had found when her lifeless remains were removed from the Long Island Rail Road tracks. Sealed evidence bags contained her dress, shoes, undergarments, bag and the contents of it. I carefully began to examine each article.

Her black party dress was simple but tasteful and carried the H&M label, which indicated that she shopped on a budget. She had been wearing a pair of pink pumps but had a second pair of black shoes in her large bag. Where was she coming from? Where was she going? It didn't look as if she was dressed for just hanging out with friends. I presumed that she was coming from or going to a party. The second pair of shoes led me to believe that she had doted on her appearance and couldn't decide which shoe looked better on her. She had a decent wad of cash in her wallet, almost two hundred dollars—mostly twenties, all fresh bills. Her wallet contained her NYS driver's license and her ID from Bennington College, her high school graduation picture, and some family pictures. Credit cards too—

Pulaski had already told me that they had been inactive since she went missing.

Unraveling the thread on a missing-persons case was never easy. The ones who were recovered early usually found a way to escape on their own. The others ... didn't usually fare as well. Famous disappearances merely hint at the tip of the iceberg. Children and adults go missing all the time. The public only hears about the media-worthy cases. Alana Moore didn't appear to be anyone's prisoner, and if she had been, I doubt she had made her escape dressed to the nines with her purse and personal effects in tow.

This one is going to take some smarts.

"What was going on with you?" I asked her photo. The case file contained the crime scene, forensic lab, and personal photos supplied by her family. Sometimes I can look into someone's eyes and read his or her story. Was she happy and content or did she have that wanderlust look in her eyes? I couldn't read Alana one way or another. Pulaski felt she'd left home on her own in order to be closer to the New York theatrical scene and had met with foul play. It was his theory ... but a theory is just a guess, and I wasn't sure if Pulaski's was accurate. I read through her case file, which made me feel more confused. I had learned just enough about this tragic woman to realize I knew nothing about her at all.

I spent a few more minutes going through the crime scene photos. Among them was a picture of a large black and white cookie with smooshed pink icing on it. I didn't know how much it had to do with her homicide, but I guess the crime scene photographer wanted to be thorough.

I decided to change direction and had just opened Sarah Fisher's case file for a first look when a shadow crossed the table. "How's it going?"

I looked up and saw newly retired Detective Sullivan Smote.

Christ on a cross—I hope he's not going to start flirting.

"Find something I missed?"

Oh thank God. "No. Actually I just cracked Sarah Fisher's file for the first time. What are you doing here? I figured you'd be in Florida by now, wooing unwitting divorcees out of their orthopedic pantyhose."

He gnashed his teeth. He had a Tony Curtis mouthful of pearly whites. "You're a real buzzkill, Chalice. You just made my golden years seem like a slow and agonizing plunge into the toilet."

Oops. "Sorry."

He pulled out a chair and sat down. "I'm not moving down there until the fall anyway. I'm going to be one of those snowbird Svengalis anyway. I'm just here to have lunch with some of the boys, but when I heard you were here ... well, you know, ego. I came in to see if you'd found something I should have caught when the case was mine. I mean, I've got a little time to kill if you need some help."

"Feeling insecure?"

"Not usually. In all the years on the force, there was only one time I walked away from a case feeling unsettled: my aunt, Celeste. I'm pretty sure she was offed by one of the kids living in her foster home, but I was never able to make anything stick."

"Sorry to hear it. I mean the victim being your aunt and all. I'm sure that one really stung."

"Still stings." He grinned sadly. "So, what about it? Did I miss anything on Sarah Fisher?"

"No such luck, Romeo. Actually, I was going to take a fast look and then bring the file with me. My family is visiting the petting zoo."

"Petting zoo? Like Blackstone's Steakhouse on a Thursday night?"

"Sorry, I don't ... Hey, what is that, some kind of vulgar reference to a cougar bar or something?"

Smote flashed his Tony Curtis teeth once more. "You *are* a bright cop."

"I wouldn't exactly call it an inspired moment. No, I mean petting zoo as in actual duckies and other soft, cuddly creatures."

"God." He shrugged. "What was *I* thinking?"

Does this guy think about anything other than scoring? "So is this a sincere offer of help or are you just hoping to catch me in a moment of weakness?"

"Somehow I don't think you have many of those."

No moments of weakness? He should see me when I'm around Nigel Twain and my legs turn to jelly. "That would be correct. How about you cast your x-ray peepers on this stuff." I handed him Alana Moore's case file and pushed the evidence box his way. "A young woman went missing from a small upstate town and was pushed to her death in front of an LIRR train. It's always good to get a fresh set of eyes on a tricky file."

He checked his watch. "Yeah sure, I've got fifteen minutes to kill. Let's see if the old dog can still hunt."

"*Muchas gracias.*" I guess Pulaski's Spanish chatter was still resonating with me. I turned back to Sarah Fisher's file and began reading the reports. I noticed that Smote had drawn simple pictures over almost every inch of the file folder. I glanced at him quickly and smirked. A diddler *and* a doodler.

Sometimes doodles can have concrete representational meanings, and sometimes they mean nothing at all. Smote doodled a lot of women in erotic poses. If this guy spent as much time thinking about detective work as he did about the ladies, we'd have both cases closed before he went to lunch.

"Anything?" I asked.

"Yeah," he replied.

I picked the right man for the right job. "What did you find?"

"This Alana, she shops on a budget: H&M dress, Steve Madden pumps. One of the pink shoes has fifty dollars written on the sole in black ink, which means she probably bought them in an off-price store like DSW or Marshalls. The black shoes are cheap too—the soles are raw leather. Swanky pumps are finished on the bottom."

And you know this how? Oh Christ, his lips are parting. He's about to tell me. Yikes!

"You can always tell if a woman has money by the shoes she wears to bed."

I pictured Smote on top of one of his conquests with her legs up by her head. *Yuck! TMI.* "You're perceptive." *Disgusting but perceptive.* "I saw the H&M label and thought the same thing. Hadn't noticed the shoes though. That's a good catch."

"Thanks." Smote turned back to the case file. He was certainly giving me my money's worth.

A sudden thought popped into my head. I checked the two different pairs of shoes and found that one pair was size seven and the other eight and a half. A half a size difference is no big whoop but a full size and a half? "Did you notice the shoes are different sizes?"

"No. What do you make of that?"

"I'm not sure, but it doesn't make sense. Even if she borrowed a pair from a friend ... I mean if she was a seven, she'd swim in the eight-and-a-halfs, and if she wore an eight-and-a-half, she'd never squeeze into the munchkin shoes."

"Maybe she's Cinderella," he quipped.

"Thanks. You're a tremendous asset."

"Her bones were all but pulverized when the train hit her. I doubt forensics could back into the victims correct shoe size by analyzing body mass—I don't even think they make that type of observation," Smote said.

"I'll make a note of it, but it's a *long* shot. Hopefully I'll find something more substantial to work with."

There were lots of pictures of Sarah Fisher. She was a cute girl, not a devastating beauty but cute with blond hair and a big, engaging smile. She was short and thin—not thin as in sleek and sexy, but thin as in she could use a little extra meat on her bones.

Where'd you go, Sarah? What's your story?

"What do make of this?" Smote asked. He held up the crime scene photo of the black and white cookie I had seen earlier.

"Anyone's guess. It said in the notes that it was photographed because it was going to dry out and crumble. The crime scene technician wanted to preserve the appearance of the evidence as it was found. I don't know if it was hers, or if it was just something lying near her on the tracks. It looks pretty smashed up."

"What's the story with the pink icing?" Smote asked.

"Some kind of design the bakery used to fancy it up I guess. Hey, was the accident before or after Easter?"

"Weeks after," Smote replied. "I remember clearly."

"There goes that theory—I thought maybe it was a pink Easter egg." I stared at the photo from across the table. "Hey, let me see that."

Smote handed me the photo.

I turned it in every direction because somehow I thought I saw something in the pink icing. "There's something here," I said. "There's an embossed figure in the icing."

"Where?" Smote stood and walked around the table to look at it with me.

I pointed to a faint outline, which was just visible in between the areas of the icing that hadn't been smashed.

"My eyes must be going," Smote said. "I don't see anything."

It took a brief moment for my brain to piece it together. "It's a bouquet," I boomed excitedly and pointed at it again. "And these are a pair of arms." I looked Smote in the eye. "I bet it's a bride holding a bouquet. It's a wedding favor."

Chapter Thirty

Kaley stepped from the shower and wrapped a towel around her head. She dried herself with an immense bath sheet that dwarfed her diminutive body and applied lotion before slipping into a pair of soft cotton panties and her flip-flops. She used a broad comb to detangle her long, blond hair, and then shut the bathroom light.

Camryn sat in a kitchen chair that had been turned to the side permitting access from the back. Like Kaley, she was naked from the waist up. Her hair was pinned up and away from her neck.

"Ready?" Kaley asked as she softly ran her fingertips along the sides of Camryn's neck. "Your neck's so long and pretty. It'll be perfect when I'm done with it."

Camryn was focusing on her iPad screen and seemed oblivious to Kaley's touch. "Did you scrub your hands?"

"Look," she replied holding her hands in front of Camryn's face before grazing her cheek. "I scrubbed them raw."

"You didn't have to. I *said* you could wear gloves."

"I don't like the way they feel. My hands get all damp and clammy." Kaley swabbed the back of Camryn's neck with alcohol and blew gently to dry it. She pressed the tiny stencil to the back of Camryn's neck just below the base of her hairline and outlined the design with ink. "I'm ready," she said.

"So am I," Camryn said without moving her eyes off the screen. "Wait!" she said abruptly and reached for a bottle of bourbon. She gulped a mouthful. "Go ahead."

Kaley dipped the tip of the tattoo pen in the deep scarlet ink and then began to trace the outline on Camryn's neck. "Hurt?"

"It's all right. Keep going."

Kaley worked quickly and was soon finished with the outside border. "How many times are you going to watch that?" she said with irritation in her voice.

"Until I get tired of it. How's it going back there?"

"Fine." Kaley said resentfully.

"What's eating you?"

"I'm jealous. Why do you watch them so much?"

"I'm getting an education. Whatever I learn from them I can do with you. There's no reason for you to be jealous."

"Are you getting tired of me?" She stared at the couple making love on the iPad. He was behind her as she purred with ecstasy. "I don't mind if you want to gag me . . . I mean, if it turns you on."

"No. Could we talk about this later when you're not poking me in the neck with a sharp needle?"

"I guess." Kaley dabbed the pen back in the ink and then began to fill in the pattern on Camryn's neck.

"And don't go screwing around and draw a pair of balls back there or something humiliating that I'll have to cover up my entire life," Camryn warned.

"Like I'd do that," Kaley said hotly. She was making fast progress. The design was small, and it wouldn't take her very long to complete.

Camryn cued the video again. It was clearly her favorite— the happy couple going at it in the privacy of their bedroom in the house they had rented from her. "Look at them, they're gorgeous. Ouch!" she snapped. "Hey watch it back there."

Kaley did not apologize. "You think you could watch something else?"

"Why? You seemed to enjoy it."

"The first time. I don't know how you can watch it over and over."

Camryn reached behind her head and grabbed Kaley's hand. "Enough! Keep whining and I'll definitely grow tired of you." She heard Kaley sniffle. "Hey, cut it out. There's no reason for you to cry."

"We'll never have what they have. We'll never—"

Camryn waited for Kaley to stop sobbing. She knew what her companion was alluding to: the secrecy Camryn demanded from her. Their life together had always been clandestine. "You know I can't be seen with you, especially now while I'm in mourning for my brother."

"I know, but . . ." Kaley lowered her head gloomily.

"I can fix that," Camryn insisted. "I'll fix it so that we won't have to hide anymore."

"How?" Kaley began to sob again. "I'm so tired of—"

Being my dirty little secret? She patted Kaley's hand. "Just have a little faith, okay?" She closed the cover of her iPad and put it down on the kitchen table.

Kaley nodded. "Okay."

"That's my girl. Now finish up back there, and then I'll do you right after, all right?"

"Yes." Kaley smiled weakly and then the buzz of the tattoo pen resumed as she quickly filled in the balance of the pattern. She stepped back to see if she had missed any spots.

"Done?" Camryn asked.

"Yes."

"How does it look?"

"It came out really good. You want to see?"

Camryn turned her head and smiled. "I'm excited," she said as a shiver ran through her. She grabbed a handheld mirror and walked into the bathroom. With her back to the bathroom mirror she looked in the handheld mirror to study Kaley's handiwork. "It's great!" she shouted.

Kaley walked hesitantly into the bathroom. "Do you really like it?"

"Like it?" Camryn said with a beaming smile. "Come here." She threw her arms around Kaley and kissed her. "It's perfect."

Chapter Thirty-One

The ticket collector tried not to show that he was staring at the two boys as they took each other's hand and disappeared into the dark corridor that led to movie theater #6.

Camryn waited until they were both bathed in darkness before she turned to Kaley and snickered.

They wore absolutely no makeup. Camryn had gone shopping in the Gap just for the occasion and had purchased matching plaid woven shirts, cargo shorts, and baseball caps, which they wore with their hair stuffed under them. The only aspect of their uniforms that didn't match was the color of their Converse sneakers. Camryn wore royal blue and Kaley wore hot pink. They took seats in the very last row of the balcony and kissed long and hard the moment they sat down.

"I'm so excited," Kaley said as she got comfortable in her seat and put her feet up on the seatback in front of her. "I've never been a boy before. This is fun."

Camryn snorted and then blew a fierce raspberry on Kaley's cheek, so loud that several of the people in front of them turned around and stared at them accusatorily.

"Stop it." Kaley giggled. "It tickles."

"Just being a dude, my *brotha*," Camryn said in a deep and manly voice. "Let's talk about boobs and pick our noses."

"Can't," Kaley laughed, "I'm too busy scratching my junk."

"Shhh," a woman in the audience said impatiently.

Camryn kicked the seatback in front of her and gave the woman the finger. She turned to Kaley. "Boys will be boys."

"I can't believe we're doing this," Kaley whispered excitedly.

"You've never seen this movie, have you?"

"*Boys Don't Cry*? What's it about?"

"You'll see. It was my inspiration, one of them anyway. I love playing dress up." She patted Kaley's knee. "I told you I'd fix things."

Kaley snuggled against Camryn. "I'm just so happy that we're out together, out like everybody else."

Out? She only thinks we're out. We're buried so deeply in the closet we can't even find the goddamn doorknob. She counterfeited a loving smile. "I told you. I told you to have a little faith."

"I can't wait to see the movie. You said it was one of your favorites."

"Hilary Swank is amazing in it." *I couldn't have given a better performance myself.*

~~~

The ending credits had just begun to roll when Camryn stood, lit a cigarette, and tossed something under one of the seats. She grabbed Kaley's hand and rushed her toward the front of the theater.

"What the—" Kaley shrieked. "Why are we—"

"Get it in gear," Camryn shouted as she ran toward the emergency exit. She pushed on the door next to the front curtain, turned around, and stared toward the back of the theater.

Kaley was out of breath. "What's going on?"

"Remember that old bat who shushed us?"

Kaley nodded while she tried to catch her breath. "Yeah but—"

"Wait for it . . . wait for it," she said with tension in her voice.

Kaley jumped as a rapid succession of small explosions filled the air. She clutched her chest. "Oh my God. What did you do?"

"Suck it," Camryn yelled toward the back of the theater. She grabbed Kaley's hand, and they raced out the door.

"What the hell was that?" Kaley asked as they raced through the parking lot toward their car, laughing and gasping for air.

"That old bitch. I lit her ass up with a pack of firecrackers. That'll teach her for messing with me."

Kaley's face was aglow. "You're so badass."

"You haven't seen anything." Camryn boasted. "Bonnie and Clyde have got nothing on us ... just wait and see what I've got planned for us next."

Chapter Thirty-Two

"The Cabernet Franc is delish," Gus said as he swirled the remaining wine in his glass to help it breathe. He was four glasses of wine into a tasting, and I could see that he was feeling a buzz. "Sure you don't want to try some?"

"No. Enjoy. I'm the designated sober parent today." Max was sound asleep in his stroller. I guess he wasn't completely thrilled to be touring a winery. Tickle Me Elmo was more his thing. I missed most of the petting zoo experience, but Gus told me that Max thought it was dope. Fortunately I arrived in time to see the piggies and piglets. Some people think that unicorns are magical animals, but I think the pig is the most incredible beast of all. Who but the pig can eat absolutely anything and turn it into bacon? Feed it a corncob and it makes bacon. An apple core ... bacon. Morels? Bacon. Who doesn't love bacon? Jesus may have been able to turn water into wine, but bacon? He may have walked on water, but he never made bacon. No wonder the big bad wolf wanted to devour the three little pigs so badly.

"Not even a sip?" Gus implored.

"No. I'm really fine." I didn't feel like I needed wine or libation of any sort. I'd just received a call from Richard Tate. The crime lab had completed its testing of the cigarettes I'd found on Bill Alden's property, and the smokes had indeed been spiked with cyanide. Alden had undeniably been puffing on cyanide-laced cigarettes. The question was for how long and who had done the dirty deed?

Hodgkin said the arsenic-laced cigarettes might have explained the high levels of cyanide in Alden's liver, despite the fact that none was present in his stomach. There was no way of telling how long Alden had been smoking the tainted cigs, but the high liver concentration of cyanide suggested that it had been going on for quite a while.

Pulaski had been assigned to the Alden homicide investigation, which was convenient because he was now my sole contact with the Suffolk County Police Department, and I found him easy to work with. I had informed him of the conversation I'd overheard at Vito's Pork Store. Sweet little Kaley ... I just couldn't imagine her messing with Alden's cigarettes, but it was an angle Pulaski would definitely have to check out. Aside from being the neighborhood saint, she was also picking up Alden's groceries. Pulaski would definitely have to question her. Unfortunately, the packaging did not contain any fingerprints other than Alden's.

"You're jazzed, aren't you?" Gus said. "You're such a bloodhound." He had a dopey expression on his face. The wine had regressed him to a little-boy state. It's a shame Max was asleep; they could've had a play date.

"I'm a little wired. I love it when hunches gel."

"I can't believe Kaley volunteered to babysit Max, and now she's a person of interest in a homicide investigation."

I thought about Kaley sitting on our sofa and bouncing Max on her knee. My stomach felt queasy. "Christ, you have to be so careful."

The restroom door opened and Ma plowed forward.

"Feel any better?" I asked. She had tasted wine along with Gus.

"This stuff ran right through me," she complained. "What's in it?"

Gus looked a little vacuous. He shrugged. "Grapes?"

"I think this place is too close to the airport," Ma commented.

"What does that mean?"

"I think the ground is saturated with jet fuel. It's given me a headache," she said, "and I never get headaches."

Egad, there must be insidious forces at work. "That's too bad. I was going to buy you a couple of bottles."

"At these prices? Bah!" she complained. "Save your money. I can buy two gallons of jug wine for what this place charges for one small bottle ... and it won't send me running to the bathroom."

"We can hit another vineyard. Maybe you'll like it better."

"And pay for another tasting? *Madonna*," she grumbled. "Stop wasting your money."

"It's okay, Ma. We're on vacation. Live a little." Ma was definitely the thrifty type. She was far from starving, but she did live on a fixed income. I tried to spoil her whenever I could, and if she didn't like the wine ... well, I'd find another way.

"I need to put something in my stomach," Ma said. "Are the two of you ready to eat?"

"I could do some damage," Gus said.

Ma and I had packed a picnic lunch: salad, sandwiches, and sides, the whole nine yards. There was also a birthday cake packed away for Gus. "Gus, why don't you and Ma take Max and find a shady spot for us to eat? I'll run back to the car and grab the goodies."

"I'll go—it's kind of a hike," Gus insisted. "I'll pick up the cooler and catch up with you on the grounds."

"Are you sure?"

"Yes, babe. I've got it."

"Sure you can find the car? You look a little out of it."

Gus patted his cheeks, pretending to wake himself up. "I'm good."

"Okay, but no peeking into the cooler, got it?"

"Sure thing. See you in a few minutes." He drained the last of his wine and headed off.

I wanted to change Max while we were close to a changing table, but he was still sound asleep and I didn't want to poke the hornet's nest. "Come on," I said to Ma. "Let's find a nice spot."

"I think the women who crushed the grapes forgot to wash their feet," Ma complained.

"Ha. I guess you really didn't like it."

"*Madonna,* twenty dollars for a few sips of wine. They've got a lot of nerve."

"It's more about the experience, Ma. It's a nice day out. You're not enjoying yourself?"

"Of course I'm enjoying myself—I'm with my family—but I could do without the overpriced wine."

One of the clerks overheard Ma's comment. I pretended not to know her. My mind was elsewhere as I pushed the stroller out of the tasting room to the back lawn. I was thinking about the party favor in the photograph and wondering if we'd be able to find the wedding or bridal shower it had come from. It wasn't the kind of thing you could run through the crime computer, so Suffolk County PD was calling all of the hotels and catering halls on the East End. The venues had to be contacted one by one to obtain the names and phone numbers for whomever had booked the affair. If we were lucky enough to find the couple that gave away black and white cookies, we'd then have to track down the invitation list, if it still existed, to see if Alana Moore had been invited to that affair. It would be a long and tedious task, but it was all we had. Alana Moore had died more than a year ago, and in that amount of time, leads have a tendency to grow very cold.

"How about over here?" Ma asked as she pointed to a shady area under a broad oak tree.

"Perfect!" I had a queen-size sheet folded up in Max's stroller. Ma helped me lay it flat, and we weighted down the corners with our shoes so that the wind wouldn't blow it away. I plopped my fanny down on the sheet facing Max and inhaled deeply. The air was fragrant. It smelled *summery.* I watched Max sleeping, his head slack against his shoulder, and his innocent baby face so perfectly content.

Ma was watching him as well. "You did good, you and Gus. You made a beautiful little angel."

"He is pretty cute, isn't he?"

"Pretty cute?" Ma huffed. "He's gorgeous! Of course, I expected nothing less with you and Gus as the parents."

I blushed. "Thanks, Ma."

She sat down next to me and put her arm around my shoulder. "You looked just like that when you were a baby. Who could've known you'd grow up to be such a terror?"

I looked at her accusatorily. "What the hell does that mean?"

She pulled me closer and kissed me on the forehead. "Thank you, sweetheart." I saw her throat begin to tighten. "I finally feel happy again."

"Stop it," I warned her. "You're going to make me . . ."

Too late, we were both weeping, tears of sadness and tears of joy. It was almost three years since my father had passed away, and there had been times when I wasn't sure either of us would make it.

"You gave me something to live for. You, your brother Ricky, Gus, and now the little one—I've got a family again. Your father would've been so proud of you, Stephanie. I just wish he were here to see it. Your father used to take me on picnics. He'd plan the trips, and I'd prepare the food. I'd fry chicken cutlets and buy fresh bread for sandwiches. We'd bring wine—not like the expensive crap this place sells. I have beautiful memories of those times."

We put our faces together and watched Max sleep. He lifted his head for a moment, stuck his thumbs into his mouth and put his remaining fingers over his nose, making a completely adorable sleepy face. *"Aw."* His weary head dropped, and he was once again in his favorite sleeping position. It seemed like a perfect moment, the kind that came along just a few times in a lifetime. I had my mother at my side, the sun in my face, and my husband . . . "Where the hell is Gus?"

"I didn't want to say anything, but that Greek God husband of yours is mighty slow getting back here with the grub, and I'm *starving.*"

I stood and dusted myself off. "Watch Max. I'll give Gus a hand. I stepped into my shoes and walked off in the direction we had parked. It was a beautiful summer afternoon, and the North Fork wineries were jammed. We left our SUV in one of the auxiliary parking fields, which was in God's country, a dirt lot in the middle of nowhere. As I walked the path in search of Gus, the noise and tumult of the winery faded into the distance. It was slow going. The path was narrow and uneven, a plowed clearing through a wooded area. I had to navigate around fallen wood, rocks, and mud puddles. *No wonder it's taking him so long.*

I walked another few minutes before the parking field came into sight. Our SUV was parked in the row of cars adjacent to the woods, smack dab in the middle of the row. "Shoot." I saw the tall roofline of the SUV, but I didn't see Gus. *I must have missed him.* The idea that we had somehow missed each other, and that I'd have to drag my lazy ass back to the picnic spot made me feel mentally and physically weary. As I got closer, I saw that one of the doors was still open. "Gus?" I called out. "Babe?" The car was unoccupied. It wasn't like Gus to leave a door open and the car not locked or alarmed. I looked all around the car—my detective's instincts just kicked in on their own. The only idea that occurred to me was that Gus had been a little tipsy when he left us and must've forgotten to lock the SUV, but as I approached the back of the truck, I noticed that the liftgate was ajar. The back of the truck was a mess, and it only took a moment to see that the cooler was still where we had packed it. I looked all around in desperation as a foreboding feeling began to creep through my veins. And then I saw something that alarmed me. Gus' cell phone was lying on the ground. As I got closer, I saw that the phone was awash with a spray of red dots.

I began to tremble.

His phone was covered with blood.

Chapter Thirty-Three

"And none of that bullshit about a person being absent for at least twenty-four hours before being legally classified as missing! Shit! I'm sorry. I didn't mean that. It's just—"

"Don't worry. I understand, ma'am." Novack, the Suffolk County cop standing in front of me, was clearly new to the job. I had identified myself as a New York City detective and was trying to stay calm but not doing a very good job of it. I could see that he lacked confidence and experience. Nonetheless he was following my instructions and making all of the calls that I requested.

I had called Tate, Pulaski, Pam Shearson, my NYPD commanding officer, and my close friend Herbert Ambler with the FBI. The latter two knew that I was not prone to undue hysterics and were scrambling to rally help. The immediate task was to convince Suffolk County PD that I wasn't just another panic-stricken wife demanding that Zeus descend from Mount Olympus to find her errant husband. I've been on both sides of the fence and knew how my requests might have appeared. Nonetheless, Gus couldn't have been gone more than thirty-minutes, and I knew that I had to stress to the locals the importance of beginning the investigation immediately. Stress? Hell, I had to demand it. I knew exactly what to do but I was out of my jurisdiction and had no authority. Somehow I had to get everyone to step in line. I figured there was a good chance that whoever took Gus was still on the road, on the way to wherever it was they intended to hold Gus captive.

The police needed to set up roadblocks and stop every car for questioning if necessary. We were on the easternmost tip of Long Island. There was just water to the east of us but to the west ... a hundred miles of densely populated Long Island towns, and if they made it past there, they'd be able to go anywhere.

"I just got off the phone with my sergeant, ma'am. He's in the car and will be here in minutes," Novack said.

"That's great. Thank you."

"A taskforce is on its way with enough men to search the winery and the surrounding area. Detective Pulaski stepped up for you and advised that we were well advised to treat your husband's disappearance as an abduction."

My mind kept circling back to the bloody cell phone—I felt certain that it was Gus' blood and that I was right about him being taken. "And roadblocks?"

"I believe they're working on it. I forwarded your husband's picture to headquarters." Novack smiled encouragingly. "Your husband may not be SCPD but we'll treat this as if he's one of our own."

I covered my mouth and fought to hold back the tears. *Deep breaths. Take deep breaths. Your husband needs you to stay calm. Focus. Get your thoughts together. Who did this? Who stands to gain the most?*

Novack's portable radio crackled. "Go ahead," he said into the radio. He listened for a moment and then turned to me. "A fellow officer located your mother and son. He's bringing them to us now."

My poor mother; God only knew the thoughts that were racing through her mind. I tried to calm her when I spoke to her on the phone but could hear the panic in her voice. Max had awoken during our conversation and was screaming in the background. "You have to keep your cool," I encouraged her. "Try not to panic Max." I told her a Suffolk County police officer would be looking for her and that she should identify herself to him and follow his instructions. Thank God she remembered to bring her cell phone because she usually forgets it at home.

Why would someone abduct Gus? I couldn't fight the feeling that I had caused Gus' abduction with all of my meddling into local homicides and disappearances. I must've gotten too close to someone and set him or her into action. But whom had I provoked? Was it related to Alana Moore? Sarah Fisher? Bill Alden? What could I have done to force someone to take such drastic action? I couldn't help but feel guilty that whatever happened to Gus was my fault.

Ma's face was pale and stricken with panic—the fear I read in her eyes cut right through me. This was the moment she had dreaded her entire life, the worry she faced everyday with my dad. She had counseled me repeatedly, "Don't marry a cop like I did." She had told me over and over again. In a way it was the look I expected to see on her face because it had been hidden there for decades just waiting for the opportunity to surface.

"Don't marry another cop." You'll never know when that call might come, "We're sorry to inform you that . . ." Ma should have been directing those comments at Gus and not at me. He was the one who had been put at risk by marrying me and not the other way around. I was the maverick. I was the one who couldn't leave well enough alone and placed her husband in jeopardy. And now . . .

Ma got out of the police cruiser with Max in her arms. "Stephanie, what's going on?" Her face was awash with tears. I took Max out of her arms and pressed him against me, his face buried in my chest so that he couldn't see the dire expression on my face.

"I don't know, Ma," I said helplessly as my own tears sprang forth. "We'll find him," I mouthed weakly. "It's only a matter of time." I forced a smile, but it didn't help her. I could see that it only made her feel worse. We stepped closer, and I put my arm around her with Max in between us. I was trying to comfort her, and she was doing her best to do the same for me.

Max looked up and took my face in his two little hands. He searched my eyes, as if wondering what was wrong, and then he babbled something. I kissed his little hand and then ... he made a sound. He was a little too young to utter his first words, but it sounded to me as if he had said, "Dada."

BOOK THREE

Chapter Thirty-Four
Search for Gus Lido: Day 1

I was sitting on a blanket at the beach with Max next to me. It was a perfect summer day. The sun was intense with low-hanging clouds drifting by every few minutes to cool me just when the heat became too strong. The water was a rich aquamarine color, and the fragrance of the sea was pure heaven. The breakers were large with frothy whitecaps. Every now and again, one would stray onto the sand when it broke, caressing my toes where they extended past the edge of the blanket.

Max was playing with a pail and shovel, no sand, just a pail and shovel. He was at that knocking-things-together-stage, and I couldn't imagine where I might find sand if I let him loose to play with it. I had him covered from head to toe so that he wouldn't get sunburned. What wasn't covered with cloth or a cap was heavily smeared with Coppertone Water BABIES. I wasn't taking a chance with my little one.

Gus walked toward the water with a surfboard under his arm. He looked back just as he hit the water's edge and blew us a kiss.

"Wave to daddy," I said. I picked up Max's hand and helped him with the gesture.

Gus pushed out his chest and placed his hands on his hips, posing as if he was a he-man superhero. He waved back and then strode into the ocean.

"Be careful," I yelled. He was just waist-deep in the water when he turned one last time and smiled a strong reassuring smile before climbing atop his surfboard and paddling out to sea. I watched him grow smaller and smaller until he was just barely visible on the horizon. It wasn't long before a giant wave rose behind him. He paddled furiously to build speed, and then the wave lifted him high in the air.

"Look at daddy." I pointed out to sea, but Max seemed to be preoccupied with his pail and shovel. He glanced up for a moment and then went back to his toys.

Gus was atop his surfboard, balancing to stay upright as the monster wave tossed him around. The wave finally broke and water cascaded down in front of him as he angled the board parallel to the shoreline to ride the pipeline. I could see him through the translucent breaker, crouched on his board, riding it out. As the mighty wave broke, it turned to white foam and obscured my view of the Big Kahuna. I adjusted my focus to the end of the pipeline and waited for Gus to emerge.

"Come on, honey," I shouted with encouragement even though I knew he couldn't hear me. "Ride it out. You can do it."

I was still watching when the wave broke and the foam dispersed on the surface of the water. *Where is he?* "Come on, babe, get up." I stood, shielded my eyes against the sun, and searched the water for him. His surfboard suddenly popped to the surface. "Thank God." It was leashed to him, and I knew I'd see him in a second but . . .

Moments passed without any sign of him. "Oh Christ." I felt my body grow numb as time ticked away. I reached down to scoop up Max but . . .

"Max?"

"We're here, ma'am."

"What?" I broke into a cold sweat.

Novack was talking to me from the front seat of the police cruiser. "Are you all right, ma'am? We're here."

I looked around frantically because I didn't know where I was. I turned to my side. Ma was next to me, holding Max. "Oh, thank God." I grabbed Max and smothered him with kisses.

"You fell asleep," Ma said. "I didn't want to disturb you." Her eyes widened. "Why, Stephanie! You're shaking."

I began to cry. "I dreamt that I lost Max."

"Okay, okay. Take it easy, Sweetheart. Max is in your arms. Take a deep breath. You poor thing, you're a nervous wreck."

"I need some fresh air."

Novack opened the door for me, and I got out holding Max. I'm sure that Max sensed that something was wrong because I was squeezing him as if he was a stuffed toy.

"You look pale," Ma said as she got out of the car. She opened a bottle of water and handed it to me. "Drink. I don't want you to pass out."

I heard car doors close. I turned around and saw Pulaski getting out of another cruiser.

We had traveled for almost an hour from Montauk to Suffolk County Police Headquarters in Yaphank, but I couldn't remember the trip. It was as if I had gotten into the car in one location and magically gotten out somewhere else.

"There's a team waiting for us inside," Pulaski said. He put his arm around me and escorted me toward the building. We were about halfway across the parking field when I saw an FBI helicopter materialize in the sky. I could just barely make out the white FBI markings on the side of the black chopper, but I knew who was inside. It was my dear friend Herbert Ambler coming to the rescue.

Chapter Thirty-Five

"Stephanie!" Herbert Ambler called to me from the far end of the corridor as he broke into a run. He was not in the greatest shape and was out of breath after his short sprint.

I threw my arms around him. "They took him, Herb. Someone took Gus." Up until now I had held it somewhat together. Now in the arms of my longtime confidant … I just couldn't hold it back any longer. I began crying on his shoulder, hysterical and out of control.

"Okay, okay," Ambler said as he stroked my hair. "It will be all right." He pulled away, just far enough so that he could look me in the face. "Remember what your dad used to say all the time?"

I shrugged—at the moment nothing was clicking.

"Let cooler heads prevail. If Gus has been taken, I'm going to need you at the top of your game in order to get him back. I need to know everything that's been going on, and I need to hear it from Stephanie Chalice the cop, not Stephanie Chalice the emotionally distraught wife and basket case." He shook me a little. "I'd rather we all have a good laugh about this after we get Gus back than cry about it now. Are you with me?"

I was panting and unable to control my breathing. I forced myself to take a couple of deep, controlled breaths and then nodded.

"Good. Are you settled enough to tell me what's been going on?"

I felt so weak, as if every ounce of life had been drained from my body. "I'll try."

Ambler's eyes widened. "Do or do not . . . There is no try," he said in Yoda's voice to make me laugh.

I wasn't able to laugh, but I was finally able to lift my head. *Baby steps*, I told myself. *Gus needs you right now. Pull yourself together.* I took a sip of water and then directed Ambler to a nearby room. "Everyone's in here."

Chapter Thirty-Six

Law enforcement folks get slammed for misconduct all the time. There are articles in the press everyday about police brutality, or profiling, or corruption. Stories about our good deeds rarely see the light of day. You can say what you want about cops but there's one thing you can't take away from us. We are the most tightly knit family in the world and when one of us bleeds we all bleed. When one cop needs help, every cop is there for him, day or night, rain or shine, no matter what the undertaking requires.

Still, I was amazed at what I saw when Ambler and I walked into the police situation room. I thought perhaps that I was in the war room at the Pentagon. Large area maps of Long Island and detailed maps of the East End towns were up all over the room. Everyone was on high alert, scrambling to track Gus before he could be taken very far. Computers were up and running, Phone lines were open. Seeing so many policemen focused solely on Gus' rescue injected me a potent ounce of hope.

"Stephanie, I'd like to make a couple of decisions for you, if that's okay," Ambler said. "It's not that—"

Ambler was far more than a friend and colleague, he was like my uncle. He and my dad had been great friends, and he had supported Ma and me emotionally ever since my father's passing. I trusted him with my life. "It's all right, Herb. I don't mind if you call a couple of shots."

"This is no environment for a child. Let me arrange for Ma and Max to be taken back to the city. I'm sure that your CO,

Shearson, will provide an escort and protection. I'll have Agent Banks at their beck and call as well.

Agent Banks was Ambler's right hand, and I knew she'd devote herself to my family's wellbeing. I thought it over and then nodded. "I agree, but I want a few minutes with them before they go back. Ricky is like a Saint Bernard; I'm sure he'll be thrilled to have Max to look after."

"I was going to ask," Ambler said. "Ricky's home alone?"

"Yes. Thank God he's so much better these days. Dr. Twain has really helped him a lot." Fresh tears began to run down my cheeks. My brother Ricky had emotional issues as a result of severe trauma. I'm so happy that he's finally starting to heal.

"It's probably not a good idea for him to know what's going on with Gus. I don't want him to get stressed out," Ambler said.

"I'll let Ma know how to play it."

Ambler checked his watch. "I arranged a sit down with the department commander. Take the time you need with your family. I'll be right back." He was not taken to shows of emotion, so I was surprised when he hugged me again and gave me a kiss on the forehead. "It'll be okay, Stephanie," he said. "Whoever did this picked the wrong cop to screw with."

Chapter Thirty-Seven

Max looked cranky when I took him from Ma. A room was set up for childcare, and we had been given access to it. "I fed and changed him," Ma said. She was bouncing him in her arms when I entered the room. "He's a little touchy. I think he's tired."

"Are you tired? Is mama's baby boy tired?" I swung him back and forth in my arms and smooched him all over his face. It made him smile, and that made me smile. "That's more like *my* little boy."

Max cooed. He may have gurgled. In any case, he made some manner of cute baby noise.

"Happy voices," I began, cuing Ma to my MO. "Herb is here. The whole place is on high alert, and I'm going to sit down with Suffolk County brass in a few minutes. Herb and I think it's best that you and Max go home."

"No, Stephanie, I'll stay here. I can take care of Max so that you can do what you have to. I promise—" She began to tear up. "I won't be any trouble."

"Come here."

Ma approached with a quizzical expression on her face.

I gave her a tight squeeze around the neck with my free hand and kissed her on the cheek. "I love you, but you have to go home. Do it for me. I need to work around the clock, and I won't feel as guilty about ignoring my son if I know that everyone is safe and that you and Ricky are watching over Max. I want you back on home turf where the police and FBI can act as watchdogs. Both Ambler and Shearson will give you round-the-clock support. And I think it's better if Ricky doesn't know what's going on. Just tell him that you took Max so that Gus and I could have a second honeymoon. He's naïve, but he'll understand what that means."

"But, Stephanie, please."

"It's better this way." We were both in tears. "So much for happy voices, huh?"

Ma sighed a long and troubled sigh. "Okay, honey. I'll do as you ask."

"Thank you." I gave her another tight squeeze. "Now take my son home. I have to go to work."

Chapter Thirty-Eight

Suffolk County Police Commissioner Joseph Bratton commanded attention when he entered a room. He was tall with thick, gray hair and a cleft in his chin deep enough to measure up to Dudley Do-Right. We were set up at a conference table in the large situation room when he entered with Pulaski at his side. Ambler and I stood as he approached.

Bratton took my hand. "Detective Chalice, I don't know what to say except that we'll find your husband and boil the son of a bitch responsible for his disappearance. You have my word."

I wasn't myself and was sure that the way I felt was obvious to anyone looking at me. Nonetheless, the time for licking wounds was over. I had to be at my very best no matter how daunting the situation was. I think in some part I was responding to Bratton's confidence. "So very happy to have you on my side, Sir."

"We're all on the same team, Detective. I take your husband's kidnapping personally. I'll treat his abduction as if someone had taken my own flesh and blood." He turned to Ambler. "Special Agent Ambler." He extended his hand. "You're in charge of the FBI's New York office, aren't you?"

"Just the criminal division," Ambler replied modestly.

Bratton grinned. "What else is there?"

Ambler laughed. "Quite a bit, I'm afraid. I only cover one piece of a very large pie."

"I have to say I was surprised to learn that you were here," Bratton said. "Any other intelligence agencies on their way?

Should I expect the NSA and CIA? How about Homeland Security?"

"No. Just me," Ambler chuckled. "This is personal. I've known Detective Chalice ever since she was a young girl. Her father worked NYPD homicide and was a dear friend of mine."

"You got here awfully fast," Bratton said.

"Chalice would have done the very same for me—I've no doubt of it. Shall we get busy?"

"Let's." Everyone sat when Bratton took his chair. Bratton faced me. "All right, Detective, why do you believe your husband has been abducted?"

I thought long and hard before answering. I'd tell Bratton everything I knew about Alana Moore, Sarah Fisher, and Bill Alden, but the only thing I could tell him about Gus' abduction came from my gut. I wasn't going to waste his time with stories about my sixth sense and so on and so forth. Bratton had acted quickly to deploy his resources, and there were already check points and roadblocks set up throughout Suffolk County. He didn't need proof. He was only looking for direction. "Okay," I began. "This is what I've got."

Chapter Thirty-Nine

As the name indicates, the Long Island land mass stretches northeastward one hundred eighteen miles from New York Harbor into the Atlantic Ocean. It's twenty-three miles across at its widest point, but splits into narrow forks at the East End. Montauk, where we were vacationing and where Gus went missing, is the easternmost town on the southern fork. Traveling west along the southern fork from Montauk to New York City there are areas where the region is very narrow. It was in these locations that checkpoints had been set up, at Napeague Harbor Road, again at Hampton Bays, and at Sag Harbor to block access to the northern fork. That being said, Suffolk County has hundreds of miles of coastline with access to the Atlantic Ocean and the Long Island Sound. The southern shore of Connecticut runs parallel to Long Island and is only a hop, skip, and a jump away, by ferry. Suffolk County PD was covering all of this, and NYPD was covering the western end of the island where bridges and tunnels provide access to Queens, Manhattan, Staten Island, Brooklyn, and the Bronx.

Ambler stood next to me after the briefing session with Bratton, studying a large, detailed map of Long Island. So far there were no witnesses to Gus' abduction, and I knew Gus would be extremely difficult to locate if we didn't formulate an efficient and expeditious plan for his recovery.

We all doubted there would be a ransom demand. The direction we were taking for now was that Gus had been taken because I had somehow poked a hornet's nest with all the prying I had done. I must've gotten close to something ... but what?

Close to whom? It was no longer a matter of one individual—me—looking into a handful of local cases. There were now dozens of investigators working on the case files of Alana Moore, Sarah Fisher, and Bill Alden. Was there a common thread? We had to find it if it existed.

"I can't believe what I've done," I lamented. "How could I have—"

"How could you what?" Ambler snapped. "Getting down on yourself isn't going to help us find Gus. You need to be one-hundred-percent. Personally I have a hard time connecting Gus' abduction with any of the cases you've been looking into. We have to consider the possibility that what happened to Gus had nothing to do with your poking around at all."

"You think it was random? You think that someone saw a six-foot-two, two-hundred-twenty-pound man and decided that he was a ripe target for abduction? No, sir, I can't believe that's what's happened. There's something I'm not seeing."

"Let's talk about the cabin fire again. That's the freshest incident, and you have some evidence to support a homicide theory. You booked this cabin, and you came out here just in time to see it go up in flames. How did you come across it in the first place?"

"We found a listing by a local vacation home rental company online and booked it. The price seemed good. It looked quaint, and we thought it would be a good spot for us to spend time with Max."

"And why did you suspect that there was foul play after the fire department investigator assured you that the cause of the fire was accidental?"

"Because they found arsenic in Bill Alden's body tissues."

"But the ME told you that arsenic is a byproduct of burning fabric. He didn't see anything suspicious, did he?"

"No."

"But you insisted on digging deeper."

"And I was right, Herb. As I mentioned in the briefing room, someone laced Alden's cigarettes with cyanide."

"The police are searching for Kaley Struthers, but she seems to be off the grid. She was the one who grocery shopped for Alden, correct?"

"Yes. Gus and I both met her. She seemed like a sweet young girl. We were told that she was very involved with the local church and does lots of volunteer work in the community." I rubbed my eyes. "She offered to babysit Max."

"So, at the moment, she's our only person of interest?"

"Yes." We had already agreed to push the story of Gus' abduction to all the tri-state news stations. Gus' photo was already on the Internet and would be on TV before the evening news broke. NYPD was offering a substantial reward for any information leading to his recovery.

"I'd like to release her photo and ID to the media and explain that she's a person of interest in the abduction. The faster we can put our finger on her, the better," Ambler said. "Let's turn up the heat. Anyone else you can think of that might have wanted to mess with Gus?"

"If you asked me that question a couple of days ago, I would've said yes, but now ... This guy who was doing work on our rental house seemed unstable to me and both Gus and I had words with him. He was showing up at the house unannounced and scaring the hell out of us. Very unaccommodating—he never came down off his ladder to talk with us, wouldn't give us the time of day. He'd sneak away when he was done with his work— a real annoying SOB."

"So why isn't he worth questioning?"

"He's believed to have died in a car fire just the other day. The body is in the morgue right now."

Ambler seemed disturbed by the news. "Another goddamn fire? What the hell is going on around here? Has the ME made a positive identification yet?"

"That's a work in progress. They're trying to make a positive ID with forensic odontology, but the ME hasn't been able to locate the victim's dental records yet."

Ambler took out his pen and pad. "Name?"

"Ray Claymore."

He closed his pad. "Look, Stephanie, I'm going to oversee the background checks on everyone even remotely connected to the abduction." He put his hand on my arm. "God forgive me for saying this, but you look like hell. You need some rest and a solid meal. I'm going to book accommodations nearby for my team and myself. I'd like you to stay with us. I know you'll be safe enough with police protection at your summer rental, but I'd rather have you close by. Agreed?"

I nodded. I was still feeling hollow inside and needed direction from my old friend. "I'll grab a sandwich and close my eyes for twenty minutes. That's the most I can promise."

He accepted quickly. "I'll take it. I know how urgent this is, but I don't want you falling on your face. An hour will give me just enough time to set the wheels in motion." He grabbed my other arm and looked me in the eye. "We've got this, Stephanie. We'll bring Gus home. Can you hold it together?"

"I have to."

"Atta girl. Now go wolf down a nice pastrami sandwich. It'll make you feel like a new woman."

Chapter Forty
Search for Gus Lido: Day 2

It was six a.m., and I was already at police headquarters searching through files. Something linked these crimes—I just couldn't see it. I found it hard to concentrate and be objective with Gus' life on the line. *My Gus.* The thought that he might be suffering crippled me—it was as if the two of us were emotionally connected. I always wanted justice. I always empathized with the victims and their families, but my family . . . I had to fight a war with my emotions every second of the day just to keep my head in the game. Gus was now gone almost eighteen hours, and I knew that with each passing minute, our chances of recovering him safe and healthy grew smaller. A full statewide manhunt was now in effect. The PBA and the Detective's Endowment Association had each kicked in additional rewards for information leading to Gus' safe recovery.

Ambler was bleary-eyed and holding a giant-size cup of coffee as he walked through the door. I glanced at my watch; it was quarter of seven. "You look like death warmed over, Herb."

"I never thought I'd say this, but you look worse." He placed his coffee cup on the conference table and pulled out the chair next to me. He took a bottle of aspirin out of his pocket, shook two into his hand, and then offered it to me. Aspirin is like the silver bullet of the pharmaceutical world. It's good for headache, pain, and fever; it thins blood, helps to prevent heart attacks, and possibly even lowers the risk for certain types of cancer. About the only thing it can't do is bring someone back from the dead. I shook a couple into the palm of my hand and swallowed them with a mouthful of coffee.

"Headache?" Ambler asked.

I nodded. I felt physically and mentally miserable, and the headache was just one item on the list. "Have we received background on Alden yet?"

"It's coming off the printer right now."

Thank God. I closed my eyes and blew a sigh of relief. "It's about goddamn time."

As if by cue, the door opened. The office admin walked in with two sets of Alden's files and placed them on the table in front of us. I read her eyes. Her smile said, *You poor thing. I wouldn't want to be in your shoes.*

"Thank you," I said. I wasn't used to appearing pathetic. *You'd better get over it, girl. Put your pain on the back shelf.*

Ambler and I dug into the file. Aside from the sound of turning pages, the room was completely silent for a full fifteen minutes. We both scribbled notes as we dug through Alden's records. The files weren't all that thick. Alden grew up in a town called Centereach, which wasn't too far from us. He had no criminal record and graduated from the State University at Farmingdale with a degree in engineering. He was married with no children and was employed by the same local engineering company most of his adult life.

It wasn't until I got to the very last page that I saw something interesting. For the last five years of his working history, he was employed in a civilian capacity for the United States Air Force. That alone was no great shakes, because the military often employs civilian engineers, but as I got to the bottom of the page . . .

Ambler must've been a few seconds ahead of me and was already reacting to what I had just read.

I pointed to the bottom of the last page.

He confirmed with a nod, reached for the telephone, and quickly punched in a number. I could tell that he was talking to one of his subordinates by the authoritative manner in which he spoke. "I'll wait," he said and covered the receiver.

I was staring at the stamp at the bottom of Alden's military transcript, where it had been officially stamped, SEALED.

Ambler jumped back on the phone and seemed to be listening attentively. I saw his face grow red. His lips were pressed together, and I could tell he was seething with anger. "Well, *wake* a fucking judge," he demanded. "It's after seven. Call one of those robe-clad assholes and tell him that I need a court order. Now!" He slammed down the receiver without waiting for a reply and shook his head woefully. "I wonder which sorry son of a bitch I'm about to piss off this time."

BOOK FOUR

Chapter Forty-One
May 10, 1985

Bill Alden found Colonel Frank Prescott at his usual picnic table at Montauk Point, eating his lunch alone under the shade of a blossoming dogwood tree.

"Frank?"

Prescott looked over his shoulder. He stared at Alden for a long moment, taking him in as he approached. Alden looked gaunt. His beard was overgrown, and he had deep circles around his eyes. "Bill," he said with surprise. He finally smiled and patted Alden on the shoulder. "I didn't expect to see you so soon. You're not supposed to report back until the end of the month."

Alden sat down on the bench opposite Prescott. "I'm not reporting back, Colonel. I wanted to catch you alone, off the base."

"Sure. Sure," Prescott said. "Want half of my BLT?"

"No thanks. I still don't have much of an appetite but enjoy your lunch. You eat and I'll talk, if that's okay with you."

Prescott popped the top of a can of Coke and took a sip. "How are you holding up, Bill?"

"Good days and bad, mostly bad. Aw, who am I kidding? Every day is just plain miserable."

Prescott looked off toward the Atlantic. The surface of the water was painted silver by the glare of the sun. His eyes clung to the image for a moment and then he sighed a troubled sigh. "So no improvement in your wife's condition?"

"Twenty-two days and counting. The machines are keeping her alive. She's still asleep and ... I don't think she'll last much longer."

Prescott looked stricken. "I'm sorry, Bill. I truly am. What about your little girl?"

"She's out of the incubator. I'm taking her home tomorrow."

"That's wonderful news. What can I do to help?"

"I'll cut right to the chase, Colonel. I can't take care of a baby, not now and maybe not ever. I can hardly—" Alden averted his eyes. "The day Caitlin went into the hospital, I was passed out in my car in the parking lot for three hours. By the time I got to the hospital, she was already unconscious." His throat tightened. "I didn't even have a chance to say goodbye to her."

"You said that you were passed out?"

"From the sessions—two years of nonstop experimentation has really taken a toll on me. I've got other stuff going on too. My stomach's a mess. If I eat more than once a day, I just give it all back. I don't sleep most of the night and then just before dawn I lie awake and hallucinate. I'm afraid I'd only wind up hurting her." His lips curled downward. "That's no life for a child."

"Do you want out of your current program, Bill? Don't worry about pay and benefits. I can reassign you to another activity, one that won't beat you up so badly."

"You'd do that?"

Prescott hemmed and hawed, shaking his head from side to side. "It's unusual, but if it'll help you ... at least until you're feeling better about yourself. Maybe all you need is to get your confidence back." He saw that Alden had a faraway look in his eyes. "Is there more?" He took a tiny nibble of his sandwich. "What else?"

"Without Caitlin ... Like I said I just don't know if I'll ever be able to take care of a child. You know my history."

Prescott seemed to be trapped in thought. He put down his sandwich. "Are you thinking about putting your daughter up for adoption? Isn't there someone in your family who can help out?"

"I'll give it to you straight, Frank." He swallowed before speaking again. "I hear talk about a program studying infants and children, the one Kleeb is trying to push through."

Prescott averted his eyes. "Where'd you hear that?" he asked suspiciously.

"Does it matter? Look, my daughter is flesh of my flesh, and there's a fifty/fifty chance that she'll be able to do what I can do. That's a far sight better than wasting your time with orphans with no demonstrated ability whatsoever, isn't it?"

"I guess there's a lot more scuttle floating around the base than I knew about. Kleeb's pretty full of himself, isn't he?"

Alden nodded.

"Still, do you know what that would mean? Do you realize what kind of childhood she'd have?"

"Not exactly, but at least she'd be close enough to me that I'd be able to keep tabs on her. If I give her up for adoption, I'll never see her again, Frank. Isn't it better that I can watch her grow up? I mean, what would you do if she was yours?"

Prescott became completely still. A long moment passed, and then he puffed out his cheeks and expelled his breath.

"Are you all right?" Alden asked.

Prescott rubbed his eyes. "I'm just tired. Look, that's a lot to chew on, Bill. I'll have to—"

"Think on it?"

"No. I mean . . . you asked what I would do if I were in your place. But, yes, I'll have to think about it." He put down his sandwich and wrapped it up.

"Aren't you going to finish?"

"No." Prescott shook his head. "I'm done."

"Do what you have to, okay? Look at me, Frank. If you were a baby, would you want this sorry mess to be your father?"

Chapter Forty-Two
September 25, 1985

Alden tapped lightly on the glass panel. The military nurse looked up from her desk and slid the glass to the side. "Can I take a peek, Margo?" he whispered.

"If you promise not to disturb her. She's got thirty minutes left on the simulator. I don't want to have to make up another cock-and-bull story about the projector breaking down again."

"I promise. I promise. I'll just watch, okay?"

Margo nodded. She slid the glass panel closed and stood. A moment later the door to the nursery opened. "She's in here."

He followed her into a darkened room where his daughter was lying in a crib. A projector positioned alongside the crib cast images onto the ceiling above her. The baby seemed captivated by the images of puffy, white clouds moving across a crystal-blue sky. Most of the clouds were amorphous in shape. Alden watched his daughter as her eyes followed the forms moving above her. Randomly a cloud resembling a smiling face would roll slowly across the sky. When it did, a lullaby began to play. The baby gurgled, making a happy sound until the smiling cloud disappeared and the music stopped.

"She's getting big," Margo said. "She's a beautiful, healthy girl." She rubbed Alden's arm. "We're taking real good care of her, Bill. We treat her like she's ours."

A tear formed in the corner of his eye. "Is she getting any fresh air?"

"I take her upstairs every day, weather permitting."

"Thank you. I don't want her thinking this is what the world really looks like. It's so dark and gloomy down here. I don't want her to know that she's below ground, under the earth, like—" He stopped and redirected his gaze back to his daughter.

The smiling cloud rolled back across the screen. The baby cooed in anticipation of the nursery rhyme music.

"She's smart too," Margo said. "She catches on to everything right away. Smartest child down here."

Bill glowed for a moment. "My little girl."

The nursery rhyme ended. "You'd better go, Bill. You know I'll catch shit if someone finds out you've had contact with her. You don't want her getting removed from the program, do you?"

"No. No. No." He blew his daughter a kiss. "Thank you, Margo. See you tomorrow?"

"We'll see," she said with uncertainty. "Now scoot!" She gave him a playful smack on the butt, sending him on his way.

He closed the door without making noise as he left.

Margo watched the promenade of clouds cross the ceiling. She had seen it often enough to know the order in which the different shaped clouds passed before the baby's eyes. There was the oblong, billowy shape, followed by a grouping of tiny poof-shaped clouds, then the long, shimmering one, and finally the smiling face with the music. As she watched, the long shimmering cloud rolled away. The baby's face grew excited. "What a smart little girl you are. You know what's coming already, don't you?"

Chapter Forty-Three
June 25, 1988

"**It's too tight.**"

"Sorry, Bill, it's got to be really snug." The technician adjusted the straps on Alden's helmet. "Any better?"

"Not really."

The technician shrugged. "Best I can do." He untangled the electrical leads and snapped them onto the helmet. "The doctor doesn't want you to get into the tank until he checks you. Just hang out a few minutes." He made a notation on the experiment chart and left the room.

Alden sat quietly in a chair, watching the shimmering water in the isolation tank. The thermometer read ninety-eight point three degrees. The saline solution in the tank had been cooled so that it was exactly the same as Alden's measured internal body temperature.

The door creaked open. Alden turned and regarded Dr. Kleeb without any emotion.

"This is the same experiment we tried yesterday, Bill, except we'd like to give you a little something to help you relax. All right with you?" Kleeb asked.

"I didn't sign up to take any drugs," Bill said flatly. "TMS and sensory deprivation are one thing, mind-altering drugs are something else."

"What's the big deal? You've been in the program for years. Have we ever done anything to put you at risk?"

"Not while Colonel Prescott was around."

"Meaning what?" Kleeb asked with insult in his voice.

"Meaning Prescott knew where to draw the line."

"And you're insinuating that I *don't?*"

"And I'm *saying* that you don't," Alden said hotly. "So back off!"

"All right, get into the tank, Alden." Kleeb went over to the medication cabinet and unlocked it while Alden slid into the isolation tank. "Be careful not to loosen the helmet."

The tank was white and shaped like a large lima bean with the ends higher than the middle. It allowed the participant to submerge up to the neck in the saline solution without covering the head. Alden was floating in the tank when Kleeb returned and set a hypodermic needle on the tank ledge even with Alden's line of sight.

"Are you kidding me? Alden said angrily. "What did I say? What did I goddamn say?"

"You think your friend Prescott was a real prince of a guy, but you don't know the half of it."

"What does that mean?"

Kleeb's lips parted, but he remained silent. A moment passed along with his nerve. "Anyway, he's gone now, and I'm in charge."

"I don't care what you're in charge of. I said no drugs and I mean it."

"You know I have complete autonomy down here and there's absolutely nothing to prevent me from booting you and your daughter out of the program."

Alden turned his head abruptly, his eyes growing wide with alarm as he and Kleeb locked gazes.

"That's right, *I know.* Prescott thought he had buried all the pertinent documents, but I did my own snooping around when I took over. All the paperwork is clean, but I know that Baby Girl Doe's hospital records have been falsified. I know everything, Bill, and I've kept my mouth shut. So don't give me your highhanded bullshit about me not being the man Prescott was. He's not the hero you think he is. I took pity on you because of what happened to your wife and son . . . tragic."

"You're a real prick, Kleeb!"

"Your daughter is three years old. I've allowed the sham to continue as long as it doesn't jeopardize the program and I've made sure that your little girl is very well cared for. I presume you'd like that to continue, wouldn't you?"

Alden bit his lip, suppressing the expletive he was about to hurl. "What's in the hypodermic?"

"That's a good boy," Kleeb said in a calming voice. "Scopolamine, just a couple of milligrams."

"At the same time as transcranial electromagnetic stimulation? Is that a good idea? How long does it last?"

"The scopolamine should wear off hours before you're out of the tank. It's a small dose. Nothing to worry about."

"Have you tried this before?"

"No."

"So I'm the guinea pig."

"That's why we pay you the big bucks, Alden." Kleeb injected Alden's arm without waiting for his approval. "You're all set. Now give us a good show." He stood and lowered the cover on the isolation tank. Alden was now enclosed in a soundproof isolation tank in a state of complete and utter darkness.

Kleeb signaled through the glass panel to the technician in the adjacent control room to begin recording data. He was stepping through the doorway when he mumbled, "Entitled son of a bitch."

~~~

"Is the man coming?" the little girl asked, her voice childlike and inquisitive.

"Your friend Bill?" Margo checked her watch. "It's kind of late—maybe tomorrow, sweetheart. Are you ready for your quiet-time bath?"

The little girl nodded excitedly. Her blond curls bounced atop her head. "Uh-huh. Can I have a *dwink furst*?"

"Sure. What would you like?"

"*Appul duce.*"

"Apple *juice*. Say apple *juice*."

"*Appul duce*," she said with an impish smile.

Margo giggled. "Okay, but tomorrow we're going to have to work on your pronunciation. Okay?"

The little girl once again shook her head happily. Margo opened the refrigerator and handed her a juice box after detaching the straw and puncturing the foil seal. "How's that?"

"Good," she said after taking a long sip. "Can I have a cookie?"

"After your quiet-bath. Now come on, let's get ready."

Margo took her hand and led her to the room with the juvenile isolation tank. It was white and shaped like a lima bean with both ends higher than the middle. She put her juice box down on a chair and took off her robe.

"Your bathing suit is so pretty," Margo said.

"*Fank* you."

"You're welcome." Margo picked her up and lowered her gently into the tank. "Is it warm enough?"

"Good," she said while nodding. "Can I play with Brynn tomorrow?"

"Of course." Margo gently pressed adhesive contact pads to the little girl's forehead and then attached electrical leads. She flipped a switch and the "Itsy Bitsy Spider" began to play from speakers located in the tank lid. "Are you comfortable, sweetie?"

She nodded enthusiastically. "I ready to get *keen*."

"Okay. I'm going to close the lid. Shut your eyes and dream happy dreams. I'll be back in a little while, okay?"

"*Kay*. You think the man will come back tomorrow?"

Margo smiled. "I think so." *I wonder what happened to Bill?* "Here we go. Sweet dreams."

"*Kay*. I *dweam* about my toys."

"That's a good idea." Margo slowly lowered the lid on the isolation tank. She set the instrumentation panel and left the room after asking one of the other nurses to keep an eye for her.

The corridors in the underground complex were long, labyrinth-like, and always chilly. She folded her arms in front of her for warmth and walked quickly toward the adult-male section of the testing area.

The testing coordinator had gone home for the evening, but the schedule was still on his desk. Margo checked for Bill Alden's name to see if he was still onsite and if he was scheduled for any tests that would run past standard hours. She noted that he was scheduled for isolation testing at ten a.m. and had signed in. Testing should have concluded at three p.m., but he had not yet signed out. Margo dropped the clipboard and ran down the hall.

When she got to the adult isolation area, she found the room empty and all the lights switched off. She flipped on the lights. All but one of the isolation tanks was empty. "Christ!" She hit the panic button and raced out of the control room. Red strobe lights flashed in the corridor, and sirens blared.

She lifted the lid on the isolation tank. "Oh my God." Alden was passed out, his head slack, his chin touching his clavicle. She unbuckled his helmet and lifted it off his head. "Come on, Bill. Wake up. Wake up." She slapped his cheeks repeatedly. "Come on. Come on." She grabbed the emergency kit and had her hand on the smelling salts when the door opened behind her.

Kleeb towered over her, his eyes beaming down angrily. "What in the hell do you think you're doing?" he shouted.

"Look!" she said with dire urgency in her voice while pointing at Alden.

Kleeb grabbed her by the shoulder and pulled her to her feet. "Get out," he ordered and shoved her toward the door.

Chapter Forty-Four
July 7, 1988

Margo waited anxiously in Kleeb's office. It was at the far end of the underground complex in the executive administration area. With the door closed, his office was like a sealed vault, silent except for the hum of the fluorescent lights and the ticking of his desk clock. Kleeb usually checked in at the nursery every day, but had avoided the children's facility since the altercation with her. She knew intuitively that the boom was about to be lowered. An official reprimand was coming—she could feel it in her bones. *But how ... how can he justify it?* "He's Kleeb, that's how," she muttered. "He can do whatever he wants."

The walls were pale blue. His desk and credenza were gray metal, like all the office furniture in the facility. Kleeb entered and sat down without making eye contact. He opened a folder and spoke to her with his eyes glued to it. "I'm shutting down the children's program and reassigning you to Female Adult." He closed the folder and finally looked her in the eye. "That's all."

"But, but ..." Margo was tongue-tied. *"Why?"*

"Progress is too slow. Our budget has been reduced again and I have to allocate funding where I can get the most bang for the buck. If I don't demonstrate sufficient progress this year, the entire facility may be closed down altogether."

"But what about the children?"

"They'll be assigned to orphanages by the state."

"That's ... that's terrible. These kids need time to adjust. The only life they've known is down here. I'm the only family they have."

"You'll have until the end of the week to prepare them. New York State Department of Social Services will be here on Monday to do the paperwork."

Margo rose abruptly. "Dr. Kleeb, these children will never be able to assimilate that quickly. Some of them—"

"Should be thankful for the time they were here, cared for and mollycoddled on the Federal government's dime. You forget that most of these children came from orphanages and state homes originally. They've been on an extended vacation as far as I'm concerned."

"You're a cruel son of a bitch, Dr. Kleeb. Is this because—"

"It's because I say so. Is there anything else?"

You piece of shit. "Can I get a little more time with them— until the end of the month at least?"

"Until the end of the week, nurse. You're dismissed."

Margo slammed the door on her way out of his office, ignoring concern for a reprimand. She had only walked a few paces down the hall when she started to cry. She slumped against the wall and dug into her pocket for tissue. *I hate him. That son of a bitch. I hate him.* She blotted her tears immediately—it was still the military despite the guise of being a government research facility, and a commissioned officer could not appear to be weak in front of her fellow officers. Her eyes were red as she continued down the corridor, when necessary dabbing at her nose with the tissue that was concealed within her closed fist.

The nursery was covered for the next hour, but she passed by on her way to the underground hospital complex just to make sure her staff was doing their job.

Access to the hospital area was restricted for all but medical personnel. She swiped her card key, and the electrical lock on the door released. She routinely visited the children's ward but needed a moment to find intensive care. "Hi, Rose," she said, seeing her friend. *God, I hope she doesn't give me a hard time.*

"Get lost, Margo? You're a long way from pediatrics."

"Just want to look in on a friend. Where are they keeping Bill Alden?"

"I didn't know you two were . . . you naughty girl," she said mischievously.

"Stuff it," Margo said, dismissing the suggestive comment. "How is he?"

Rose laid her head on clasped hands, pantomiming to indicate that he was asleep. "Still in a coma, Betty Boop. He won't have a clue that you're here."

Margo sighed. "So it's okay if I look in on him?"

"Of course."

"Thanks." She stepped closer to her friend. "Look, this is just between you and me, okay? I don't want that son of a bitch, Kleeb, to know I looked in on Bill. Okay?"

"*Please.* You're kidding right? Like I'd tell that creepy bastard anything other than to take a hike."

"Thanks, Rosie. You're a doll."

"I am, aren't I?" she said as she cracked her chewing gum.

The ICU was about thirty feet long and contained six beds in a row, each separated by a privacy curtain. She found Alden in the first one. He looked pale, but the dark circles he usually bore were gone from around his eyes. He looked peaceful and appeared clean and well cared for. Oxygen was being fed into his nostrils. Margo checked his IV bag. It contained saline and glucose. She checked the output level of his urine to make sure that he was adequately hydrated.

"So still." She tried to repress the thought that he appeared deathlike, like someone who had passed, been embalmed, and been made up for showing at a funeral. She sighed and stroked his hair but remained verbally silent. *I'm so sorry.* She owed him nothing, nothing save the pleasure of serving as mother to his little girl for the past three years. *I love her too. You poor man. That little girl is all you have left and now . . . you won't even know she's gone.*

Alden didn't respond to her presence or her sentiment. He lay perfectly still drawing even, measured breaths.

She sniffled. *I did my best, Bill. I really tried.*

"Hey, Margo, are you all right?"

She turned and saw that Rose was walking toward her.

"Come on, I've got to get you out of here. Dr. Jerkoff usually makes his rounds about now."

"Thanks." She turned back to Alden. *If you could just wake up.* She kissed her fingertips and touched them to his forehead.

"What's with the kissy-touchy? You one of those gals who likes banging coma patients?" Rose cackled.

"Take a leap, will ya?"

"Hey, I hear the nursery is shutting down. Is that true?"

Margo frowned. "News travels fast."

"Are you getting reassigned?"

Margo nodded.

"Tough break for those little kids. Tough break for you—I know how much you liked that job."

"Thanks, kiddo." Margo hit the release button, and the hospital door swung open. "Remember," she said. "Mum's the word."

Chapter Forty-Five
July 11, 1988

"What's this one's name?"

"Raven. Raven Gallagher," Margo said proudly.

Celeste Thax peered at the little girl through veiny, milky-white eyes. "Raven? That's a name?" Behind the cataracts, her irises were cat's-eye green. "She's tiny like a bird."

Raven tugged at Margo's sleeve. "Why she has whiskers?" the child whispered.

"Shhh. Be polite," Margo said. "This is the nice lady who's going to be taking care of you from now on."

Raven stomped her foot, *"No!"* Her protest was both childish and resolute at the same time.

A child wearing a stained, broadcloth dress and white Mary Janes ran down the stairs and hid behind Thax, peering out at the two strangers.

"And who's this pretty girl?" Margo asked.

"That's Kim," Thax said bluntly.

Raven tugged on Margo's sleeve again. "Why Kim smells like pee?"

"I've got a lot a cats," Thax explained. "Maybe the kitty litter needs changing." She looked down at Kim. "Change the kitty litter before you take your bath. You didn't take one last night, did you?"

Kim shook her head, cowering from her caretaker.

"I didn't hear you," Thax snapped.

"N-n-no." Kim said, her voice trembling.

"It's no wonder you stink." Thax looked up at Margo. "You try to teach these brats good hygiene, but they just keep running around like wild Indians."

"Not want to live here," Raven sulked. Her eyes grew red.

Thax sneered at her. "Well, ain't that just tough titty. Listen, your highness, beggars can't be choosers."

"*What* did you just say to her?" Margo said with outrage.

"What's the matter, sister? Got a hearing problem?" Thax said resentfully.

"My head *huwts*." Raven rubbed her temple. She frowned and began to sniffle.

Margo knelt alongside her. "What's wrong, sweetheart? Do you have a headache?"

Raven nodded and continued to cry. "Since I got shot."

"Listen to the brat," Thax laughed. "Kid, if you got shot, you'd have much more to worry about than a headache."

Margo shot Thax a scalding glance then looked back at Raven. "What shot?" she asked.

"Dr. *Kweeb* give me shot. Now my head *huwts* and my cheeks burn."

Shot? Kleeb, you son of a bitch. She placed her hand against Raven's forehead. "Maybe you're coming down with something. You feel a little warm." She picked up Raven's coat. "Put this on, honey, I'm taking you back to the base."

"What's the big tadoo? A couple of Excedrin, and she'll be right as rain."

"You don't give Excedrin to a three-year-old. Come on, Raven, we're going."

"Why not?" Thax asked. "I give it to all the brats."

"Why am I not surprised?"

"Come. Go. Stay. Whatever," Thax said highhandedly. "The state is paying me whether she's here or not. Bring her back when she's fixed up . . . or not."

Chapter Forty-Six

"**Half a milligram of scopolamine three times a week?** Are you out of your mind?" Margo shouted as she burst into Kleeb's office, waving Raven's medical chart in the air. She was still wearing her coat when she slammed it down on his desk. "Why wasn't I told that you've been medicating my kids?"

"Come in," he said sarcastically. "Make yourself at home." He put down his pen and sat back in his chair. "Anything else you want to say?"

"Half a milligram? That's more than the maximum pediatric dosage."

He picked up the medical chart and weighed it in his hand. "Just what part of experimental government program don't you understand, Nurse Atwater? We're developing techniques to control the human mind. The Army and the Air Force sanctioned this program. You're a military officer, for Christ's sake. Pull yourself together."

"Raven has headaches and a rash. Her father is in a coma. Doesn't that matter to you? She's a child, not a soldier."

"Do you know Bill Alden's story? Maybe I should tell you. Did you know that his wife died during childbirth?"

Margo sighed a long and troubled sigh but said nothing.

"Alden fell apart and voluntarily asked the great Colonel Frank Prescott to enroll his child in the program because he couldn't take care of her. So why am I the bad guy? He was in the program almost two years when all this happened. It's not as if he had any misconceptions about what happens down here—we test and we experiment. We poke, pinch, and prod. There's nothing cruel or unusual going on down here. It's just science. I'm a doctor, a doctor paid to run a government research program and develop vital initiatives for the military. We were getting nowhere fast, and I made the decision to introduce psychoactive medications into the program. Aside from a control group, psychoactives are being used on everyone in the study at this point."

"Including the children? We have absolutely no idea what the effects of long-term scopolamine usage will be. These kids are being exposed to high-energy electromagnetic radiation, isolation therapy, subliminal imagery, and God knows what else. What are the chances of these kids having any type of normal life?"

Kleeb stared at her blankly. "Where are you going with this? These kids were orphans. They were homeless. We cared for these kids. We fed them. We clothed them and gave them shelter. How many times do I have to repeat myself? Maybe if we hadn't pampered them so much, I wouldn't have had to terminate the program. Maybe if you saw these kids as experimental subjects . . ." he huffed. "The children's program is dead now. Raven and every other child in the program is now in the care of New York State."

"Care of the state? What a joke. I brought Raven back with me. I wouldn't leave my worst enemy in that foster home. The woman who runs the place is an animal. The house is filthy dirty and it smells like urine. I'll never bring her back to that place."

"That's too bad. Should I write you up for insubordination now or would you like a few minutes to think it over?"

"What?" Margo pressed her lips together until they turned white. "You'd do that?"

"You're giving me little choice, Nurse Atwater." Kleeb checked his watch. "Raven can stay the night, but she goes back to the foster home in the morning. With or without you."

"You're such a shit."

"The choice is yours." He opened his desk drawer and pulled out a pack of cigarettes. "Is there anything else?" he asked impatiently.

Margo jumped up. "I won't stand for this. If I have to I'll adopt her myself."

Kleeb smirked. "Knock yourself out, but no matter what, Raven will be dropped off at the foster home in the morning." He lit a cigarette and blew a cloud of smoke across his desk. "Anything else?"

Chapter Forty-Seven
January 1991

"**Raven. Raven! Get your boney little keister down here right now.**" Thax plopped into a recliner and put her floppy-sock-clad feet up on the footrest. She picked up the remote, clicked on the TV, and surfed channels until she found something she liked. A talk show host was interviewing a TV star who had long outlived her fifteen minutes of fame. Thax lost patience with the show after a few minutes and clicked the remote again. "Raven. Raven! I'm waiting."

Raven stood atop the stairs looking down at the old woman. She sighed before taking the steps down to the first level.

"What is it?" she asked as she approached Thax.

The old woman grabbed one of her loose-fitting socks at the toe, yanked it off, and wriggled her toes.

Raven cringed at the sight of Thax's feet. *Ooh. Gross!* "Already?"

"Yes, already. You're six years old. How long are you going to bellyache about it?" Thax picked up a mug and sipped the head off her beer, leaving a white, foamy mustache on her upper lip.

Raven couldn't help but giggle at her, because she thought that Thax looked like a cartoon character. With her mustache and chin whiskers, Thax was just a hat and sunglasses short of a bad disguise.

"I don't get you," Thax said. "One minute you're pissed off and the next minute laughing. I think you're turning into one of those schizos." She picked up the nail clipper and held it out for Raven. "And careful this time. I'm too old to lose a toe." Her toenails were thick and gray. The nail on her big toe was chipped.

Raven accepted the clipper and sat down cross-legged on the floor at eye level with Thax's hammertoes. She focused on Thax's feet to avoid seeing her fat, fleshy legs, which extended past the hem of her housecoat. She held her breath so as not to gag from the smell. Starting with the pinky toe, she worked her way from small to large because the nails were thinner on the smaller toes and easier to clip. She needed to put both hands on the clipper to cut the big toenail. A nail fragment shot off and hit Raven on the chin. "Ugh."

"Hurry up," Thax complained. "My feet are getting old." She took a big gulp of beer and redirected her attention to the TV. Rosie O'Donnell was being interviewed on a talk show. "No. I hate this Bozo." She clicked the remote again and again and . . .

Raven waited until Thax was completely mesmerized with one of the TV shows and then jabbed the point of the clipper into the old lady's big toe.

"Ouch! You clumsy bitch," she shouted as she rubbed her big toe. "It's bleeding. Get some Mercurochrome out of the medicine cabinet."

Raven popped up and raced to the stairs. "Sorry," *you old nag.* "I'll be right back."

"You'd better be sorry. Get your ass back here on the double."

Raven used a stepstool to reach the medicine cabinet. Finding the Mercurochrome, she fished a booger out of her nose and stuck it on the end of the applicator. She giggled before returning to Thax. Her booger had turned reddish orange from the antiseptic. She smeared it across the punctured wound and recapped the bottle.

"That burns," Thax complained. "Better be more careful with my other foot."

The other foot was far worse than the first. Thax's nail beds were yellow with fungus. Raven kept her mouth closed and did her best not to breathe the foul odor. She made quick work of the second foot and stood to go.

"Not so fast," Thax said with spitefulness in the tone of her voice, "For nearly cutting off my toe off, you get the honor of cleaning the toilet today."

"But it's not my turn," Raven protested.

"And you can do it tomorrow also."

Shit! "Can I have lunch first? My head hurts a lot." She pouted sadly, hoping to elicit sympathy from the wretched old woman.

"Playing on my good nature, are you? There's bologna in the refrigerator. Make me a sandwich too. I'm hungry."

"Thank you." Raven's arms were plastered to her sides as she hurried toward the kitchen.

Kim was sitting at the table eating corn flakes and water.

"That looks like vomit," Raven said. "No milk?"

"Not for days."

"The witch wants a sandwich."

Kim's eyes lit up. "Can I help?"

Raven nodded gleefully. "One topping each." She took the white bread out of the breadbox and removed four slices of bread. She made her own sandwich, first adding bologna without any condiments and cut off the crust with a sharp knife. Thax took all of her sandwiches the same way, with mustard and tomato. Raven squeezed mustard into a small dish and added a hefty shake of Bon Ami cleansing powder. Kim approached the table with an impish smile. From behind her back, she produced a cat turd, which she had removed from the litter box.

Raven snorted.

They both giggled while Raven blended it in with the mustard.

Raven placed the sandwich on a snack tray. She squeezed her eyes shut suddenly, looking uncomfortable.

Kim recognized the expression on Raven's face. "Another headache?" she asked.

Raven nodded without opening her eyes. It took a full minute before she was able to continue. She picked up the serving tray and forced a smile. "I hope she eats the whole damn thing."

~~~

"You still have to scrub the toilet," Thax said without looking at Raven, who set the snack tray next to her recliner and topped off her mug with beer.

"Yes, ma'am," she said politely. She turned and fought to hold back her laughter as she joined Kim behind the stairs to watch Thax eat her cat's shit.

Chapter Forty-Eight
May 2000

Thax moved slowly, taking an inordinately long time to get into her bed. She had just gotten home from the hospital and now had two amputated fingers to go with her three amputated toes. Her skin was yellow and covered with bruises—cirrhosis and diabetes, not a great combination.

"Stop scratching," Raven insisted. "Your skin is raw."

"I can't stop," Thax said. "It's driving me out of my mind."

"No. It's driving me out of *my* mind."

Thax was a big-boned woman, but had wasted away and was now down to a mere ninety pounds. Stretched out on the bed with her bloated belly and spindly arms, she looked like a frog pinned to a dissection tray. Her chin whiskers now extended down past the base of her neck. "The pain is killing me, Raven. Did you refill my prescription?"

"You know I did," she replied impatiently. "I'll go get it. Beer chaser?"

Thax nodded. "Yes, honey, and please hurry. I can't take it anymore."

Raven walked purposely out of the bedroom and down the stairs to the kitchen. She picked up an amber prescription bottle and read the label again, even though she'd read it three times since returning from the pharmacy. *OxyContin: one pill orally as indicated for pain.*

"Finally!" She had been waiting many long years for this moment—ever since the day Nurse Margo dropped her off at Thax's foster home. She crushed ten pills with a mortar and pestle and dissolved the powder in a glass of beer. She shook one additional pill into the palm of her hand and went upstairs.

"Oh good, honey." Thax eagerly picked up the pill, placed it on her heavily coated tongue, and washed it down with a gulp of beer. Raven had been abusing Thax's food for years, adding in almost anything she could think of in order to get even with the woman who treated her like the dirt beneath her fingernails. At first the infusions and mixtures were harmless but grew more insidious over the years.

How does the old bitch survive? "That's a good girl, drink it all down. You have to stay hydrated."

The old lady's appetite was nothing like it had been. Thax forced down the rest of the beer and was breathing heavily by the time the glass was empty.

Not this time, Raven swore to herself. *Die, you old bitch. Die!*

Thax began to yawn almost immediately.

"The surgery has taken everything out of me," Thax said. "I think I'll close my eyes." She began to snore in less than a minute.

Raven watched the old woman attentively as she walked out of her bedroom. She took the beer glass downstairs to the kitchen and washed it thoroughly before placing it in the rack to dry. She wiped out the pestle and put it away in one of the cabinets. She checked the time and then went inside to turn on the TV. A half hour had passed before she realized that she was not paying attention to the program.

Raven knew that Thax's time was running out, but how long would it take? Raven wanted closure and she wanted it now. She turned off the TV and went back upstairs to check on the old woman. Daylight was ebbing. Thax looked as if she was dead, but the faint sound of air whistling through her nostrils told Raven that she wasn't. She stood around waiting and hoping that the sedative would do the work on its own.

But it didn't.

Several minutes passed. Raven put her ear to the old woman's mouth and heard the faintest sound of breathing. She jostled her shoulder, but Thax did not stir. "Goodbye, you miserable old monster. This is for all the years of hell and all the years of being your slave." She pressed a pillow over her face, not hard enough to bruise her, just hard enough to suffocate a weak and heavily drugged old woman. It didn't take long. Raven held the mirror from Thax's compact over her mouth to see if it fogged. She found the carotid artery and checked the pulse on her neck. "Burn in hell, you old misery!"

Raven took a moment to prepare herself and then began to scream. Almost immediately she heard doors opening and feet on the stairs. "Oh my God," Raven stammered as soon as one of the other foster kids entered the room. "I think she's dead."

Chapter Forty-Nine
May 2000

The medical examiner sat on a stool next to the autopsy table where Celeste Thax rested. He picked up a microphone and began to dictate his findings.

"These are the autopsy notes for Celeste Thax, identification number 336754. The individual is female. Her age is seventy-three years old as ascertained by public records. A study of the internal organs shows that—"

The door to the morgue swung open. A clean-cut and immaculately dressed man walked briskly through the door. He was carrying a soft-sided leather briefcase. "Hi, Doc," he said as he pointed at the body of Celeste Thax. "I caught you just in time—I see you've got my Auntie Celeste on the table."

"Detective Smote," the ME said, confused. "What's going on? Are you related to this woman?"

"My mother's older sister." He crossed himself and looked toward the sky. "Now they're together," he said with a frown. He examined the body. "God, I haven't seen her in years. She's withered away to nothing. Except for the whiskers ... they're long enough to string a Fender guitar."

The ME chuckled. "Eighty-seven pounds exactly."

"What did you find?"

"Her medical history is well documented—advanced diabetes, advanced cirrhosis of the liver. Her heart arrested following a surgical procedure. She died in her sleep. All in all, not a bad way to go. She wouldn't be in the morgue at all if she hadn't just had a surgical procedure."

"Any serology or toxicology studies?"

"I didn't plan on doing any."

"I think you should," Smote said with a note of certainty in his voice.

"And why is that?" The ME sounded as if he was curious and irritated at the same time.

Smote reached into his briefcase and removed a white porcelain mortar and pestle contained in a plastic evidence bag. "Routine sweep of the kitchen." He handed the evidence bag to the ME. "Opiate residue on the tip of the pestle, I'm sure of it."

"The police report stated that she was taking OxyContin for pain. Maybe she had trouble swallowing the tablets."

"Maybe and maybe not. Auntie Celeste was a bit of nasty bitch. She ran a foster home, and I'm sure any number of her kids would have loved to see her dead. I'm going to drop this off at the crime lab. If it tests positive, I'm going to open a homicide investigation."

The ME rubbed his chin. "No problem, I'll run blood and tissue studies just to play it safe."

"Thanks, Doc. I appreciate the help." He winked at the ME and then stuffed the evidence bag back into his briefcase. *Now who'd want to go and kill old Auntie Celeste?* he mused. *I guess just about anyone.*

Chapter Fifty
June 2000

Terry O'Neil was busy pressing his suit slacks. It was the third time he'd hit the creases with steam, and when he finally lifted the pressing cloth, the creases in his slacks were razor sharp. He slipped into them while they were still warm and was buttoning his shirt when the doorbell rang. He stepped into his wingtip shoes and walked to the door without tying the laces. "Yes?" He pulled aside the white, lace curtains and looked through the glass door panel. A man held up a gold shield. O'Neil opened the door with urgency.

"Is everything all right?" he asked.

"Mr. O'Neil?"

"Yes."

"Detective Sullivan Smote. Can I come in?"

"Of course." O'Neil's eyes were wide as he stepped aside to give Smote room to enter his home. "What's going on? Did someone get hurt? One of my kids?"

"No. The kids are fine as far as I know, Mr. O'Neil. This is in regard to another matter."

"Oh thank God. You'll have to excuse me," O'Neil said. "I was in the middle of getting dressed." He shut the front door and gestured to the sofa. "Have a seat, Detective." He sat down in a side chair and tied his shoelaces. "How can I help you?"

"I'm investigating a homicide," Smote said.

O'Neil's mouth opened. He covered it with his fingers. "My God. Who?"

"You may not remember the victim's name but she was a foster parent like you, a woman named Celeste Thax. One of the children from her home is living with you now."

"That's terrible. You think she was murdered?"

"Possibly, not definitely, but I have enough evidence to conduct a homicide investigation. There were six girls living in her foster home. I'm making the rounds, talking to all of them." He flipped open his notepad. "The child's name is Raven Gallagher."

"Raven?"

"You seem shocked."

"I am. I've only known Raven a short time, but she's a real sweetheart and doesn't give me a lick of trouble. She's out shopping, running errands for me right now—very helpful girl."

"Out, huh? When do you expect her back?"

"An hour or so. Shouldn't be longer than that."

Smote smacked his lips. *"Okay."* He seemed displeased as he reached into his pocket and handed O'Neil his business card. "I have three more girls to talk to today. I'll come back. Call me as soon as she returns.

"Yes, of course," O'Neil said in a cooperative manner. "I'll get in touch the minute she gets back."

"Great." Smote was clearly unhappy. He stood. "Hush, hush on this, understand? I prefer to question persons of interest without giving them time to prepare for me."

O'Neil nodded. "I understand."

Smote saw himself to the door and left.

Chapter Fifty-One
Raven: January 2003

Terry O'Neil crossed his legs and picked up a rainbow cookie. He nibbled at the corner of the confection and then dabbed the corners of his mouth with his napkin. He checked his slacks to make sure that he hadn't dropped any crumbs and brushed them with his hands. He was sipping at his tea when the doorbell rang.

"Mr. O'Neil?"

"Yes?"

"Paul Bisbay," the visitor announced. "Suffolk County Department of Social Services. I made an appointment to see you. I'm the new case officer."

"Oh yes," O'Neil said with a wide smile. "Do come in." He saw Bisbay into his home and closed the door. "I was just having a cup of tea. Would you like some?"

"No thanks. I'm going to grab lunch as soon as we're finished."

He watched Bisbay from behind as he walked into the living room. Bisbay was short, with a large paunch, and pants that bagged beneath his rear end. *Eww.* O'Neil pretended to shudder. *Not with Donald Trump's dick.* "Help yourself to some cookies. I bought them for you." *Chubby.*

"Rainbow cookies," Bisbay exclaimed as he glanced down at the coffee table. "I love these. How did you know?"

"Everyone loves rainbow cookies."

Bisbay sat down and immediately picked up a cookie. "These are too good to resist. Thanks." It took but a moment for the first cookie to disappear. "Is Mrs. O'Neil home?"

"No. She's out at the moment, but I'm sure I can answer any questions you might have." Mrs. O'Neil hadn't been home in years, not since Terry began to indulge his sexual curiosity. She was living with a fisherman in Naples, Florida. She and Terry had never officially divorced so that Terry could continue to run the girls' foster home and collect revenue from the state. O'Neil sat down and crossed his legs. "Now how can I help you?"

"Just checking in," Bisbay said as he released the clasp on his briefcase. He opened a portfolio and clicked his ballpoint pen. "I'm taking the opportunity to visit all the foster families that have been assigned to me." He shuffled through his folders until he found the one he was looking for. "Here it is: O'Neil, 88 Leeward Lane. So how are you doing with the kids, Mr. O'Neil?"

~~~

Raven opened her eyes when she heard the front door close. It was after eleven, but she was still in bed, groggy with sleep. She and O'Neil had been up late, smoking pot and screwing. The frilly undergarments and stocking that O'Neil had worn were on the bed beside her. They were both into role-playing and gender experimentation. Dressing as a woman while being with a woman was one of O'Neil's favorites. Raven was into just about anything that was fun. She put O'Neil's discarded underthings on beneath her jeans and T-shirt and went into the bathroom to make sure that she looked presentable. She had a command performance to give to the caseworker, and she did not intend to disappoint.

~~~

"Are you ready to take in more children?" Bisbay asked.

"Maybe in a few months. The three girls keep me pretty busy," O'Neil said.

Bisbay flipped a few pages and looked up. "You do know that Raven Gallagher will be aging out of the system soon. Her ninety day notice will be going out any time now."

O'Neil saddened. "Raven is aging out?"

"Yes. She'll be too old for foster care and will have to transition to living independently. I assume that you know how it works."

"Can't she stay here a little longer?" O'Neil asked.

"Not on the state's dime." He flipped a few more pages in his portfolio. "She'll have to find a fulltime job and a place to live."

"Can she stay with me if I stop billing social services for her care?"

"Yes, of course, but I don't recommend it, not long term at least. It's better that they learn to take care of themselves. Delaying the process isn't going to do her any good."

"But it can be done?"

Bisbay nodded. "Yeah. I guess so."

O'Neil heard footsteps on the stairs. "Here's Raven now," he said with joy. "I'm so glad you'll have a chance to meet her." He turned toward the approaching teen and smirked. "Raven, tell Mr. Bisbay just how well we're getting along."

Chapter Fifty-Two
Raven: February 2004

Margarita Tejada stood in front of 88 Leeward Lane readying herself to ring the doorbell. She had been recently promoted and had only made a handful of onsite inspections. The process still intimidated her. The last home she visited was a mess, and she wondered how her predecessor had allowed it to keep its state charter. The house itself was in shambles. It was filthy and, in her mind, presented an unhealthy living situation. The foster parents did not keep adequate records and didn't seem to know where any of the children were. By contrast, 88 Leeward appeared to be a well-maintained property. *I hope this one's not a zoo like the last one.* The house was quiet when she rang the bell.

It took a moment for the door to open. The woman who answered the door appeared young, perhaps still in her teens or early twenties. She was dressed in jeans and a pretty top. Her hair was short and brushed to the side in a sweep. Her makeup was dark and dramatic. "Hi, can I help you?" she asked.

Tejada handed the young woman her business card. "I'm Margarita Tejada with the Department of Social Services. I'm here for a scheduled inspection."

"What happened to Mr. Bisbay?"

"Paul's been reassigned," Tejada said.

"That was quick—I think he only started last January."

Tejada shrugged. "I'm really not sure. And you are?"

"I'm *Ray-lene*," the young woman announced as a flashbulb went off in her head. "Terry's daughter. Come on in." She showed Tejada into the living room. "Have a seat. I hope you like rainbow cookies. They're my dad's favorite."

"I'm not hungry, but it's hard to say no to one of these."

"Something to drink?"

"No thanks. Is your mother or father around?"

"My dad will be right down. He's just washing up."

Tejada looked around while she munched on her cookie. "This is a lovely home. Most of the foster homes I visit aren't as well maintained."

"Dad's very handy," Raven said. "And he's got great taste."

"Do you live here, Raylene?"

"No. I'm just visiting."

"Hello," O'Neil said from the top of the steps. He descended holding onto the oak banister. He was dressed in a charcoal gray three-piece suit and a white shirt. He carried a tie in his other hand. "Sorry to keep you. I was just about to put on my tie." He extended his hand. "Terry O'Neil. So nice to meet you."

Tejada stood and took O'Neil's hand. "Margarita Tejada. I'm Paul Bisbay's replacement. So nice to meet you."

O'Neil's eyes widened. "Replacement? That wasn't long at all."

Raven put her arm through O'Neil's. "That's what I said, *Daddy.*"

Tejada smiled. "Your daughter Raylene is delightful. She's been very welcoming."

O'Neil's eyes twinkled at Raven's quickness. "I'm glad. So, you were saying something about Mr. Bisbay?"

"It's the old social services slip-and-slide, Mr. O'Neil. Paul has been reassigned to a different area. By the way, thanks for the cookies. They're delicious."

"Everyone loves rainbow cookies," O'Neil said with confidence. "I just adore them."

Raven kissed O'Neil on the cheek. "I'm gonna run, Daddy. I'll call you later." She turned to Tejada. "Nice meeting you." She grabbed her bag and went out the front door.

"Lovely girl," Tejada said. "Is she in school?"

"Not right now. She's kind of in between things." He sat down on the sofa and crossed his legs in an elegant manner. "I'll look forward to your visits, Ms. Tejada. Where do you want to begin?"

Tejada opened a folder. "I told your daughter that it's a pleasure to see a foster home that's as nice as this one. The one I just came from was a real pigsty. I don't know how Paul allowed it to stay open."

"I've heard about some of those places," O'Neil said. "I'm just trying to provide a nice home for a few needy kids. I'm not interested in running a dormitory."

"That's good to hear, but I do hope I can talk you into taking on a few more." She smiled at O'Neil trying to coax him into agreement. "You're down to just two."

~~~

The apartment that O'Neil had arranged for Raven was only a few blocks away from his home. "I'm on my way over," O'Neil said over his cell phone. "The social worker just left."

"Did she give you any trouble?"

"No. Your name never came up." O'Neil replied.

"I'm looking forward to your visit, *Daddy,*" Raven said toying with O'Neil. "Who would you like to screw today?" she giggled. "Raven, Ray, or Raylene?"

Chapter Fifty-Three
Raven: April 2007

Kim stood at the bar in a dance club with two of her friends. They were all wearing tube dresses and platform shoes. Their hair was teased and heavily sprayed. They wore their makeup heavy, almost circus-sideshow heavy. They were practically carbon copies of each other. In fact, it looked as if a 3D printer had produced three identical bimbos.

Kim looked nothing like the little girl who Celeste Thax dressed in rags and ordered about like an indentured servant. She was tall and thin with sultry brown eyes. She had aged out of the social services system and was now sharing an apartment with her girlfriends. She was making money working in the cosmetics department at Macys but not enough for the tempting frock and pumps she wore, which she had borrowed from Bebe. The price tag was still on and the dress was going back after the weekend.

"*Hey*, you look familiar. Do I know you?" Kim said to the guy standing next to her at the bar.

One of her girlfriends nudged her shoulder, drawing her attention away from her new acquaintance. "Ready?" her friend asked.

Kim nodded and the three girls dropped layered shots of Jameson and Bailey's into their Guinness lager. They simultaneously hoisted their glasses and chugged. Kim couldn't get it all down and giggled as the concoction dribbled down her chin.

"Boilermakers?" he asked.

"Irish car bombs," she replied with an embarrassing smile on her face. She grabbed a napkin from the bar and dried her chin. "Classy, huh?"

"Looks like you're having fun."

"Fun? Oh yeah, tons of fun. I don't know why you look so familiar." The club was dark. Strobe lights flashed over the dance floor backlighting the stranger and making it difficult for Kim to see his face clearly. She squinted, trying to get a better look.

He shrugged. "I don't know. I guess I just have one of those faces. Can I buy you another car bomb?"

"Really?"

He nodded.

"Are you going to do one too?" she asked.

"Absolutely!" He called to the bartender and ordered a round for everyone.

Kim introduced her friends to him. "And what do they call you, mystery man?"

"Ray," he said most matter of factly. His eyes widened. "Here they come."

The bartender placed a tray on the bar and served the four glasses of stout and paired shots.

The girls looked from one to the other, their expressions saying, *are we really going to do this again?* One of the other girls shouted, "Let's get crazy!" They all dropped the shots and chugged with determination.

Kim only made it halfway before she paused to take a deep breath, but Ray coaxed her to finish. She drew a few deep breaths like someone preparing to hold their breath underwater and then finished off the brew. She was breathless by the time she put her empty glass down on the bar. "That's insane," she said. "Did you like it?"

Ray grimaced and rubbed his forehead.

"Brain freeze?" she asked.

"Migraine," he replied. "Been getting them since I was three years old."

"Will it go away on its own?"

"Eventually."

"Can't you take something for it?"

Ray's eyes widened. "Another car bomb?" He nodded enthusiastically and summoned the bartender. "Hit us again."

"Are you kidding?" the bartender asked.

"One last time," Ray insisted.

"You're insane," Kim said teasingly. "I . . . I can't."

"Don't wimp out on me now," he said, daring her to accept the challenge.

"But—"

"No buts."

The third round was placed on the bar, and the ritual was repeated. "I'm going to throw up," one of Kim's friends said. "I'm going to the bathroom—time to cop a squat."

"Me too," the third girl said. She turned to Kim. You coming too?"

"In a minute," Kim said. "I'll catch up."

The two girls were drunk and wobbly on their feet. They had to walk arm in arm to keep from teetering. "I think she likes you," one of the girls whispered in Ray's ear, with a silly expression on her face.

"Come on," the other girl insisted and yanked her friend away from Ray.

Kim smirked as her friends staggered away. "They're wasted." She blinked in an exaggerated manner. "You know what? So am I." She tottered and grabbed Ray's arm for support. She buried her face in her hands. "All of a sudden, I—" When she looked up her eyes were bloodshot, and it was an effort for her to focus on Ray's face. "Christ, my head is spinning."

He looked around the room and then led her by the arm. "There's a chair. Come over here."

~~~

When Kim awoke it was morning. She had no sense of where she was or how she'd arrived there. The bedroom was bright with sunlight, bright enough to sting her eyes. Her head was still spinning, and her stomach burned. In the next moment, she realized that Ray was lying next to her in bed. She gasped with worry before realizing that they were both still fully dressed and lying on top of the blanket. *Oh my God*, she thought, rubbing her eyes, hoping to clear the cobwebs from her mind. The evening's events started coming back to her. She heard the sound of snoring coming from the next room. She sat up in the bed and looked around until she saw one of her friends passed out on the sofa and the other asleep in a recliner.

She took a few deep breaths, and her pulse slowly returned to normal. Looking at Ray, she realized that she knew nothing about him. *What was I thinking? I was with him less than half an hour before . . .* She pressed her memory. It was blank. *I must've passed out.* It then dawned on her that Ray had seen all of them safely back to his apartment.

Gee, what a good guy.

She searched his face. Something about him still reminded her of someone she knew. She stroked his hair and his eyes opened. "Thank you," Kim said.

Ray was still half asleep. For a minute it looked as if he might go back out again, but then he smiled. "For what?" he asked in a sleepy voice.

"For getting us all—"

Ray was out again, snoring lightly.

Kim smiled. *This one just might be a keeper.* She watched him sleep, noting the contours of his face. There was something about his eyes that was familiar to her. His lashes were very long, and there was a delicate slope to his nose. *He looks more like a—*

Her breath caught in her lungs, and her eyes widened alarmingly. *Can it be? The headaches . . . that face. Oh my God.*

"Raven?"

Chapter Fifty-Four

"Okay, see you later." Kim waved to her friends from the doorway of Raven's apartment. She watched until they were all the way down the stairs. A few seconds later, she heard the heavy apartment house door slam shut.

"Thanks for staying," Raven said. "I guess we've got a lot to talk about."

"Ya *think*? Jesus, Raven what's going on?"

Raven closed and locked the door to her apartment. She looked at Kim and shrugged. "I don't know. It all happened pretty fast."

"For God's sake, Raven, we were in bed together."

Raven smiled softly and ran her fingers through Kim's long hair. "It's not the first time, now is it?" she said with a smug smile.

"That was different," Kim exclaimed. "We were kids then. Kids do that kind of thing, especially when there's no heat and you feel like you're going to freeze to death."

"I know. The old battle-axe was pretty cheap with the heat."

"This is unbelievable." Kim stormed off and sat down on the living room sofa. She tucked her dress under her legs for modesty. When she looked up, Raven was sitting down next to her.

"So let's talk," Raven said. She looked into Kim's eyes. "Okay?"

Kim nodded.

Raven continued, "We've both been through a lot. I don't know how we survived those days living with Thax. She was such a monster."

"We looked out for one another," Kim said. "You were all I had. Things were actually worse before you moved in. I think that in some way you kept Thax on her toes."

"Me? How did a three-year-old scare a snarly, old ogre like Thax?"

"By putting flour in her coffee instead of creamer and by putting ants in her underwear drawer. She knew better than to mess with you." Kim became quiet. "You know she's dead, don't you?"

"Know? I was still living there the day she died."

Kim's mouth dropped. "Get out of here . . . really?"

"Yeah, she was falling apart bit by bit. Her liver was going and the diabetes . . . they had just chopped off two of her fingers the day she died."

Kim shuddered. "So she died in the hospital?"

"No. She made it home."

"So what happened?"

Raven looked at Kim and then averted her eyes. There was a long guilty pause before she answered. "I told you," Raven said with modest irritation. "She was really sick."

"Oh . . . I see."

"You're lucky you got reassigned to another home when you did. How long has it been?"

"Got to be six or seven years." Kim thought for a moment. "I think I was fifteen when they moved me out of there."

"Looks like you turned out okay." Raven's attempt at a segue was clumsy and obvious.

"Thanks." Kim blushed. "Where'd you go after Thax's home closed?"

"O'Neil's."

"Any better than Thax?"

"Miles better. O'Neil's a really good person." Raven became pensive. "He made me really happy."

"But . . . why are you dressed like a guy?"

Raven shrugged, her guilt apparent in the expression on her face. "I don't know. My life has been so confusing. One day I want to be a boy, the next day I want to be a girl. O'Neil helped me to find out some stuff about my family—some pretty terrible stuff."

"What kind of stuff?"

"Like my mother died from a complication of childbirth."

Kim recoiled. "Raven, I'm so sorry."

"As if I wasn't crazy enough before. Do you have any idea how guilty that made me feel? O'Neil helped me to cope with all of my issues."

"But it wasn't your fault, Raven. How can you blame yourself?"

"There's more." Her throat tightened. "I had a twin brother, only . . . no one knows what happened to him. He was born with all kinds of problems and was put into a special care facility. I haven't given up, but that's all I've been able to find out so far."

"That's terrible. Really terrible," Kim said with compassion.

"Yeah, it's pretty messed up. Hey, it's been so long. Let me buy you some breakfast. I'd like to catch up with you."

"Maybe," Kim said warily. "But first answer one question: bumping into me at the bar, was that by accident or was it intentional?"

Kim knew the answer before the words left her mouth. Raven's expression was a dead giveaway.

Chapter Fifty-Five
April 2007

Kim waited for more than hour for Detective Smote to return to the police station. She rubbed her hands together nervously while she passed the time. The desk officer glanced at her every few minutes; it didn't help to make her feel any more at ease. *It's the right thing to do,* she told herself. She sighed nervously.

When the door opened, Smote burst in to escape the wind and rain that pursued him through the parking lot. He was dripping wet, and his gray trench coat was so completely soaked that it appeared black in color. His umbrella had turned inside out. He pulled on the edges until it snapped back into shape and then tamped it on the floor to remove the excess water. He wiped the rain from his face and turned toward Kim. "Sorry I'm late."

Kim waited patiently while Smote removed his coat and stomped his feet on the floor. She was surprised to see that his suit was dry beneath his saturated coat. His wet shoes squished on the vinyl tiles as he approached.

"Thanks for coming in," he said. "It's been years." He looked her up and down. "You certainly grew up."

She blushed.

"This way," he said and motioned for her to follow.

She followed him into an interrogation room and sat down while he neatened his coat and laid it on an empty chair.

He shuddered. "I'm frozen," he said. "Coffee?"

"Thanks. That would be great."

"Milk and sugar?"

"Just milk."

"Make yourself comfortable. I'll be right back."

She began to tremble when the metal door clanged shut, and again sighed nervously. *This is it.* She wrung her hands together. *There's no turning back now.* She looked around the room. It was painted two-tone green, light green from the ceiling to just past the top of the door and dark green from there down to the floor. There were no windows, and the requisite one-way mirror reminded her of an episode of *Law & Order, Special Victims Unit*.

Smote had been gone for a full ten minutes. *Is he doing it on purpose? Is he watching me through the mirror? You haven't done anything wrong. Take a deep breath and relax.*

She jumped in her chair when Smote returned. He placed her coffee on the table in front of her. His feet still squished on the linoleum, but he looked otherwise dry.

"That's better," he said as he gulped his coffee and sat down in a chair. "I take it you've got something to tell me?"

Smote was now in character, poker-faced and intent. His eyes were cool and unnerving, as she had remembered them from their last meeting all those years back. "Did you ever find the person you were looking for, the one you thought killed Mrs. Thax?"

"No. There haven't been any new developments since then. I'm actually very surprised that you're coming forward now. As I told you, Celeste Thax was murdered or committed suicide. The level of OxyContin in her system stopped her heart. I interviewed all of the children who were living in the foster home at the time, as well as some like you, who no longer lived there, but had been in the victim's care for a long time. Everyone was capable of poisoning her, and from what I've learned, they all had sufficient motive to want her dead. You yourself told me that Thax was a nasty foster parent who pretty much cared nothing for the children she was responsible for. So short of a *Murder on the Orient Express* explanation, I've never been able to prove who did it. It's been years, and no one has talked." He took another gulp of coffee.

"What do you mean by a *Murder on the Orient Express* explanation?"

"Jesus. What do people your age read these days?" Smote asked rhetorically. "It's a classic novel—thirteen suspects on a train . . . they all did it. They all took turns stabbing the victim."

"Oh."

"So why are you here today?"

"Did you question Raven Gallagher?"

"I certainly did."

Kim searched his eyes. They were all business. "My two friends and I went out the other night, and we met this guy. We all hung out for a little while, and he bought us drinks."

"Yeah. So?"

"Well, we all got pretty shit-faced." She looked at Smote apprehensively.

"Go on, Kim. You're not the first girl who went out and had too much to drink. Tell me about this guy, the one who bought the drinks."

"Well, that's just it. I can't remember what happened after that, but we all woke up in his apartment."

"Do you think he drugged you?"

"No. That's not the point. The point is that when I woke up I realized that this guy was Raven."

"Whoa." Smote looked at her disbelievingly. "And you had no idea until you woke up?"

"No! The club was dark and my head was spinning from all the alcohol."

"All right, whatever. So you woke up and then what?"

Kim rubbed her forehead. "I hadn't seen Raven in like seven years, but I was sure it was her. She had her hair combed like a guy, and she was dressed like a guy, but I knew it was her. I stayed with her after my friends left the next day, and we talked. I asked her if she knew that Thax was dead and—"

"Did she admit to killing her?"

"No, but . . . I could tell that there was something she wasn't telling me. She just seemed so damn—"

"Guilty?"

Kim nodded. "Oh God, I hope I'm doing the right thing."

"Drink your coffee. You're doing exactly the right thing."

"God I'm so nervous. I didn't know what to do, but her bumping into me like that . . . well, she admitted that it wasn't a coincidence and the whole dressing up like a guy thing . . . She made me feel really uncomfortable and I mean, if she did kill Thax . . ." Kim was rambling and finally looked into Smote's eyes, confessing, "We all hated Thax so much. We'd put stuff in her food."

Smote narrowed his eyes. "Poison?"

"No. No," Kim said nervously. "Just kid stuff like cat poop and stuff like that." A tear drizzled down her cheek. "She was so mean to us."

"Take a deep breath. I'm not going to arrest you for a prank."

Kim sniffled. "I'm just so afraid. If she killed Thax, do you think Raven would kill me too?"

BOOK FIVE

Chapter Fifty-Six
Search for Gus Lido: Day 2, Afternoon

"How's Max doing?"

"He's fine," Ma said over the phone. "Ricky just fed him and is about to take him for a walk in the stroller."

My throat tightened. "Are you telling my men that I love them?"

"Every chance I get, honey. Now tell me what's going on over there? Give me some good news."

"The good news is that every cop east of the Hudson River is out looking for Gus, whether they're getting paid for it or not. The bad news is that we still don't have anything solid to go on."

"Nothing?"

"No. Nothing."

There was silence on the line. Ma, who usually had something to say about everything, was at a complete loss for words. What could she tell me—that she was angry Gus hadn't been found yet ... or just keep my chin up? The tension was so thick you couldn't cut it with a blowtorch. "I'm sorry, honey. I just don't know what to tell you."

"You don't have to tell me anything, Ma. Just take care of my little boy. I'll bring his daddy home." That was the mother and wife in me talking. The cop knew that precious seconds and minutes were ticking away, and with each passing moment, the chances of successfully recovering Gus grew smaller and smaller. I couldn't imagine a future without my husband. I tried desperately to keep from getting morose. Whenever a bad thought popped into my mind, I did my best to switch gears. I was doing a pretty good job of staying productive. I just had to make the time count. "I really have to go, Ma. I have to go out and knock down some doors."

"I know you do, Stephanie. Just be smart about it. Don't do anything..."

She didn't have to finish her sentence. "I won't. Love you, Ma."

"Love you too, sweetheart. I'll talk to you later."

I disconnected and turned to Ambler. He was crouched over, talking on the phone. I could tell by the shade of red on his face that things were not going well. He slammed the receiver down on the cradle. *That confirms it.* "What happened?" I asked.

He looked over his shoulder and then stood. His skin looked hot to the touch. "The son of a bitch JAG wouldn't accept our subpoena. They won't unseal Alden's record."

"Why not? I mean, can he do that?"

"It's the goddamn military, Stephanie. It's like another civilization. The bottom line is that whatever Alden was involved in must have been pretty important stuff. That's the only reason I can come up with for them not cooperating. I mean, for God's sake, this took place more than twenty years ago. Even JFK's records are a matter of public record now.

"Yeah, JFK's records are out there, but not the truth about his murder."

Ambler shook his head woefully "I hear you, kid. I just don't know what to say." He took off his glasses and rubbed his eyes. "What's your game plan for today?"

"I'm heading over to Kaley Struther's place. We just received a warrant to go in."

"Good."

"Honestly, I was going in one way or another. I just can't wait anymore. I have to make something happen."

"I know what you mean. I'm not exactly feeling patient myself. I think I'm going to take a jet down to Randolph Air Force Base in Texas. I've got a good buddy down there who might be able to help. If I leave now, I can catch up with him for dinner and fly back first thing in the morning."

"You think he'll help?"

"I think it's worth a shot. Jack Bancroft is a good man and a dear friend. I just hope he's at the base."

"Well then, get your ass down to Texas. You're no help to me here, walking around with your red face and piss-poor attitude." I kissed him on the cheek. "I love you, Herb. Thanks!" A tear popped from my eye. "I'm out of here. Call me if you get through to Bancroft."

"Will do." I could tell he wanted to say something to boost my spirits, but he didn't. He sat down and got back on the phone.

Chapter Fifty-Seven

I was hurrying to my SUV when I noticed a familiar face approaching. "Smote?"

"Chalice, hi. Hey look, I've got time on my hands, and I'd like to help. Do you mind if I ride shotgun? I hear you're on your way over to this Kaley Struthers' house."

"Yeah. The warrant just came through. We've been searching for her, but she's completely off the radar. I have to tell you, the judges out here have two speeds: slow and slower."

"Agreed. Do you think Struthers' absence means she's with your husband?" Smote's question could have been taken in two ways. "Um . . . you know what I mean." He wasn't suggesting that Gus was being unfaithful.

"Yes. I know what you mean, and yes the thought has crossed my mind. If she is involved in Gus' abduction, there's a very good chance that's exactly where she is. Get in. I'm driving."

We spent all of five seconds waiting to see if Kaley was home and would answer the door. The police detail assigned to us surrounded the property. Pulaski gave them the nod, and the door was taken off the frame. Police officers poured into the house. I was accustomed to leading the way, but I had no official jurisdiction in Suffolk County, so I had to wait outside until the coast was clear. The Boys in Blue didn't keep me waiting long. Pulaski reappeared at the doorway in less than thirty seconds and waved me in. "The place is empty," he said. "No sign of Struthers."

It was one thing to search a home for clues, and it was another to desperately comb through every scrap and detail, knowing that your husband's life might hang in the balance. *How can I be sharper?* I wanted to be supersensitive, and needed to kick my sixth sense into top gear. I was going through the contents of her desk when Smote came over to me, holding a small stencil.

"What do you make of this?" he asked.

I had seen it before. It was a ring with an arrow sticking out at two o'clock, a cross below six o'clock, and an arrow with a slash through it at ten o'clock. "It's a tattoo stencil. There are tattoo pens in the desk."

"Is it some kind of symbol?"

"Ya. The arrow represents man. The cross represents woman, and the third is a combination of the two. It's a transgender symbol."

"A transgender symbol?"

"The transgender community is more outspoken in the city than I imagine it is out here. I see this from time to time. It's a symbol of solidarity for their community."

"By transgender you're referring to—"

"Anyone, Sully: transsexuals, bisexuals, transvestites, cross-dressers ... it's pretty much a catchall for any sexual alternative."

"So Struthers may fall into one of these categories herself."

"That's one theory. Judging by the basic tattoo equipment I found, it looks like she only does this as a hobby."

"There's another possibility," Smote said. "She may be too embarrassed to go to a tattoo shop. If that's so, she may be trying to keep her sexual preference a secret."

"I hadn't thought of that, but you're right. In any case we should take a look at all the tattoo shops out here to see if her name pops up. It's a pretty basic design—she may have created it herself, or she may have purchased it from a tattoo shop or an online store."

"I'm on it," Smote said. "I'll brief Pulaski."

Smote hustled into the next room, and I sat down at the desk. *What are you hiding from me, Kaley? What don't you want me to see?* Other than the tattoo paraphernalia, I didn't see much of note. I didn't see a physical address book, but our warrant also gave us access to her cell-phone account. If she had an address book on her phone, it would be ours shortly.

I found an iPad charger, but no iPad. I searched everywhere in the room, but it didn't turn up.

Something occurred to me then. *How stupid.* When she was in our rental house, she had given me her phone number in case we needed a sitter for Max. She had sent her contact information from her iPhone to mine, including her address, phone number, and email. She wasn't answering her phone, but her house had Wi-Fi, so I picked up my cell phone and FaceTimed with her using her email address. I heard the familiar iPad notification jingle in the next room. I flew out of my chair and into her bedroom. I repeated it again and found her iPad buried in the bottom of her sock drawer. It wasn't passcode protected and when I flipped the cover shocking images filled the screen. The wallpaper was a montage of snapshots, two women making love, Kaley Struthers and Camryn Claymore.

~~~

Pulaski marched into the bedroom with Smote at his side.

"Chalice," Pulaski announced as he approached the doorway, "we found a wireless CCTV link in the upstairs closet, closed circuit TV."

Pulaski and Smote looked at one another and rushed toward me.

"What's wrong?" Smote asked.

I covered my eyes and tried to hold back the tears, but it was no use. There was a video stored on the iPad. It was a video of Gus and me . . . making love.

Chapter Fifty-Eight

"It's only good for short-range transmission," the crime scene officer explained.

"How far?" Pulaski asked.

"Half a mile . . . one kilometer max."

I was shaken. Having spent the night in a hotel room I had completely forgotten that our summer rental was a mere stone's throw from Kaley's home. I couldn't believe Kaley had been watching the two of us during our most intimate moments. I felt violated and dirty. I couldn't believe I let her touch my baby. I wanted to strangle her so badly I could almost feel my hands around her throat.

Smote sat down next to me and handed me a bottle of juice. He hadn't seen the video, but I had explained to him and Pulaski what was there. "Crime scene techs are at your rental now. I'm sorry, Chalice," Smote said. "This is a sick, sick, sick world."

The iPad was already on its way to police headquarters. Like it or not, every fragment of data on that machine was going to be viewed, analyzed, and catalogued. Police personnel were going to watch the two of us together. I couldn't imagine walking back into police headquarters not knowing who had seen the videos and who had not. *You've just got to be strong. Hold on*, I told myself. *You've got to fight. Gus needs everything you've got, all that and more.*

A text message came in from Ambler: *On my way to the airport. Meeting Bancroft for dinner. Talk later.*

He didn't know what had just happened, and I wasn't in a rush to tell him or anyone else for that matter. I was wounded, fighting not to collapse. I didn't have a clear direction, but I knew I couldn't stay in that house any longer.

"I'm going across to the rental," I told Smote. I handed him back the bottle of juice."

"Let's go," he said. "But drink the juice." I took the bottle and sipped as we walked through the woods to the house. I could see the rooftop as soon as I left Kaley's place. It was on higher ground, almost in line of sight from Kaley's front porch. "Christ, she could see us anytime she wanted to." I pointed to our bedroom window for Smote's benefit. "But that wasn't enough. She had to stick a camera right up my ass."

"Okay, Chalice. Definitely justified—I completely understand but try to cool down. You're not doing yourself or Gus any good fuming the way you are. You've—"

I'd stopped dead in my tracks.

"What's the matter?" Smote asked.

I pointed. A tech was on a ladder just outside my bedroom window, prying a wire out from beneath the vinyl siding. A lump formed in my throat. I remembered awakening from my dream about Nigel Twain to the sound of hammer thuds and my son screaming. I awoke to find Camryn's brother, Ray on a ladder outside my window. I stood motionlessly for a moment trying to picture Ray outside my bedroom window. The more I stared, the clearer his image became. An idea popped into my head, a strange one admittedly but one I couldn't dismiss. *Nah, it couldn't be.* And then suddenly I was sure ... The person up on the ladder pounding nails into the house was Camryn Claymore, dressed like a man.

Chapter Fifty-Nine

Commissioner Bratton strode into the conference room and pulled up a chair next to me. Pulaski sat down across the table from us. "Pulaski just briefed me, Stephanie. Now I want to hear it from you. What's your take on this? Why do you think Struthers was spying on you and your family?"

The crime scene team had pulled apart the rental house and found cameras in almost every room—pencil cameras, tiny enough to be hidden in the smallest most undetectable places. Selected video segments had been stored on a computer in Kaley's basement. There were random snippets of the family, not only Gus and me, but Ma and Max as well—those were few and far between. The only "feature-length" videos were of Gus and me making love. I spent the late afternoon watching us together. Beautiful moments Gus and I had shared were now something tawdry and cheap. We were no longer a loving couple—we were victims, and our most private moments had become evidence.

"Why, Commissioner? I don't know why. I'd say it was because I took it upon myself to look into matters that didn't concern me ... but we had met Camryn Claymore days before everything began. Was it a coincidence that we happened to meet her in the MTK Café right after Bill Alden's house burned to the ground? I don't know. If I had to guess ... Camryn and Kaley are probably into kink. They're into these spy videos, and Camryn saw a couple she thought she and her gal pal could get off watching."

My thoughts ran to Kaley, Ms. Sunshine and Sweetness, the girl who allegedly volunteered at church, as holy and pure as Jesus himself. How the two of them must have laughed at us. Kaley had shown up at the front door our first morning in the house. She said that finding her new neighbors was happenstance, but now I had to consider the possibility that Camryn had tipped her off to visit us. "Check out this couple," Camryn must have said. "Two rubes with hot bodies. I can't wait to watch them ..." But Kaley had said too much. She was just making conversation when I asked about Alana Moore and Sarah Fisher. I don't believe she had any clue that she was laying out a trail that I would be compelled to follow.

"Stephanie? Detective Chalice, are you all right?" Bratton's hand was on my shoulder.

I shook my head. "Sorry. I must've zoned out."

"No apology necessary," Bratton said. "I can't imagine what you're feeling. It's amazing you're able to work through this at all."

"Camryn and Kaley are definitely in this thing together." I pictured Max on Kaley's lap and shuddered. "Why this blew up the way it did ... I don't know. Maybe they're two sex-crazed women who saw Gus in action and wanted him for themselves; or maybe it's because I got too close to something and taking Gus is their way of getting back at me."

"Pretty brazen," Pulaski said. "I mean, abducting a cop? That takes real balls."

"Camryn knew we were cops. It didn't stop her from watching the two of us in our bedroom. I think brazen barely sums it up. I think they're full blown sociopaths, and somehow they're connected to Alden's death and maybe the other two cases I've been investigating. Camryn's brother Ray burned to death in that car fire right after I called to complain about him. Maybe in some weird way she holds Gus and me responsible ... I don't know." My head slumped. I felt weak and nauseous.

"A warrant to search Camryn's home will be here within the hour," Bratton said. "We'll add her face to Struthers' and get her profile out on the media." He lifted my chin. "We're close. You just don't want to admit it to yourself because you're afraid of getting your hopes too high. No self pity now, okay? We'd be nowhere if it wasn't for your strength and perseverance. It's only a matter of time until we tighten the noose around their necks. I guarantee it!"

"Thanks. I'll be okay in a minute." I could sense Bratton's strength and commitment, and it helped to buoy my spirits. I had a sense that he was one of the great ones, great in the spirit of my father and Chief of Detectives Sonellio. Men whose hearts were as pure as gold. I had to fight to keep myself from languishing in despair.

He's right, I told myself. *We are getting close.*

Chapter Sixty

CRACK. The doorframe shattered. Wood splintered and flew in every direction. The police team entered and cleared the house quickly and efficiently. I was right behind them as we filed into Camryn's home. The temperature was ungodly warm. It seemed incongruous to me that a woman like Camryn wasn't running her air conditioning day and night during the heat of the summer. There was also a light film of dust on the highly polished wood floor.

"Doesn't look as if anyone's been here for the last couple of days," I said to Pulaski. I quickly walked into the kitchen and looked around. I opened the refrigerator. It was pretty sparse—no milk, only half a stick of butter and three eggs. There were several bottled items, but nothing much that needed to be freshly bought like fruits and vegetables. "Almost two full days since Gus was taken. No one's been here in at least that long."

Pulaski's cell phone rang. "It's Bratton," he said and ducked into the next room to take the call. Our task force was growing. Investigators were already in every room of the house looking for evidence. A female tech entered the kitchen and began going through the cabinets. I pulled open one of the drawers and started to sift through it. It was filled with basic kitchen hardware, a potato peeler, a meat thermometer, etc. I shuffled the items around and moved onto the next drawer. *What in the world?* The next drawer was filled with cutlery, nothing surprising, except that several of the spoons and forks were bent. *Who does this?* My mind raced back to Bill Alden's backyard where I found the cyanide-laced cigarettes. An old bent fork was lying on one of the Adirondack chairs. At the time I didn't think anything of it but now ... It was one more connection from Camryn to Alden, but it was one that I didn't understand.

Pulaski returned and gave me a reassuring thumbs-up. "Fucking A," he began. "Bratton just got approval from the governor—hundreds of law enforcement officers are being bused onto Long Island, the National Guard too. They're going to begin going door to door. Bratton said he'll check every house on Long Island if he has to."

I started to cry. I dug into my pocket for a tissue and blotted my eyes as quickly as I could. Pulaski put his arm on my shoulder. "Deep breaths," he said. "Put your game face on. No let-down until we recover your husband."

I nodded with conviction and took a deep breath. "I'm okay. Thanks."

"What the hell?" Pulaski was staring into the flatware drawer. He picked up a couple of spoons and examined them. "This strike you as odd?"

"I saw a bent fork at Bill Alden's house too."

"It may not be a coincidence then."

"Maybe not but I don't understand the connection."

"Yeah, me neither. I'll have all of it dusted for prints, but I don't know if it'll prove worthwhile."

"I agree. Do it anyway, okay?"

"Sure." Pulaski called over the crime scene tech who was in the kitchen and gave her instructions.

"Pulaski," one of the other officers called through the house. We marched out of the kitchen and encountered a crime scene officer on the stairs who signaled for us to follow him to the second level. We entered the bedroom and walked toward the closet. The hanging contents of the closet had been pushed aside and the crime scene officer illuminated the back of the closet with his searchlight. Three driver's licenses were stapled to the back wall.

Chapter Sixty-One

It was late in the day before Trent Summers finished his homework and had the opportunity to go out hunting. Twilight hunting was more dangerous than hunting in daylight hours, but he was accomplished at the sport and liked to go out when the nocturnal creatures were beginning to stir. He killed raccoons and opossums mostly—just for fun after a day glued to the books.

"Come on, boy." Rusty, his coon dog stirred at the first sound of his voice. His tail wagged excitedly as he walked over to his bowl, expecting to be fed. "Not yet, boy." He gave Rusty a Milk-Bone, threw on his backpack, and slung his birthday present over his shoulder. The .17 HMR smelled from solvent and gun oil. The fragrance resonated with him making him eager to fire it.

He waited until Rusty emptied his bladder before starting down a familiar path into the woods, which divided into two trails. He usually took the west fork, which brought him up to the high ground, but he hadn't had much luck there lately, so he decided to take the east fork that traveled downhill until it ran parallel with the Hoosick River.

The river was just mildly illuminated by the reflection of the setting sun when he got down to the bottom of the hill. The air was moist, and Rusty was already intently sniffing the odors of the forest floor. Almost immediately, he got low on his haunches, a telltale sign that he was stalking a critter.

"Whatcha got, boy?" Trent whispered. He stood motionlessly watching Rusty slink away. He took his rifle off his shoulder and looked through the scope. The area was dense with trees, mostly pines and oaks, and the lighting was poor, which made it difficult for him to spot his prey until a sudden rustling in the leaves drew his attention.

"Yes!" he whispered with exuberance. It was the rarest find of all, a woodchuck. They hibernated through the fall and winter and were only active during the summer months.

Rusty stopped and lay down. It was a signal to Trent to take the shot. He aimed and fired. The bullet whizzed through the air. He was hoping for silence, but instead he heard the loud whistle of the woodchuck warning his colony of danger. He lowered his rifle just in time to see the woodchuck tunneling into a plunge hole.

Rusty closed in on the animal just as its tail disappeared into the hole. Rusty was barking and scratching at the hole, trying to get at the woodchuck when Trent arrived. Trent looked up at the darkening sky. "Give it up, boy. He's not coming out of there." But Rusty was committed to the task. He continued to scratch, digging up roots and soil.

"It's okay, boy. Come on, let's get some dinner."

Rusty understood the word dinner very well. He stopped for a moment to look up at Trent and then continued to bark at the hole with persistence. He had widened the hole so that the opening was now double the size it was before he started. Trent looked down and saw white boney fingertips protruding through the earth. He felt the blood drain from his face as understanding kicked in. He leashed Rusty and ran home as fast as his legs would carry him.

Chapter Sixty-Two

Three driver's licenses: one for Sarah Fisher, one for Joshua Dane, and one for Camryn Claymore. The face I was familiar with was present on both Camryn Claymore's and Sarah Fisher's licenses. I pointed at them, for Pulaski's benefit. "Two different driver's licenses with the same face on both."

"Yeah," Pulaski laughed. "Shoddy work," he said as he looked at Joshua Dane's driver's license. "Must have been done by the same character who forged the driver's license for McLovin here. How do you think this guy fits in?"

"Only time will tell." Finding a man's driver's license did not fit in, and I was none too pleased by the new twist. Were men being targeted as well as women? I saw Gus' face and an ache grew in my gut.

I was on pins and needles while we waited for the laminated driver's licenses to be fingerprinted; the minute hand on my watch ticked by from one agonizing minute to the next. "I knew that Camryn had something to do with Sarah Fisher's disappearance." Finding her driver's license in Camryn's closet only further cemented my theory.

"But Alana Moore's license isn't here," Pulaski noted.

"No. It was in her purse at the time she was killed by the LIRR train. So . . ."

The fingerprinting was finally complete. I was itching to examine the licenses up close, not so much Sarah Fisher's, but the second one. Why would Camryn's driver's license be stapled to the wall along with the others?

I had but to hold it in my hands to understand.

The picture belonged to the woman who had rented us our vacation home, but her date of birth struck me like a lightning bolt to the head. There was absolutely no way the woman I had met on two separate occasions was anymore than thirty years old, and by the date listed on her license, Camryn Claymore was forty-four years old.

My cell phone rang. I'd lost track of the time; it was already quarter of nine. As if by cue, my stomach grumbled. *You'll just have to wait.*

It was Ambler. "Herb, speak to me. What did you get from Bancroft?"

I heard Ambler exhale long and hard through his nostrils and I knew that it wasn't good news. "Very little, Stephanie. Jack's a good man, but there are matters even he's not willing to talk about."

"You're kidding, aren't you? Gus has been missing for two full days, and this Air Force muckety-muck can't talk to you about a matter that might mean the difference between life and death? This goes back decades. What the hell could be so important? Come on, man, really? I mean, if he won't step up for someone as high up on the FBI totem pole as you . . . Jesus, I've had it," I said with resignation in my voice.

"Okay, my dearest, chill out. I said he told me very little. I didn't say he told me nothing at all. Have you heard of Camp Hero?"

"No. What the hell is Camp Hero?"

"Camp Hero used to be called the Montauk Air Force Station. It's a defunct military installation not far from where you are right now, right near Montauk Point. At one time, it was a strategic outpost and radar station that protected the east coast from enemy attack up until about 1981, when it became obsolete. There's huge machinery in place over there, radar towers and artillery guns. It's all been decommissioned, but it was too expensive to tear down, so the site was abandoned. You can Google it if you want more details."

"So what's the great big secret? I mean if it's on Google, it's not exactly a state secret."

"It's like Area 51 in Roswell, New Mexico."

"Are you trying to tell me that aliens are buried there?"

"No. My point is that conspiracy theorists believe, in its latter years, secret government research was conducted by the military in an underground complex at the site. So in that sense, the truth is classified, just as it is with Area 51 in Roswell. No one can talk about it and that includes Bancroft. That's why the Air Force Judge Advocate General wouldn't release Bill Alden's file."

I slumped into a chair and rubbed my temple. "I guess some good can come from this. Bratton and the governor are sending an army of cops and military here to look for Gus. I'll pass along this information, so they can make Camp Hero their first priority."

"I've got more," Ambler said in a robust voice. "Grab a pencil. Bancroft gave me the name and phone number of the officer who was the base commandant during the time Alden was hired on as a civilian. His name is Frank Prescott and he lives in Hog Creek about a half hour from you. I just spoke with him."

"That's terrific, Herb." My throat tightened again. "Thank you."

"Stop wasting time lollygagging with me. Prescott knew Alden, and he's willing to talk to you about him. He just put on a pot of coffee, and he's waiting for you at his home. Anything new on your end?"

"Yes, we're pretty sure that Kaley Struthers and a woman named Camryn Claymore, the realtor who rented us the summer place are behind this. I'll fill you in later. I don't want to keep Prescott waiting. I love you, Herb."

"And I love you. Our boy's coming home," he said to reassure me. "I can feel it in my bones."

Chapter Sixty-Three

Pulaski was tired but far from quitting for the night, determined to work as long as it took and then some. I was running on vapors, both physically and emotionally, and so very glad to have him along for support.

It was almost ten p.m. when we pulled up to Prescott's home, a modest ranch set on large acreage in front of Gardiners Bay, one of the bodies of water that separates Long Island's North and South Forks.

"Let's do it," he said. We traded yawns and got out of the car. Prescott was waiting for us on his front porch.

A silvertip Lab sat obediently by his side. The playful animal grew more and more excited as we approached, and I could see that it was a real effort for the Lab to sit still. *"Stay,"* Prescott commanded as the Lab got up on all fours. "Stay, Montana." Montana sat, fighting every ounce of his innate desire to be playful. "Are you okay with him?" Prescott asked.

"I love dogs." I smiled at Montana. "Come here, fella." Montana looked at Prescott for approval and then leapt off the porch. He was a big boy. Despite the strain I was feeling, I grinned as a hundred pounds of unconditional love flew through the air. He gave me a couple of quick sniffs and then he was up on his hind legs kissing my face. For a brief moment, I was caught up in Montana's spell, which washed away some of my pain and anguish. I don't know what it is about dogs and the magic they possess, but I could almost feel my heart lighten. In some way, I guessed he could sense that I needed his love. I hugged the warm furry beast, and then he was off to greet Pulaski.

Prescott was smiling at me as I walked up the porch steps to greet him. "You passed the Montana test," he said as we shook hands. "Frank Prescott. Thanks for coming by to visit. Your last name is *Cha-lee-see*, correct?"

"You nailed it. Please call me Stephanie, and thanks for seeing me. I know it's late."

"No formalities required," Prescott said. "I'm glad to have the company. The powder room is the first door on the right as you walk in. Go ahead and wash the doggie slobber off your face. I've got hot coffee and pie from Briermere Farms waiting on the kitchen table."

I wasn't familiar with Briermere Farms, but Pulaski hooted an enthusiastic, *"Nice!"* as he fended off Montana's high-spirited assault.

Cleansed of dog dribble, I made my way into the kitchen. Pulaski was already halfway through a slice of what looked like blueberry cream pie. A second slice was waiting for me. The kitchen was air-conditioned cold, and steam rose from the mug of coffee Prescott had poured for me. The coffee aroma smelled sublime.

Montana pegged me as the weak link, the human most likely to sneak him a scrap, and sat down under the table with his snout in my lap. Despite the tiredness and strain, the atmosphere in Prescott's home boosted my spirit. I knew it would be short lived, but I was grateful for a moment of happiness all the same.

"I'm sorry to hear about your husband's disappearance," Prescott began. He was up there in years but looked vital. His ruddy complexion contrasted greatly with his lustrous, silver hair. "Tell me what I can do to help you. I understand that you have questions about Bill Alden?"

"Correct," Pulaski said. "Without getting into a lot of detail . . . Alden recently died in a fire, and we suspect foul play."

Prescott gritted his teeth. "Oh. I'm sorry to hear that. Poor Bill, he didn't have an easy life."

"In what way?" Pulaski asked.

Prescott puffed out his cheeks. "God, where do I begin? I met Alden when he applied to participate in a paid long-term research study conducted by the Air Force. He was about forty, and his life wasn't exactly a bowl of cherries."

"What kind of research study are we talking about?"

Prescott shot me a quick glance, his expression indicating that this was where things became difficult. "When I was discharged from the service, I signed a document stating that I would not discuss the nature of the work going on at the base, but I know this is important so . . . well, I'll have to tread lightly."

"We understand. Anything you tell us is more than we know right now."

"First off, you have to remember that this project began in the sixties. The cold war was raging, and the Soviet Union was a real threat to our national security. Most Americans feared that the Russians would pull the trigger, and then we'd pull our trigger, and the world would end in a nuclear holocaust. If war broke out between the two super powers, the best we could hope for was, a traditional war: air strikes, infantry, and naval, but no nukes. Because of this, the military was investigating alternative military strategies. One of the strategies was mass mind control."

"Mind control?" Pulaski smirked. "What is this, *The Twilight Zone*?"

"More like the *Outer Limits*, Detective," Prescott replied. "There is nothing wrong with your television set. Do not attempt to adjust the picture. We are controlling transmission."

I presumed that this TV program Prescott alluded to had aired way before my time because I had never heard of it, but Pulaski was immediately up to speed. "We control the horizontal. We control the vertical."

"Exactly right," Prescott continued. "Remember, we didn't know what we know today. Technology was a million years behind where it is now. Computers were the size of ballrooms and were as slow as molasses. Those monstrosities were far less capable than the smartphones we carry around in our pockets these days. So we had what we had—theories and an endless list of willing guinea pigs to experiment on."

"That's horrendous."

"By today's standards, yes, certainly, but back then it was the status quo. There was no such thing as animal or civilian protection groups, and the military pretty much ignored civilian law anyway."

"So what kind of experiments did you conduct?" Pulaski asked.

"That's classified," Prescott explained. "All I can tell you is that some of the tools we used were high-energy electromagnetic radiation, isolation therapy, subliminal imagery, and mind-altering medications. We did our utmost to maintain safe conditions for our subjects."

"And Bill Alden was one of these subjects?"

Prescott nodded. "Yes he was."

I shook my head in dismay. All the happiness Montana had lavished upon me melted away.

"You haven't touched your pie," Prescott said. "You'll be sorry if you don't at least try it."

I ate a piece of pie not so much because Prescott suggested it, but because I was starving and had been suppressing hunger pangs for hours.

Montana sniffed me while I chewed.

"That's really good." I washed the pie down with a sip of coffee. "Let's go back to Alden. You said he was in bad shape when you met him."

"Yeah. From a medical perspective he was physically healthy when I first interviewed him, but mentally . . . He lost his civilian job because he couldn't focus on his work. Today they would have simply treated him for ADHD, but back then ... he had money problems, and his marriage was shaky. He and his wife were never able to have kids. Back in more traditional times, that alone could break up a couple. Add in financial woes and ..."

"So no children."

Prescott shot me that glance again, the one that said, *things are about to get rocky.* "About a year after we enrolled him in the study, he came to me and told me that after many years of trying, his wife finally managed to get pregnant and with twins to boot. I tell you he absolutely became a new man. He was happy and full of vigor. He volunteered for more testing and was just full of life."

"So what happened?" Pulaski asked.

Prescott shook his head unhappily and sighed. "His wife and son died shortly after childbirth. Bill crumbled again and was never the same."

"Oh my Lord. That's terrible."

"He couldn't take care of his daughter. Hell, he could hardly take care of himself." Prescott paused. He looked worried. "This is where I'm really going to need your discretion."

"Just tell us, please. I'm only interested in finding my husband."

"We weren't making fast enough progress on the mind-control studies so one of my colleagues, a venomous piece of shit by the name of Kleeb, asked for and received authorization to expand the project to include infants and children to see if we'd have better results working with young minds." Prescott blew out a deep sigh. "Alden begged me to take his daughter into the program. He said he'd have to put her up for adoption if I couldn't help him."

"And you agreed?"

"I did. Reluctantly of course, but Bill ... I was afraid he'd kill himself or do something terrible. He really needed my help."

Prescott looked at me for a third time, but this time his expression said, *May God forgive me.*

"You have a good heart, Frank," I said. I took his hands in mine. "What else can you tell us?"

"We accepted Alden's daughter into the juvenile program as an infant, but because our charter only allowed one participant from any given biological family, we had to perform a little monkey business. We pulled some strings and his daughter's birth certificate was altered to read: Baby Girl Doe, as if the identities of her biological parents were not known. As a condition of the study, the baby lived on the complex twenty-four/seven. In effect, she was an orphan who belonged to a military program. All in all, she was a pretty happy kid. Bill asked that we name her Raven, which was the name his wife had picked out for her.

"One of the nurses, Margo Atwater took a real shine to her and cared for her as if she was her own. Bill had the ability to keep tabs on her and watch her grow up, but I guess . . ." Prescott paused, and I could see that his emotions were getting the better of him. "That poor little girl. Kleeb closed the program about a year after I retired and all the children were shipped out to foster homes. Like I said, the man was a venomous piece of shit."

"I have to ask you, Dr. Prescott, with all the baggage Alden carried around with him, why did you ever accept him into the program," Pulaski asked bluntly. "And why on earth would you compromise your position in the military by altering records and taking in his little girl?"

"Because he needed help and no one else was stepping up to do it, damn it. And . . ."

"And what?" Pulaski said pushing him.

"Alden wasn't exactly your everyday candidate. He had a rare gift you find in maybe one out of a hundred million. He was legitimately psychokinetic. He could do things with his mind practically no one else could do. He could move and alter light pieces of metal."

"He *what?*" Pulaski cried. "This was no trick, something done with smoke and mirrors?"

"No trick whatsoever," Prescott said soberly. "We had many uniquely talented subjects in our program. He was just one of them. Believe me when I tell you he was the real deal."

The three of us sat quietly for a moment. The image of a drawer of bent flatware came into focus in my mind.

Chapter Sixty-Four

"Cam, do you think this is a good idea? I'm really nervous." Kaley tugged down on the brim of her baseball cap and looked in the car vanity mirror as she fidgeted with her long, blond hair until it was all contained within it. She turned to Camryn, who sat behind the wheel of the car performing exactly the same task. "Cam? I mean, really, can I get an answer? I see our faces every time I turn on the TV. Half the cops in America are searching for us."

"Would you relax? They're looking for two women, not two guys having a few pops at the local watering hole. Would you prefer that we tuck ourselves away like a couple of moles? He's not going anywhere. We took plenty of precautions."

"How much longer are we going to hold him? I've never done anything like this before, and I'm scared to death they'll find us and then . . ."

Camryn adjusted her cap and gave Kaley a smooch on the cheek. "It will be over soon. I'm just tying up a few loose ends." She looked at Kaley pointedly. "And then we'll do what we have to do."

"Holding a cop hostage is not a loose end. If they catch us—"

"They won't! By tomorrow night we'll be on a plane to Dubai, and all our worries will be over. I told you we're just buying a little time while the cops are out chasing their tails. I'll take care of the last item on my list tomorrow, and from there on out, it's clear sailing."

"What is this list of yours? You go out. You come back. I'm your partner. Shouldn't I know what's going on in your life? What's with all the secrecy?"

"You don't want to know."

"I do!" Kaley's eyes filled with tears.

My life has been a fucking mess, and now I'm getting even with everyone that screwed me over, including that nosy cop and her husband. I'll fix her wagon. I'll fix it good. Camryn reached down deep and found a smile to mask her true feelings. "I'll tell you everything—all in good time."

"I still don't get it. Why are we taking a chance like this, knowing that we're leaving the country?"

Camryn's eyes glazed over. *None of this would have happened if you hadn't opened your big mouth and told them about Alana and Sarah. You idiot, you sweet oblivious idiot!* "You want to go back to the marina? Go ahead. But I'm walking into that bar and getting hammered. I need it."

Kaley wiped away her tears. "You promise?"

"Promise what?"

"That you'll let that cop go home unharmed. They were so nice to me, Gus and his wife." Tears sprang forward. "They let me hold their baby."

"Yes, we'll let him go." *Whatever you need to tell yourself.*

Kaley stared at her doubtfully. "Promise!" she insisted.

"Yes, I promise," Camryn said, bringing forth all the false sincerity she could muster. She pulled the door release handle and stepped out of the car. She leaned in before shutting the door. "Coming?"

Kaley huffed loudly before unbuckling her seatbelt. "I'll hate you forever if something goes wrong."

"Yeah, yeah, yeah," Camryn said as she sauntered through the parking lot with Kaley a few steps behind. *Sure I'll let him go—over my dead fucking body.*

Chapter Sixty-Five
Search for Gus Lido: Day 3

I didn't want to go to sleep, but I forced myself to lie down knowing I'd fall on my face if I didn't. I went out hard but was awake by five a.m., my mind frantic with the idea that Camryn Claymore was Bill Alden's orphaned daughter.

I showered and dressed and was about to rally the troops when Ambler knocked on my door carrying coffee and what smelled like a fried egg sandwich. He reached into his pocket and handed me a half dozen packets of Heinz ketchup, so I knew that my instinct was correct—if nothing else at least my sense of smell was up to snuff (no pun intended).

Ambler had flown in late the previous evening. He hadn't gotten much sleep either, but that's standard operating procedure for him—it's as if he runs on batteries or something.

"You look better," Ambler said.

"Yeah, it's amazing what half a night's sleep will do for you." I sat down at the desk, and Ambler plunked down on the edge of the bed. I gulped down some hot coffee hoping the caffeine would charge through my bloodstream like Usain Bolt on a one-hundred-meter sprint.

"Bring me up to date. What did you learn from Prescott?" he asked.

"I'm pretty damn sure that Camryn Claymore is not who she says she is. We found two women's driver's licenses stapled to the back wall of her closet. One belonged to Sarah Fisher, the girl who at one time lived in the house we're renting, the girl who went missing. The other one was Camryn's. The picture was accurate, but the date of birth makes her forty-four years old, and I can tell you straight out the woman I met is years shy of thirty. I think the driver's license has been altered."

"Not uncommon. So who do you think Camryn really is?"

All of a sudden I was ravenous. I tore the aluminum foil, uncovering half the sandwich and doused it in Heinz. "All right, follow me—when I was at Alden's house, I saw a bent fork and thought little of it. When we went through Camryn's house, I found a drawer full of bent flatware."

"And?" Ambler was looking at me as if I was crazy. Perhaps I was.

"Alden had a bad life. I mean this man had seen some *shit*. After years and years of trying, his wife finally got pregnant but—" I had to catch my breath. I was talking and wolfing down my food too quickly. "His wife and son died soon after childbirth; only his daughter survived."

"Jesus," Ambler swore. "Talk about being born under a bad sign."

"The poor guy couldn't handle being a father and convinced Frank Prescott to take his infant daughter into the Air Force program. They fudged the baby's records, and she became part of the government's experimental program. Her birth certificate was altered to read Baby Girl Doe."

"You've lost me, Stephanie. What do bent forks and spoons have to do with this child?"

"Prescott struck me as a straight shooter. He looked me dead in the eye and told me that Alden had genuine psychokinetic powers."

"What?" Ambler grimaced expressing doubt. "I've seen that kind of stuff on TV but I'm sure it was all fake. You're telling me he was able to bend spoons and forks with his mind?"

"Yes, and if I'm right ... so can his daughter who I think is Camryn Claymore."

Ambler ran his fingers through his short stiff hair. "That's a lot to swallow, Stephanie. Even if this psychokinetic stuff is true, how do you tie her to the abduction?"

My head dropped. So much had happened that I'd forgotten or perhaps had intentionally forgotten to tell Ambler about the spy cams and videos. It violated me so deeply. I just wanted to forget about it and pretend it never happened. I reluctantly related the details to Ambler and watched him fume. Ambler was unmarried and without children of his own. I was the closest thing to a daughter that he had ever known. He was so hot I think he would've killed Kaley and Camryn if he could've gotten to them. It took a while, but he eventually cooled off.

"Do we know what happened to this child after the government shut down the program?" he asked.

"Not yet. Prescott retired when the baby was two. The project was taken over by a guy named Kleeb, a guy Prescott described as a 'venomous piece of shit.' This all happened last night—Detective Pulaski is trying to locate the child's adoption records." The egg sandwich was gone, and I busily licked ketchup off of my fingertips, after which I raced into the bathroom to wash my hands. My cell phone rang. "It's Pulaski," I announced as I answered the phone. It was barely six a.m. and Pulaski was already hard at work again. I was proud to be a part of this strong cop family.

"Steve, I'm here with Ambler. I'm going to put you on speaker. I guess the early bird catches the worm."

"Not the early bird, Chalice . . . the coon dog," Pulaski said.

"It's too early for me, Steve. What are you talking about?"

"Some kid was hunting upstate. His dog chased a woodchuck into a hole and scratched up a human skeleton. Hoosick Falls, Chalice. Do you remember who came from up there?"

"Moore, Alana Moore, but I thought—"

"Right, that she died when someone pushed her in front of the Long Island Rail Road train. This only happened yesterday, but I got a call from a detective who was working the case all through last night. He said the skeleton has distinguishing characteristics: healed compound fractures of the ulna and radius. The train victim's skeleton was completely pulverized on impact, so we couldn't check for the identifying fractures. They're bringing in a forensic odontologist to see if dental records match. It's not conclusive, but I thought you should know."

"Thanks, Steve. That sounds important."

"No sweat. I'll call you after social services locates the other records we're looking for." Pulaski hung up.

"You heard?"

Ambler nodded and then placed the heel of his hand against his forehead. "Sometimes I wish I was smarter. What the hell does any of this mean? Can't someone just draw me a map showing where we can find Gus?"

The G-Man, as I affectionately called him, was not prone to frustration, but I understood that he was feeling a measure of the same fragility that I was feeling. "Keep cool, my friend. You're all that's separating me from a rubber room."

My phone rang again. I had the sense that I was about to hear something vital even before I checked the caller ID. Like a safe cracker with his ear to the door of a safe, slowly turning the dial in one direction and then the other, I listened for the tumblers to fall into place.

It was Pulaski again. He had just received a fax with a list of invitees to the wedding of Lindsay Rothchild and Ryan Michaels, the couple who had given black and white cookies to their guests as wedding favors. Alana Moore was not among the list of invitees, but Sarah Fisher was.

CLICK!

Chapter Sixty-Six
Raven: April 2013

Sarah Fisher gazed up at the heavens and saw stars blazing vividly in the dark sky above her. A crisp breeze ripped by—it felt cold against her cheeks as it rushed toward the East End of Long Island. She checked the length of the train platform and saw that there was no one around. She didn't like being alone in such a secluded place and her heart was beating quickly from nerves. She looked down the line, hoping to detect the muted glimmer of the train's headlamps in the distance. There was only pitch black in that direction, an immense rift that separated East Hampton from New York City. The breeze died suddenly, and the night became silent. It was so quiet that she noticed her ears were still ringing from the loud music that had been played at the wedding. She checked the length of the platform again and saw that she was still alone.

Or was she?

~~~

Raven had been watching Sarah for several minutes, hidden by the shadow that covered the platform staircase. There was something about Sarah that fascinated her enough to make her want to act out. She focused on the contour of Sarah's nose and cheek, which were softly illuminated by the station lamplight. *She's so pretty.* A moment passed while she evaluated the opportunity. She extended her hand past the shadow so that lamplight fell on the printed train schedule and read that the next train to New York was just minutes off. Her heart thumped, and it seemed like seconds passed before it beat again. She looked around and saw that no one else was on the train platform with them.

Raven gazed across at the barren parking lot to make sure that no other cars were approaching the station. Off in the far distance, the glimmer of approaching train lights came into focus. She felt uncertain and tentative—her hastily formulated plan required bold action. *Now*, she thought, *go now*. But she could not will her feet to move. She had killed before, but those acts had required much more premeditation. A moment passed and she still had not ventured out of the shadow. The overhead clock ticked off another minute—a minute lost forever. Would she allow them all to tick away? *Now!* It was the blast of the eastbound train whistle on the opposite track that finally set her in motion.

The eastbound train had taken Sarah by surprise, Raven noted as she approached. Sarah had jumped nervously, which made Raven snicker quietly. *A bundle of nerves, are we? Perfect.* "Hi," Raven said in a timid manner.

On edge already, the sound of a stranger's voice startled Sarah and stole her breath for a moment. "What the hell?" Sarah clutched her heart. "You scared the shit out of me."

Raven did the same, pressing her hand to her chest mimicking the action of her intended victim. "I'm so sorry," she said. "I didn't mean to ... I'm just happy that I'm not alone. I tried to catch you on the way out of the reception hall—I thought we could share a cab to the train station."

"You were at the wedding?"

She nodded. "Uh-huh. I thought you'd never leave."

"Excuse me?"

"If there was an Olympic event for saying the longest round of goodbyes at a wedding, you'd be a gold medalist."

Sarah's cheeks rose and formed a smile that replaced the look of apprehension on her face. "I'm happy to have company. It's a little creepy out here ... I'm Sarah."

She studied Sarah's face while she thought about the name she would offer her in return. She had not been given a name at the birth. Her birth certificate had simply read: *First Name: Baby Girl. Last Name: Doe.* She had gone through most of her life as Raven Gallagher, but had spent the last several months posing as Alana Moore, a college student from upstate New York.

"Call me Alana. I'm a friend of the groom. Oh my God, it was *such* a gorgeous affair. I can't believe that I was invited to a Hamptons wedding. Everything was so beautiful. Do you believe how many guests they invited? There must have been five hundred people at least."

"Lindsey and Ryan make such a great couple, don't they? I feel like they were meant to be together," Sarah said. "It really was an incredible wedding. I guess what they say is true: *it's good to have money.*"

Raven shrugged. "I wouldn't know."

"I know what you mean—I won't be home until after two in the morning, and I have to be up early for work tomorrow. No rest for the weary, I guess." Sarah was quiet for a moment, as if deciding whether or not to say what was on her mind. Finally, she added, "I have to tell you, Lindsey's father really surprised me."

"What do you mean?"

"For a man with so much money . . . I mean he really doesn't make much of an appearance."

"I know what you mean—he's not the best looking."

Sarah nodded. "Best looking? You're being polite. He looked so sloppy . . . and that beard?" She rolled her eyes. "He looked like he should be swinging from a tree."

Raven giggled. "Eccentric people. I guess you can't judge a book by its cover. Look at that Richard Branson guy."

"The guy who owns Virgin Airlines?"

"Virgin everything—throw some pelts on his back, and he's a Neanderthal."

Sarah chuckled. "Oh my God, I just pictured him—you're so right." Sarah turned and saw the New York-bound train lights in the distance. "Oh great, the train is coming. I thought there would have been more people headed back to the city after the wedding, but I guess they're all staying over for the night."

Raven forced herself to sigh—she nodded simultaneously. "Thank God it's on time. I hear the Long Island Rail Road is always late, especially on the weekends."

"True that," Sarah said. "The LIRR sucks. So you're Ryan's friend?"

"Yeah. We went to school together. Can you believe how well he's doing, marrying into all that money like that? Meanwhile, down on the farm ... I'm still working at a temp agency and looking for my first real job. *"Good, you're doing good,* Raven thought. *Your bullshit is killer.*

"He's a great guy and *so* focused—he'll rule the world one day," Sarah said. "I don't remember seeing you at the wedding— which table were you at?"

"Oh, I was at the orphan's table. You know, the one reserved for the distant friends ... the ones they never expect to attend. Actually, I spent most of the night on the dance floor. The band *rocked.*" She paused for a moment as if uncertain as to what to say next. "*You* certainly stood out. Your dress is fabulous, and I love the pink shoes. You have to tell me where you got them; they're to die for."

"DSW."

"You're kidding, the discount warehouse? Those? Really?"

"Yeah, they sent me a coupon for my birthday— it was too big a bargain to resist, and they dress up the cheap outfit."

"I have to learn where to find the bargains—I'm only in the city a couple of months. I'm crashing at a friend's place on Bleecker until I can afford a place of my own."

"You're in The Village? It's so fabulous down there—I wish I could afford a place downtown. I'm in a basement apartment right near the entrance to the Queens-Midtown Tunnel on 34th. It's a rat hole, but at least I'm in the city."

"No roommates?"

"No. It's just me. I'm from out here, but I moved to the city last year. I'm trying to spread my wings a little."

"I'm envious—you have your own place *and* your privacy. What more could a girl can ask for? I'm from the sticks, and my roommate is a party monster. She's got something going on every night. I can't get a minute's peace."

"Oh, I have privacy all right. I hardly see anyone. My apartment is like a bunker. So, where are you from?"

Where am I from? Raven thought. Her mind raced through possible scenarios. She recalled a road trip and visualized a nondescript section of countryside that bordered the New York State Thruway. "Upstate," she said. She smiled sweetly. "I'm a country girl."

"Oh that's right; Ryan got his bachelor's at Bennington—got it. I hear it's a great school."

She shrugged. "Yeah, not bad. You know what I mean. I wanted to go to Marist, but it wasn't in the cards. Bennington was across the Vermont border, but close enough to home that my parents didn't need to spring for my room and board."

Raven saw the westbound train lights getting closer. *Maybe a minute away,* she thought. She lifted her foot and rubbed her ·heel. "These heels are killing me. Thank God I brought another pair of shoes." She opened her bag and took out a pair of flats. She tried to balance on one foot while she changed out of her black pumps but lost her balance. "Say, would you mind—"

"Holding your bag? Sure. No problem." Sarah held Raven's bag while she walked a few steps across the narrow platform so that she could steady herself against the railing to change her shoes.

"I'm a dummy," Sarah said, "I didn't bring a pair to travel in."

Raven was in the shadows while she changed her shoes. She wriggled her toes and smiled contentedly. "That's *so* much better." She waved to Sarah. "Come over here, okay?" she said, "I don't like standing so close to the tracks."

"Sure." Sarah shrugged and walked closer to Raven. She continued to hold her bag while Raven slipped her black pumps into it.

Raven lifted her foot and deliberately dragged the sole of her shoe across the top of one of Sarah's pink pumps.

The lighting was poor but not so poor that Sarah could not see the fresh smudge on her shoe. "Hey, what the—I love these shoes." She bent over and tried to remove the spot. Only part of it brushed away. "That was pretty rude." Sarah looked up unhappily. "Why'd you do that?"

"They make you stand out." Raven looked through Sarah as if she wasn't there. The train was approaching fast. The whistle blew to announce its imminent arrival. "You wore them to stand out and now look at what's happened. You're so pretty, but in a minute, I'll be the pretty one."

"What do you mean? What the hell is wrong with you?" Sarah asked. She attempted to hand Raven back her bag. "Here," she said. Sarah's expression showed that she couldn't wait to get away from Raven. "Nice meeting you. Good luck finding a job." *Why am I being polite?* she thought. *What a crazy bitch.*

Raven reached out but instead of grabbing her own bag grabbed Sarah's. "Now I'm you."

"The hell is wrong with you?" Sarah said. She tightened her grip on the handle of her bag and tried to wrestle it away, but Raven's grip was incredibly strong.

Raven grinned wickedly when the railroad crossing arms lowered, and the warning signal began to clang.

Sarah jumped when the train whistle blew. She could feel the platform rumble beneath her feet. "Let go!" Sarah shrieked as she tried again to yank her bag free.

Raven stomped down on Sarah's foot.

Sarah cringed and looked up in horror. "Get off of me," she demanded. She tried to free her foot, but Raven pressed down with her full weight, pinning Sarah's foot to the platform.

Sarah tugged one last time, lost her balance, and teetered.

Raven angled her head until her eyes bore into Sarah's. *She mine.* "You're clumsy, Alana."

"What? Why did you call me Alana?" Sarah asked with bewilderment. *"Help!"* Her scream echoed and then disappeared into the lonely night.

~~~

A chill raced up Sarah's spine as she looked into Alana's cold and lifeless eyes. *She's crazy.*

Sarah's face contorted with panic and then she went numb as she sensed what was about to happen. She tried desperately to free her foot as the multi-ton train rumbled toward the station with devastating velocity. She began to tremble, and the hairs on the back of her neck stood on end. "Don't," she pleaded. "Please don't." Sarah searched Raven's eyes for a sign of human compassion, hoping against hope, knowing that she was about to die. It felt as if the blood had drained from her heart. It felt hollow and lifeless.

Sarah heard the girl's hateful tone as if she were far away: "Is that all you've got? You should be happy I'm taking over now—I'll do a much better job with your life than you did." Sarah's mind then went completely numb, her ears filled with the echo of those words as the train . . .

She watched in horror as the girl thrust out her hands and pushed.

Chapter Sixty-Seven

I spent the morning poring over Baby Girl Doe's social services records. She was the girl I believed had grown up to become Camryn Claymore or whatever her real name might have been. According to the records, the child's name was Raven Gallagher. Raven started her life as a guinea pig, and it only got worse from there. The stars were most certainly out of alignment the day this child was born. Looking through her file, I tried to imagine myself in her place but couldn't begin to contemplate the misery she had known. She had been orphaned, experimented upon, and raised in a foster home by an appalling human being, a woman who treated her like an animal. It was no wonder she had grown up to become a deviant. There was no doubt in my mind that she was behind my husband's abduction and the string of murders that was unraveling before my eyes. I made a list of some of the essential individuals in the case, as potentially connected to Raven.

Bill Alden: presumed biological father, dead from poisoning
Celeste Thax: foster parent, dead from poisoning
Alana Moore: victim, dead
Sarah Fisher: victim, missing and now presumed dead
Ray Claymore: true relationship uncertain, dead, car fire
Joshua Dane: relationship uncertain, under investigation
Camryn Claymore: relationship uncertain, under investigation
Margo Atwater: nurse during military testing, under investigation

"Take a look at this list, Herb. I think Joshua Dane and the real Camryn Claymore are dead too. If that's true then this woman, Raven Gallagher, has killed at least seven people over a period of roughly a dozen years. We should hear something about the last three names on the list within the hour, and I just got approval to test the train victim's DNA. Smart money says that the victim is Sarah Fisher and not Alana Moore."

Ambler scanned the list. "Why am I never surprised when I learn about something like this? It's frightening when you think about how many serial killers there are walking among us that we don't even know about. Were you able to get a hold of Smote?"

"Not yet. I tried him three times, but the calls go straight to voicemail."

Ambler grinned. "If he's anything like you told me, he's probably with a couple of women getting himself into a heap of trouble."

"You mean knocking boots?"

"Nothing quite that elegant."

I smirked.

One of the more surprising details to come out of Raven's file was that she was twice questioned by Smote in connection with the murder of her foster parent, Celeste Thax, once shortly after Thax's death and once several years later. Smote wouldn't have had any reason to bring up this information before, but now with the possibility of an old murder suspect and Camryn Claymore being one and the same . . . I needed to speak with him to find out why he was never able to make a case against her.

It was barely eight a.m. Smote was officially retired and had every right to sleep in, either alone or in the company of anyone over the age of eighteen. He probably turned his phone off when he went to bed, and I can't say that I blamed him.

Smote had questioned all of the children living in Thax's foster home at the time of her demise. I read his report twice, and there was no mention of him suspecting Raven more than any of the others girls. There was a note, which referenced an interview with one of Thax's former foster kids, a girl named

Kim Phillips years after the initial investigation. We were in the process of retrieving those records from the archives. It was the old waiting game—anything current would have been available with the click of a button, but older files and cold cases took much longer to retrieve.

Pulaski raced into the room like a bat out of hell. "Here's the scoop," he said. He pulled up a chair and sat down without looking at us. His eyes were on a printout he held in his hands. "All right, Joshua Dane, resident of Schuylkill Haven, Pennsylvania. Twenty-one years old with a list of minor offences in various counties in Pennsylvania, New Jersey, and New York. Mostly penny-ante stuff: minor drug possession, disorderly conduct ... petty theft." Pulaski rolled his eyes. "Never did any jail time. Some public service though."

"Sounds like a lost soul," Ambler said. "A transient."

"Yeah. Agreed," Pulaski said. "Next. Camryn Claymore." He looked at me pointedly. "I think your hunch was right, Chalice. Forty-four years of age. Last known residence, Rego Park, New York. Last tax return filed in 2010. No police record. We called her last known employer, Coldwell Banker Real Estate. They haven't seen or heard from her in years. They said she just stopped coming to work." He handed us a DMV printout of Camryn Claymore's drivers license as it was originally issued. The picture was of a different woman, a woman who appeared much closer to the stated forty-four years of age.

We glanced at each other knowingly. I posed the question, "Burned or poisoned?"

"Poisoned," Ambler guessed.

Pulaski flipped the page. "I could flip a coin, but I'm going with burned ... We ran Raiden Claymore and every possible variation of the name. No one living or dead matches."

"My God, Pulaski, could you please give me something to work with?" I begged.

"Absolutely. Margo Atwater, the nurse who cared for Raven Gallagher, is alive and kicking and lives nearby in Amagansett.

She received an honorable discharge from the Air Force and retired with full benefits. No criminal record."

"I'll take that one." I stood and grabbed my bag. "Address? Phone?"

Pulaski handed me the printout with her information on it.

"Can you do some additional looking into Camryn Claymore and Joshua Dane?"

"I'll see if I can track them down," Pulaski said.

I turned to Ambler and raised my eyebrows, asking silently, *And you?*

"Camp Hero," he said. "I'll get a status on the search for Gus. It's a massive complex. I hope they're coordinating the search efficiently."

I was so focused on solving the case that for a short time I had lost sight of the real mission, recovering Gus. I felt an ache in my chest. "Thanks, Herb. Keep me posted, okay?"

"You bet," Ambler said, and with that, we all went our separate ways.

Chapter Sixty-Eight

"Ms. Atwater? Margo Atwater?" The woman who answered the door looked to be in her sixties. Her hair was short and dyed in a pinkish hue—likely not purposely chosen. She wore a polo shirt and Capri pants. "I'm Detective Stephanie Chalice. I called."

"You're the wife, aren't you?"

"Yes. It's my husband Gus who's gone missing. Can I come in?"

"Well, of course." Margo said pleasantly and stepped aside for me to enter. "I don't know how I can help you, but ... Can I get you something to drink?"

"No thanks. I'm fine."

She closed the door and led me to the kitchen table. "Are you sure, dear? I make a wicked sweet tea."

"Tempting but no thanks."

"Well then, just how do you think I can help you? I don't see how I'd—"

"Tell me about Raven Gallagher, Ms. Atwater."

"Raven?" Margo's mouth opened wide, and I could see that she was searching way back in her memory. Her mouth tightened suddenly, and she reached across the table for a box of tissues. "Why?"

"I know it might be tough for you to make the connection, but there's a possibility that Raven is one of the persons of interest in my husband's abduction."

"No," she said as if to correct me. "The news mentioned two women, but neither was named Raven."

"These women might not be using their real names. Please, Ms. Atwater, I need to know everything you can tell me about Raven, and I need to know right now."

"Oh. Okay. Where should I begin?"

"With Bill Alden. Start there."

"Bill?" A tear ran down her cheek. "I hope he's all right. That poor man."

I wanted to tell her that Alden was dead and likely murdered, but I knew she would've gone to pieces, so I bit my tongue. "Tell me what you know . . . please."

"Do you know about the program that was going on at the Montauk Air Force Base?"

"I've been briefed. I spoke with Frank Prescott last night."

"Frank." Her eyes glazed over. "How is he?" she asked in a detached manner.

"He appears to be well. Now please, you were telling me about Bill Alden."

"I met Bill when he joined the program. He was a nice man, but he was always so sad. I'd see him in the hallways and in the testing rooms, and you could just see that he was hurting. I didn't know if he was always like that or if it was the toll the testing had taken on him. A lot of the subjects couldn't handle the strain of the experiments and would drop out suddenly."

Margo paused and her expression brightened. "And then his wife got pregnant and everything changed. He began to walk around with a smile, and he'd stop to make conversation. He was so happy about becoming a father. He was on cloud nine." Her eyes began to drift. She seemed to be going to another place in her mind, and then her throat tightened. "That only lasted about six months." She looked into my eyes. "You heard what happened, didn't you?"

I nodded.

She shook her head sadly. "Tragic, so terribly tragic. He never recovered from the death of his wife and son. It's an awful thing to say, but he was like the walking dead. The only time he was happy was when he stopped by to see his little girl. I wasn't supposed to know she was his, but I knew. I figured it out." She paused, letting loose a deep sigh. "Can you imagine living for those few precious minutes a day when you could see your child?"

"Did he ever tell you why he gave her up?"

"No, but he didn't have to say. He was a mess, widowed and bereft of his son. The program took a terrible toll on him: terrible headaches, internal bleeding, nausea, and vomiting ... insomnia too. Especially after Frank Prescott retired. The man who replaced him, Kleeb, was a cruel son of a bitch. He'd do anything he wanted to the subjects. Poor Bill was in a coma when—"

I took Margo's hands. "When Raven was put into a foster home?"

She nodded and dabbed at her eyes. "I tried to stop it. I even thought about adopting her but Kleeb threatened to bring me up on charges of insubordination. I don't know where that man is today, but I hope he's burning in hell. He never brought any charges against me but from that day on he made my life a living hell." She drifted again. "Poor Bill, so sad, so loyal—I don't think he ever knew that little girl wasn't his."

"What?" My mouth flapped open in disbelief.

Margo nodded. "I don't think he was the father. He and his wife had tried to conceive for years and years. You think it was a miracle she got pregnant after all that time, and with twins no less? We're talking almost thirty years ago. Today they can make just about anyone get pregnant, but back then ... I think that's why the Lord took her life. Poetic justice, isn't that what they call it?"

I thought about the bent forks and spoons—Raven had to be his daughter. "I'm not sure you're right. You think she had an affair?"

"Yes," she said confidently. "I suspected that she did. I loved that little girl, but when I looked into her eyes, I could see who her real daddy was."

"Who?" I said as I heard a knock at the front door. "Are you expecting someone?"

"No. I wonder who it is." She seemed surprised as she stood, walked to the front door, and pushed aside the curtain that framed it. "Frank?" she exclaimed with shock. She unlocked the door and pulled it open. Frank Prescott was standing on the other side.

Chapter Sixty-Nine

Frank Prescott looked more surprised to see me than Margo was to see him and far less happy about my unexpected presence in her home. His head dropped the moment we made eye contact.

His visit also took me completely by surprise. It occurred to me that something said during the previous night's meeting must have prompted his visit to Margo's home. But exactly what? I smiled to break the ice. "Colonel Prescott, we've got to stop meeting like this."

He smiled back, feebly.

There was something off in Margo's expression as well. I assumed that she would've been delighted to see her old acquaintance, but that seemed hardly the case.

"Frank," she said "What a wonderful surprise," but reading between the lines her greeting translated more like, *What are you doing here?*

"Can't I drop in on an old friend?" It was a good extemporaneous cover-up story but far from the truth.

"Come in and sit down," Margo said. "I understand you've met Detective Chalice."

"Yes. I—" Prescott froze dead in his tracks. We were still standing in the foyer with the door open when his face took on a grave countenance. "No. No games." He turned to Margo. "Did you tell her?"

I had a good idea about what he was going to say. "No. She didn't tell me anything, Colonel. I'd rather hear it from you."

We continued into the kitchen where the three of us sat down at the table. "I'm the woman's father," he said courageously, "this Camryn Claymore you're looking for. I was up all last night thinking about it—it's got to be true." He turned to Margo with somber eyes. "This is what happens when you don't tell the truth the first time around." He swallowed with difficulty and turned back toward me. "Raven Gallagher is my daughter. Gallagher was Caitlin Alden's maiden name. After I took her into the program I named her Raven because I knew that it was the name her mother had picked for her. Bill made the same request of me but it was redundant. I've tried to forget my sin most every day for decades, but I just can't, and now ..." He broke down and was on the verge of tears. "This is what happens when you're weak."

Prescott certainly wasn't the first man to ever commit adultery, but after last night's conversation with Pulaski and me, he couldn't deny the truth that Camryn Claymore and Raven Gallagher were the same person, the person suspected of multiple homicides and the abduction of a New York City detective. Prescott had engaged in an affair with Caitlin Alden, an affair that led to her death and the death of his infant son, an affair that gave life to a child who had been abused and mistreated her entire life. That reality carried devastating weight, and I could see that Prescott was succumbing beneath its crushing force.

"I have a question." A spoon was lying on the kitchen table. I picked it up, holding it between my thumb and forefinger. "I found several bent forks and spoons in Raven's kitchen, and I found a bent fork at Bill Alden's home." The spoon suddenly felt malleable in my hands. I watched to see if it would bend but wasn't quite sure if it did or didn't. I looked up to see Prescott staring at it with great concentration. The spoon felt weird between my fingers so I released it and let it clatter onto the table. "You too?"

Prescott nodded. He had a sad expression on his face. "That's why I began studying psychokinetics in the first place. It's no surprise that my daughter is able to do it as well."

I had connected Raven with Bill Alden because of their rare gift, but I had assumed too much. The gift was so extremely rare ... how could I have guessed that Prescott shared the same talent?

"Why, Frank?" Margo asked. "That little girl looked just like you. Why didn't you come forward and fight for that child? I almost adopted her myself just to get her away from that dreadful foster woman, but the courts dragged it out forever and I couldn't afford to keep going with it. How could you let her undergo testing for the military? How could you let her go into that awful foster home? Bill couldn't take care of her. He was hospitalized and in a coma. When he finally came out of it he was more of a zombie than a man. He couldn't take care of himself, let alone fight a battle to rescue his daughter." She shook her head disapprovingly. "You saw her almost every day for two years. You knew she was yours and yet you let Bill believe she was his daughter. She had your eyes."

Trembling, Margo continued, "Is that why you retired at the very first opportunity you had? What happened? You just couldn't bear to look at her anymore, could you? After you left, that monster Kleeb was unstoppable. He treated the test subjects like animals. That's why Bill lost his mind." Her voice modulated and was no longer controlled. "You left and turned your back on both of them. How could you?" she screamed. "How could you? I thought you were a decent man but—" She began to sob uncontrollably.

"I didn't know what to do," Prescott explained, pleading with Margo. "Yes, I had an affair with his wife but ... Bill was so fragile. I thought he would've killed himself if he knew his wife had been unfaithful. I watched them both—Raven and Bill— every day. I couldn't decide if it was better to rescue my daughter or save my friend." He shrugged. "So I did nothing," he lamented.

I went to the sink and filled two glasses of water. I needed more information from both of them, and I needed them to calm down so that we could get back to work. But when I turned around . . .

Chapter Seventy

Both glasses of water slipped through my hands and shattered on the tile floor. The spoon I had dropped on the table was curling up. My mind refused to accept what I was seeing. A long moment passed before I noticed that someone was standing in the kitchen doorway. *The door,* I thought. *Christ, Margo left it open.*

"Raven?" Margo's face was ashen white. Somehow she knew that the woman standing in front of her holding a gun was the little girl she had cared for at the underground military installation.

Prescott looked as if he had seen a ghost. An expression of incredulity was chiseled into his face. His hands began to tremble.

"Raven," I began in a soothing voice. "Please put the gun down." I could see that she was visibly shaken—who could blame her after the confession she must have overheard? She no longer looked like the hotshot realtor she had portrayed to Gus and me a week earlier. She was dressed like a man in jeans and sneakers with her hair up in a baseball cap. She looked like a broken little girl playing dress-up, the very last person I wanted to see holding a gun.

"How long have you been standing there?"

Margo stood.

Raven whipped the gun in her direction.

"Sit down," Raven ordered and took turns pointing the gun at each of us. I could see that she was not real comfortable with a gun in her hand. Bullets were not her MO. Poison was more her thing—drop something in a glass and wait for the victim's heart to stop. It was slower, but she didn't have to see the internal organs turning into mush, and was spared the devastating impact that occurred when a bullet struck and ruptured flesh and blood. I suspected that death by gunshot was far too violent and instantaneous for her—Most were unprepared for that level of extreme horror. Yes, even a serial murderer like Raven Gallagher.

"I heard it all," Raven said. The gun began to shake in her hand.

"Raven please put the gun down," I repeated. "You don't want it to discharge accidentally."

My logic must've appealed to her on some level but instead of lowering the gun as I had hoped, she brought her left hand up to steady the one which was shaking.

Prescott was frozen. His mouth was open, and his gaze was fixed on his daughter.

Margo was still crying. "I'm so sorry sweetheart," she said. "I tried to stop them from putting you in that foster home, but—"

"I came here to kill you," Raven shouted at Margo. "I killed my father for being such a worm, and I came here to kill you for putting me into foster care and turning your back on me." Tears began to drizzle down her cheek. "You were all I had, Margo. You were everything to me." She aimed the gun at Prescott. "But I can't blame her, can I? Not when this is all on *you*. I killed my father because of you. I waited years because I pitied him, but it was you who took everything away from him ... his wife, his children, and his self-respect. My father loved me in spite of all he suffered through, and I never even knew it. *You're* the one who turned him into an empty shell. So many people have died because of the way my life turned out, but they really died because of *you*." She turned the gun around, the barrel just inches from her face. Her hands were trembling and out of control as she pulled back the hammer. "May God forgive me." She closed her eyes and steadied her thumb on the trigger.

"Raven," I pleaded. "Put the gun—"

Prescott leaped from his chair, his arms outstretched, reaching for the gun. She had hesitated just long enough for her father to grab the weapon before it discharged. The gun fired as they tumbled to the floor together and came to rest on it, motionless with blood pooling beneath them.

Chapter Seventy-One

No wonder she wanted to be someone else, anyone else.
Oh my God, that's what this is all about. The other girls: Alana,
Sarah, and Camryn—she was living their lives because anyone
else's life was better than hers.

She killed Alana and became her, and then she killed Sarah
and became her, and then ... I think she even masqueraded as
her brother Ray. Neither Gus nor I had ever seen him closer than
from the top of a two-story ladder with a hat pulled down over
his face, and Pulaski reported that there was no record of
anyone named Raiden Claymore living or dead. My guess was
that Joshua Dane was the one who actually died in the car fire,
because Raven needed to kill off the character of Ray Claymore,
a brother who had never truly existed. It appeared that she was
tying up loose ends. The question was, why now? Why after all
of these years?

One bullet discharged, two people down. A single bullet had
gone through her jawbone and cheek before entering her
father's skull. She had taken the life of the man who had given
life to her, the man who had sent her on a lifelong journey of
torment, loneliness, and suffering.

EMS techs had packed her jaw so that she could travel, but I
could see that her open mouth was hanging askew and limp. She
had passed out and was still unconscious when the EMS techs
carried her out of Margo's house. I was in the EMS van, hoping
that she would regain consciousness, hoping she'd come to soon
and tell me where my Gus ...

My cell phone rang. "Herb? I can barely hear you."

He raised the level of his voice substantially. "I'm underground," he said. "At Camp Hero." I thought the signal was lost, but it was just an uncomfortable pause. "Gus isn't here, Stephanie." He sounded disappointed, disconsolate, and beaten. "We've searched every square inch of the complex."

"We've got Raven. She tried to take her own life, and we're on our way to the hospital."

"Raven? You're with her?"

"Yes. It's a long story."

"Did she talk?"

"Not about Gus. I'm hoping she'll regain consciousness."

"Shit! Which hospital? I'll come right away."

I called to the EMS driver, "Where are you taking her?"

"Southampton Hospital," the driver replied. "We're less than a minute away."

"You heard?" I said into the phone.

"On my way," Ambler said. "Call me the moment she comes to."

Chapter Seventy-Two

Ambler was in a full run when he caught up with me in the hospital waiting room. "Is she awake?" He was panting as he asked, but his face already bore a look of disappointment. He knew that I wouldn't still be hanging around the hospital if I had discovered Gus' whereabouts.

"She actually did come around for a moment but passed out again as soon as she tried to speak. Her jaw is shattered."

"So we wait."

"Yes." I began to mist up. I hadn't been able to hold my husband in days and was praying to God that he was still alive. Herb was one of the few people I could allow to see me with my guard down. I buried my head on his shoulder. "Hold me, Herb. I'm scared to death."

"Hey!" He shook me. "We've got this. I know we have to wait, but she'll come out of surgery, and then we'll know where Gus is being held."

"God, I hope so. I'll die without him."

"Hey!" he said forcefully. "No one's going to die! Now show me what you're made of, damn it." He lifted my chin and stared at me with unwavering confidence. "Take a moment and then get your shit together. You can go to pieces after Gus is safe and sound, all right?"

I nodded.

"Good." He looked around. "Where can I get a cold-friggin' drink?" He looked past me and must've seen a vending machine. "Sit down. I'll be right back."

I found a chair, sat down, and took a few deep breaths to calm my nerves. *In and out. In and out.* My phone rang, but my mind was a million miles away. The call was just about to go to voicemail when I finally reacted to it. "Hello."

"Chalice, it's me. Sully."

"Sully? You have news?"

"No time for details. I'm at the Westlake Marina in Montauk. I think your husband may be here. I followed two guys here last night. One of them left a couple of hours ago, but the other one's still aboard a yacht, a Carver C40 named *Cornucopia*."

"And you think—"

"I was out having a drink last night when these two young guys came in. The bar was dark so I suppose the dim light and alcohol made them feel at ease and they got a little loud. It didn't take me long to realize that they both sounded like girls. I moved in for a closer look and noticed that they both had that transgender tattoo on the back of their necks. This is going to sound crazy but one of them looked like that foster kid I questioned years back, Raven Gallagher, the one I most suspected of killing my aunt. Anyway I followed them to the yacht. How long before you can get down here?"

"Montauk? Damn it. I'm about an hour away."

"Well, call the cavalry and haul ass, Chalice. I don't how much longer this one will stay put or when the other one will return."

"The other one's not coming back," I said.

"What?" Sully asked. "How do you know?"

Now I understood why Raven had shown up at Margo's home dressed like a guy. I'm sure that she expected Margo to be alone when she came to kill her. If witnesses saw her, they would report they saw a man coming and going from Margo's house.

"I just do," I said to save time.

Ambler was on his way back, holding two cans of soda.

"Hold on," I said to Sully. "Herb," I called out. "Can you get a chopper out here PDQ?"

Ambler saw that the light was back in my eyes. He nodded eagerly.

"Stay put, Sully," I said into the phone. "I'm on my way."

Chapter Seventy-Three

At one hundred twenty knots air speed, it took less than fifteen minutes for the FBI chopper to cover the thirty-mile stretch from South Hampton to Montauk, cutting thirty to forty minutes off our travel time had we taken a car along the congested two-lane Montauk Highway.

We were high enough for me to see both land and sea as we flew east along the South Fork. There was no question that tactical forces were racing toward Montauk. Law Enforcement vehicles of every description were speeding east along Montauk Highway with their lights on and sirens screaming.

As we hovered over the Marina, I could see that policemen had been posted strategically around the area. A SWAT van was pulling up to the marina just as we arrived. Sharpshooters poured out of the van and took positions as directed by their commanding officer.

It was hard for me to accept that Gus was being held captive by someone as diminutive as Kaley Struthers. To me, that meant Gus had been drugged or the two women had not acted alone. Either or both were possible. Neither mattered at the moment. The only thing that counted was that we would find Gus unharmed in the yacht below us. I was looking beyond the moment of rescue, and in my mind, he was already back in my arms.

To the untrained eye, it might've seemed that nothing was going on, but that was not the case. I knew how these rescues worked. The commanding officers were discussing strategy and the coordination of each police unit. It was slow and steady all the way, as they would do nothing to risk Gus' safety. Ambler and I waited patiently in our perch in the sky as police boats filed into the marina, preventing the possibility of the yacht escaping by sea.

I heard the voice of the officer in charge thundering over the bullhorn, "Ahoy, *Cornucopia*. This is the Suffolk County Police Department. You are surrounded. Come out with your hands up."

Within moments, Kaley appeared on the deck with her hands up in the air. We were close enough to see that she was trembling. In an instant, she was surrounded by police officers and then the rest of the tactical team boarded the boat.

My heart was pounding wildly in anticipation of seeing Gus appear on deck. It seemed like an eternity from the time the yacht was boarded until an officer surfaced from within. He shook his head in an exaggerated manner and my heart sank. Gus was not aboard.

Chapter Seventy-Four

Kaley's head dropped as I approached the police car she was locked within. I was so furious that I wanted to reach through the window and strangle her with my bare hands. I tried to control myself, but I couldn't. "Kaley! Where is my husband? Where is Gus?" She actually shuddered from the intensity of my voice. "Hey! I asked you a question."

Ambler was by my side. "Easy," he said. "She's scared to death. Take it down a notch. You know," he whispered, "more flies with honey..."

A crime scene officer rushed toward us holding a Ziploc bag. It contained small syringes marked 3/10 mL/cc, and a bottle of etorphine.

My eyes widened and my nostrils flared as I read the label. Without thinking, I reached for Kaley's neck. "Animal tranquilizer? You used animal tranquilizer on my husband?" I was still screaming as Ambler yanked me away from the police car. I heard Kaley retching from inside the car.

"She'll talk, Chalice," Ambler said. "You've got her so scared, she can't breathe."

"Etorphine, Herb? It's fatal to humans." A lump formed in my throat, and I began to mist up, fearing that Gus' abduction had become something much worse, something irreversible. "He could be dead, Herb. He could be—"

"It's only fatal when used full strength. You saw the tiny syringes. That's the only way two women were able to handle Gus. They must have crept up behind him and dosed him with a small amount of fast-acting tranquilizer. I'm sure of it."

"Are you?" I cried with contempt. I tried but I couldn't find my humility. It just wasn't there. *"Fine."* I said with disgust. "You talk to her."

"Thanks," Ambler said. "Give me a minute."

I walked a few paces away and was within earshot but unable to hear what Ambler was saying to her. I was desperate and unable to control the way I felt. It seemed as if Ambler was talking to her forever, but in reality, only a few minutes had passed. "It's Raven's brother," Ambler said. "He's got Gus."

"What brother?" I asked, frantically. "There is no brother."

"There is," Ambler said assertively. "There is."

BOOK SIX

Chapter Seventy-Five
Raiden: 2000

"Hey, stop wasting the trash bags," Ray said as he pulled a white t-shirt over his head and rushed down the steps of the foster home.

Mica looked up as Ray approached. Ray was skinny, and his jeans were baggy around the legs. His hair was long, and it glistened with the luster of youth.

Mica said, "I just do what they tell me. The man says, 'line the trashcan,' I line the trashcan."

"Man, I'm going to need some of them for my getaway," Ray said. "Don't be wasting that fine foster-home luggage on food scraps and junk. The raccoons just knock the cans over and eat through the bags anyway. The sanitation guys always shovel it up—that's what they get paid for, isn't it? Besides, it's dark already. No one's going to come out and check." He reached for the unused trash bag. "Give me that. I need it."

"Take it—less work for me anyhow." Mica snatched a half-smoked cigarette from behind his ear. "Got a light?"

Ray reached into his pocket. "Ever know me not to have matches?" He struck a match and lit the stub.

"So what's with this getaway?" Mica asked as he puffed on the cigarette.

"Told you. I'm busting out. I can't be dealing with this lame foster-ass living anymore."

"Where do you think you're going to go, some swanky resort in the Swiss Alps?"

"I got a plan. Hey, give me tug on your ciggy," Ray said.

Mica pinched the cigarette by the end of the filter so he wouldn't burn his fingers as he handed it to Ray. "Don't smoke it all," he said.

"Relax," Ray said as he took a long and satisfying drag. "I've got a couple of butts in my pocket." He took one out and lit it from the one he held between his lips. He handed the fresh stub to Mica. "You got any chores you gotta do?"

"No. I'm finished for the day. What about you?"

Ray's expression said, *don't be ridiculous.* "I forgot that you're new here. I don't do chores."

"What do you mean you don't do you're chores? Everybody—"

Ray exhaled, blowing the smoke skyward. "Nope. Not everybody." He flicked away the cigarette butt and watched as the orange embers glowed in the dark. "Hey, check it out." He slid a small can of Zippo lighter fluid out of his back pocket and squirted the liquid close enough to the smoldering butt for it to catch fire.

"Cool," Mica said. "Where'd you get it?"

"I stole the old man's lighter fluid." Ray shrugged. "I mean it's not like I've got money to buy stuff."

"You'd better put it back before he knows it's gone," Mica said.

"Why? What's he gonna do about it?" Ray spotted a water bug emerging from the sewer drain. His eyes sparkled with an idea. "Watch this." He traced a wide circle around the water bug with the lighter fluid and then connected it to the burning cigarette butt, encircling the giant insect in a ring of fire. "He's trapped," Ray said gleefully. The water bug raced away from the flame only to find that there was nowhere for it to escape. He traced a smaller concentric circle within the larger one, drawing the flame closer to the doomed insect. The bug raced frantically in scattered directions. A third concentric circle trapped the bug, giving it almost no room in which to move.

"That's mean, man," Mica said. "Just burn it already."

"Not yet." He watched as the bug repeatedly moved an inch in each direction, repeating its unsuccessful attempts to escape. He finally squeezed the can, dousing the bug in lighter fluid. He smiled as the bug caught fire, burned, and crackled. "Let's go find more stuff to burn."

The door to the foster home opened and Old Man Forrester slowly stepped outside. "Mica? Ray?" The old man squinted, trying to see the boys in the darkness. "What the hell are you two up to?"

"Shit. Run!" Ray grabbed Mica's arm, and they ran off down the block. The sign at the end of the street read: No Trespassing, NY State. They easily scaled the chain-link fence and landed in the water collection sump.

Ray became hysterical with laughter.

Mica had difficulty catching his breath. "Damn. We'll catch all kinds of shit when we go home later."

"You worry too much," Ray insisted as he sat down on the ground. "Here, take these." He showed Mica a prescription bottle and shook some of the pink capsules into his palm.

"What are those?" Mica asked.

"The old man's pain pills. I took them once, and they made me feel really good." He put two of the capsules in his mouth and swallowed. "Go ahead, try it."

"Are you sure it's okay?"

"Yeah. It's not much stronger than a beer buzz."

Mica put a couple of capsules in his mouth. "This better not mess me up."

"Just swallow them," Ray insisted. "Don't be such a pussy."

Chapter Seventy-Six

When Mica's eyes opened, he realized that he was lying outdoors on the cool ground. The grass around him was damp, and a field mouse scampered by, not two inches from his arm. His head ached and his vision was blurry.

"What the hell?" He rubbed his aching forehead and turned on his side. Three cigarette butts lay on the ground where Ray had been. "What?" The cicada's song built to a deafening level while he looked around for Ray. He called out, "Ray? Hey, Ray, where you at, man?"

He stood up and scanned the area around him. The sump was level ground for about ten yards and then dropped suddenly into a deep basin used to funnel rainwater into the ground. Mica stood at the edge of the basin and looked into it. It was very deep, too deep and dark for him to see the bottom.

Where the hell is he?

"Hey, jackoff, it's not funny. Where'd you—"

"*Boo!*"

Mica clutched his chest and sucked in a chestful of air. He looked back over his shoulder. Ray was standing behind him, laughing hysterically.

"Asshole!" Mica shouted. "What the hell is wrong with you?"

"You should see your face," Ray said with his finger pointing straight at Mica's nose. "You look like you just saw a goddamn ghost."

"Yeah, very fucking funny, Ray. You scared the crap out of me."

"Aw, relax and stop acting like such a chump. I'm just having a little fun, that's all."

"Have fun with someone else." Mica glared at Ray and marched over to the chain-link fence.

"Hey! Cool down," Ray shouted. "Why are you so mad? You had a good time, didn't you?"

"Piss off, Ray."

"Man, I got you stoned. We had some laughs. What've you got to complain about?"

"I said piss *off.*" Mica got a toehold in the chain-link fence and boosted himself up.

Ray grabbed him by the belt.

"Hey! Get off me," Mica protested. "Don't you know when it's time to quit?"

"Get back down here, you scared little bitch." Ray yanked him off the fence.

Mica clenched his fists and spun around. Before he knew what hit him, Ray pressed his lips against his mouth.

"*Ugh!*" Mica made no attempt to conceal his disgust. "Are you nuts? Are you, a fucking homo or something?"

The sudden yelp of a police siren made both boys jump. A police car stopped just outside the sump. The beacon from the police car illuminated them. "Freeze!" an officer called out.

"Oh shit," Mica said. "Look what—" He stopped when he realized that Ray was pressed up against him. "Ray," he whispered, "what's wrong with you?" He shoved him away just as the policeman approached.

"That's enough," the policeman said. He approached holding a searchlight above a drawn automatic. He shone the searchlight beam in Mica's face and then Ray's before his focus settled on Ray. "Not you again. Jesus, you've got to be kidding me." He shook his head unhappily, took a step back, and ran the beam up and down over Ray, from head to toe, and then over Mica. He shook his head again this time in dismay. "All right, you two. Get down off the fence, and don't try anything stupid." He stepped back to give the two boys room to get down off the fence, but continued to hold the automatic beneath his searchlight. "Turn around, both of you—hands against the fence, feet spread." He waited for both of the boys to comply before holstering his weapon and securing his searchlight. He handcuffed them both. "Wait right here," he said to Mica and led Ray to his squad car. He opened the back door. "Get in there, you skinny little twerp." He turned toward Mica the instant the back door was locked.

"Turn around. What's your name, son?" the police officer asked.

Mica's face was drenched in sweat. "M-M-Mica," he stammered.

"Mica what? You got a last name?"

"Mica Hollister, Sir."

"Calm down, Mica. I want to ask you a few questions."

"O-okay."

"How old are you?"

"Fourteen."

"Do you live at the foster home down the street?"

Mica nodded. "Yes."

"I haven't seen you before. Are you new?"

"Yessir, only been living there about a month."

"No one warned you about Ray?"

"Warned me?" Mica seemed confused. "About what?"

"All right, son, I'm going to cut to the chase. Were you and Ray having sex in there?"

Mica gulped. "Sex? No. No, Sir. Why? Why do you ask?"

"Because it looked as if the two of you were kissing when I pulled up. Were you?"

"Kissing? No. No, Sir."

"You sound nervous, Mica. Tell the truth, were you and Ray kissing?"

"No."

"Then why do you have lipstick all over your mouth?"

"I . . . what?" Mica's eyes widened, and he dragged his hand across his mouth. He stared at his hand in the moonlight, trying to see if the smudge he saw there was red. "I-I-I don't know how it got there."

"Well, I do. You're not homosexual are you?"

Mica shook his head frantically. "No."

"Do you want to press charges against Ray?"

"Charges?"

"Sexual assault."

"Why would I—"

"You do know that your fly is wide open, don't you?"

Mica's eyes dropped. He stared at his gaping fly in disbelief and then quickly zipped. His throat tightened, and he looked to be on the verge of tears.

"Did Ray make you have sex against your will?"

"No. He gave me some pills, and I fell asleep."

The police officer formed a knowing expression. "They weren't pink capsules, were they?"

Mica nodded. His upper lip broke out in dabs of sweat.

"It's all right, son. Turn around." The police officer removed Mica's handcuffs. "I'll take you over to the hospital, and we'll get you checked out."

Chapter Seventy-Seven
Raiden: 2012

Alana Moore dropped a pile of textbooks on the counter. She smiled at the guy behind the cash register as she opened her bag and removed her wallet. She pulled out her student ID card and placed it atop the stack of books.

"That's quite a pile of books you've got there."

"Who'd have thought there'd be so much to read about acting theory?" Alana replied. "Acting isn't feeling all that glamorous to me right now."

Everyone working at the Bennington College Bookstore wore the college colors and a bookstore nametag. Ray wore a blue vest over his white t-shirt. He began to look at the pile of books. "We've got a couple of used copies of the Saint-Denis book if you want to save some money."

"I looked," Alana said. "I didn't see any."

"Really? I know I saw at least one when I straightened up the stock this morning. I'll show you. Come on."

Ray stepped out from behind the counter.

Alana seemed happy to follow him as he squeezed through the narrow aisles of eight-foot-tall metal shelving. "I haven't seen you here before. Are you new?" she asked.

"No." Ray said without turning around to make eye contact. He seemed intent on finding the used book for her. "But this is the first time I've worked on campus."

"You don't sound like you're from around here. Where are you from?"

Everywhere and nowhere. He turned and smiled this time, he smiled for all he was worth. "Long Island. Why, do I sound weird?"

No. You sound cute... She wasn't normally attracted to slight men. *But that smile. Yummy.* "You just sound different, that's all. I mean it's not a bad thing."

"Thanks." Ray looked through a stack of books and quickly found the one he was looking for. "The old one has a different cover," he said as he handed the book to Alana. "That's probably why you missed it."

"Oh, that's great." She checked the price which was written in pencil on the inside back cover. "Twelve bucks cheaper." She wasn't much of a flirt, but she was interested in him and hoped that it showed. "How can I thank you?"

"I don't have a car, but if you're not turned off by public transportation, we could go into town and grab a bite."

She was happy to be hit on and blushed. "This fortuitous meeting may just work out very well for you."

"What do you mean?" Ray's eyes grew large with excitement.

"Don't get carried away with yourself. I drive because I don't live on campus. I commute."

"That's great. Really, you drive?" *That's it. Tell me everything I need to know about you. Go ahead, I'm listening attentively.*

"Yes, *I drive*," she said.

"Oh that's cool. I heard Kevin's Pub serves a great burger."

"Yeah. They *really* do." They were less than five minutes into their relationship, but Alana already sensed the chemistry flowing between them. He seemed very easy to talk to. "So it's a date?" She smiled prettily, while clutching the large textbook to her stomach.

"Works for me. Of course, it would be nice if I knew your name," he said once again lighting up the smile billboard.

"Eek!" *Overanxious much? Gee whiz, girl. Don't be such a klutz.* "Alana. I forgot that you're the only one wearing a nametag. Mine should read: Ditzy."

Ray laughed a bit louder than he normally would have in response to her mediocre joke, as she smiled broadly.

"You're a fellow carnivore, I trust?" he asked.

"Are you kidding? I'm from Hoosick Falls. Where I live, if you don't eat cow, you just plain don't eat—it's as simple as that. I grew up on steak and potatoes."

Ray chuckled. "When's the last time you checked your cholesterol?"

"The point is moot. My mother thinks if you serve steak well done, it no longer counts as red meat."

"I'm gonna go out on a limb here—did you grow up on a farm? Are you a farm girl?"

"Milking cows and feeding chickens—that's why I'm a theater major. I'm only in my twenties, but I've already had enough reality to fill a lifetime. Believe me there's nothing quite as invigorating as slogging through a barn filled with cow manure and carrying a metal bucket at four in the morning to start the day off right. Now you know everything about me. That's why I'm studying so hard . . . It's bright-lights-big-city for this girl."

"Who's going to milk the cows while you're gone?"

Alana tilted her head to the side. "Machines do it. *As if* you really care."

"Not so. I'm *udder-ly* committed to the humane treatment of all farm animals."

"That was incredibly lame. Maybe I ought to think twice about going out with you."

"How about tonight?"

"Tonight?"

"Yeah, unless you're worried about the cows or something. We'll go to Kevin's—you drive, I'll treat."

Alana pretended to ruminate for a moment. "Okay, let's do it," she said with a girlish lilt in her voice. "I'll pick you up here at—"

"I get off at six."

"Six is good for me too." She turned and walked toward the register. "Well, Ray, are you going to ring me up? I don't have all day you know," she said teasingly.

~~~

You do have all day but that's about all you've got. Tonight I'll treat you to your last supper. He rang up the sale and continued to smile at her while he contemplated how she would die.

Chapter Seventy-Eight
Raven and Raiden: 2012

Raven reached out and reluctantly took Alana's bag from her brother. "Do I have to?"

"You know you do," Ray said. "You think I went to all of this trouble for nothing?"

"But is she—"

"Look, the less you know the better. This is what you wanted, isn't it? This is why you tried so hard to find me. You don't want to be Raven Gallagher any longer, and I don't want to be who I am either. This is how we get to do it."

Raven took the wallet out of the handbag and began looking through it. She examined Alana Moore's ID. "She looks nothing like me."

"It doesn't matter. She's blond and you're blond. You're about the same age. That's all it takes."

"And no one's going to ask questions?" she asked pointedly.

"No one's going to ask questions? Are you nuts? There'll be a million questions," he blurted. "There will be a police investigation. I killed her, for God's sake. I killed her for you."

"But—I didn't think—"

"Right, you didn't think. More like you didn't *want* to think. You thought someone was going to say, 'Totally, take my identity. I want to disappear anyway.' This is how it's *done*, Raven. This is how it has to be done. This is the legacy our father left us when he turned you into a lab rat and stuck me in a retard home. The motherfucker," he swore angrily. "This is the first step. It's drastic I know, but there's no other way."

"Did you have to kill her?"

"Yes, Raven, I had to kill her." He took hold of her arms. "She died so that you can live. She died so we can *both* live. Are you going to fall apart on me?"

"Ray, this is bad. It's so fucking bad."

"Look!" he yelled. "We've suffered our entire lives and for what? Our father was a spineless worm who couldn't take care of his children. I want him dead and everyone else who screwed us over. It took us over twenty-five years to find each other, and now that we have ... Look, I love you, Raven and I'm going to take care of us. We'll go back to Long Island and no one will be the wiser. Alana Moore, the bumpkin farm girl ... she's just collateral damage."

CONCLUSION

Chapter Seventy-Nine

"But I thought—"
"That he died at birth?" Ambler asked.
"Yes."
"I guess that's what everyone was led to think, but Struthers is telling me he's real and that he played a big role in Gus' abduction." Ambler sighed, looked around, and then brought his focus back to me. "I believe her. I think she's just a dumb kid who got caught up in a plan of revenge. She and Raven—"
"I know. They're lovers."
Ambler shrugged. "Why else would anyone get involved in all of this stupidity? Only for love or money, and money doesn't seem to be part of this equation." Ambler shook his head woefully.
"They both have transgender tattoos. I guess to show they're a couple. They also dressed as guys but I'm not sure if they did so because they are into cross-dressing or to disguise themselves.
A police officer sat in his car waiting for his onboard computer to spit out information on Raven's brother. Multiple searches had already been run with variations of the name Raiden Claymore to no avail, but now that we had some hard details . . .
I prayed that the police computer would spit out an address.

Chapter Eighty

Gus' eyes opened when the car bounced off the curb and hit the pavement. It was pitch black and it took a full minute for his head to clear sufficiently for him to understand that he was locked in a trunk with his wrists and ankles bound. The effects of the sedative were still working on him. His eyelids felt like lead and they continued to close even as he fought to awaken. *Christ, I'm so woozy.* He was bound tightly, and there was barely any room for him to move around within the tight confines of the trunk. He shook his head violently to get his blood pumping. *Think. Damn it. Think. What did they give me?* He rubbed his face on the abrasive trunk liner, anything to stir the senses and get himself going. The car hit a pothole, and he smacked his head on the trunk lid. His head stung like hell but the blow succeeded in bringing him around where his other attempts had failed.

He knew that newer model cars have glow-in-the-dark trunk release handles. Gus searched within the confines of the trunk and found it. The cable had been clipped, and the handle was lying on the floor of the trunk—useless. His eyes closed in despair, but only for a moment. The car bounced again, and this time his back pressed against the corner of the trunk support bracket. He squirmed until he was able to bring his wrists in contact with the unfinished steel bracket and rubbed his twine restraints against it.

~~~

I got excited when my cell phone rang. A call was coming in from Pulaski but the call dropped before I could answer it.

"Shit!" I called him back, dying on the inside as the phone rang. "Pulaski?

~~~

Pulaski stepped through the front door and checked his cell phone to see if he had better reception outside than he had within the house—still no signal. He began walking down the block. One bar appeared. He dialed and continued to walk in the direction of the strengthening signal. "Chalice, the house is empty, but Gus must have been here. I found a pair of shackles around a support column in the basement, and there are injectable sedatives in the kitchen. Hold up." A full minute passed before he came back on the line. "That was one of his neighbors. He said a car pulled out of the garage about fifteen minutes before we arrived. He didn't know the make or model but he said it was a gold sedan."

~~~

Gus felt the steel bracket cutting through the restraints and into his skin. He pulled against the restraints as best he could and heard some of the fibers begin to pop. *Thank God.* He continued to rub against the metal bracket, distracting himself from the pain by thinking forward to what he would do when his hands were finally free.

~~~

"That would put them about thirty minutes ahead of us," I said over the phone to Pulaski, screaming so that he could hear me above the infernal chopper noise. "The only real ground route off the island is west on Route 27. Any other direction and they have to cross water."

Ambler relayed my comment to the chopper pilot.

"We've got all the ferries and marinas covered, correct?"

"That's affirmative, Chalice. Every water route is covered, one hundred percent," Ambler said.

~~~

POP! Gus's wrists were free. He tried to untie his legs, but there wasn't enough trunk space for him to reach down by his ankles with both hands, and he couldn't untie himself with just one hand. He had formulated a plan and was now ready to carry it out. He listened for road sounds while he got his hands into position. He could hear the noise of the car on the road surface and the hum of the running gear, but not the rumble of trucks, which meant that the car was moving rapidly but was not on a major expressway like the LIE.

He was becoming more and more awake with every passing second. He pried up the trunk mat and cover, which contained the spare tire and tire-change equipment. He could not lift the cover fully because he was lying on top of it but he pulled with all of his strength and the cover snapped. He removed the jack and jack handle.

~~~

We were flying at high speed over Route 27—any faster and we wouldn't have been able to identify the cars as we shot past. A dozen law enforcement helicopters were in the air, scouting various routes. Kaley's last call was made just minutes before she surrendered at the marina, a tipoff to Gus' captor that she had been found. The call was traced to the location Pulaski had just called from.

All eyes were on the road as we tried to identify a gold sedan. We were so close to Gus I could feel it, but at the same time, I also felt an undercurrent of tragedy that wouldn't be lifted until Gus and I were once again together.

~~~

Gus tried to pry the trunk latch free with the jack handle, but he could not get sufficient leverage to muscle it open. His movements were limited only to what he could accomplish with wrist movements. *Think, Lido. Think! At least my hands are free. If he comes at me with a syringe again, I'll ... Wait a minute. Got it!*

There was just enough room for Gus to insert the jack handle into the jack. Using small wrist movements he was able to ratchet the jack open until he had it tightly wedged between the steel trunk liner and the trunk latch. With each click of the ratchet, the force required to expand the jack grew greater and greater. The jack was almost fully expanded. With the jack at near maximum extension there was just enough light spilling in around the trunk seal for him to see the remaining notches on the jack—there were only two left. He worked his forearms with every last ounce of strength. The jack ratcheted up another notch, one from the last. *Shit!*

~~~

There were only about two miles to go before tributary roads would branch off Route 27 and lead to major parkways and expressways. *And then what? He'll slip through our fingers again? Please, God, no.*

I was becoming discouraged again and was fighting off tears when I saw a car's gold roofline in the distance.

"Is that it?"

Both Ambler and the pilot trained their eyes on the gold sedan. Just as they did, the trunk popped open and I saw him—I saw Gus. "Oh my God." I could see the strain on his face as he sat up and tried to untie the rope around his ankles.

The chopper pilot was on the loudspeaker instructing the driver to pull off to the side.

Ambler was on the phone calling for backup.

Chapter Eighty-One

The sound of police sirens filled the air as the chopper descended onto a field just north of the roadway. The door opened, and the driver ran from the sedan. I had the chopper hatch open and was out the door before the chopper touched down. I hit the ground running.

The driver had taken off and was heading south of the roadway, across an open field.

I saw Gus and choked up realizing that I couldn't go to him yet. *I'm sorry. Just a few more minutes. I'll wrap my arms around you after I see this all the way through.* I ached so badly. I wanted to run to him and hold him but I couldn't. I had to end this thing now.

Most of the cars had slowed but not to a full stop. I zigzagged between the two opposing lanes of traffic as I gave pursuit.

The driver was in a flat-out run, but I was not going to be beaten. Not now, not with Gus' captor in sight. I reached down deep and found an extra gear, one that I didn't know existed. I was running so fast, I felt as if I could take off. I was closing in on him: two yards behind . . . one . . .

I lunged and took him down by the ankles. As he attempted to kick free, I pounced upon him, fists flying. I hauled back and was ready to pummel him when I froze. *"You? It's you?"* The face I was about to strike was one I had seen before. This man was the one who told me there was absolutely nothing suspicious about the fire the day I first inspected the remains of Bill Alden's cottage. Two bodies, burnt beyond recognition—now I understood who would use that specific MO. *Dummy, you couldn't make the connection?*

It was the fire inspector, Jay Charnoff.

"You son of a bitch." I heard the sound of others running toward me, but my fist was clenched.

"Chalice, we've got him," Ambler said. "Don't!"

There was no force on heaven or earth strong enough to keep me from striking him, this man who had turned my family's world upside down and put my husband's life at risk. I drove my fist into his jaw and heard it crack. I was ready to hit him again when someone grabbed my arm. I looked up and saw Gus. His cheek was swollen, and there was dried blood on his face.

"Thanks, babe," he said, "I'll take it from here."

Chapter Eighty-Two

"Stephanie, I want to go home."

"Tomorrow, babe, the doc says you've got to stay overnight."

"But I'm fine," Gus frowned. "I want to see the little guy."

"Me too, but you're dehydrated and they have to make sure all the sedatives have been flushed out of your system. You need your fluids and a good night's sleep."

He flexed, making a point of his rock-solid bicep. "I'm strong as a bull. I can take on a toddler."

"Max isn't walking yet."

"Your point?"

"He's not a toddler yet. He sleeps, crawls, poops, spits up, gushes, and laughs . . . those are your options."

"Seriously?"

I snuggled close to Gus on his hospital bed. "I'm so glad the doctors finally left you alone. All that poking and prodding . . . that's my job." I gave Gus a big kiss on the lips and then I just couldn't wait any longer. "I hope you're up to this." I probed his mouth long and deep. He seemed to enjoy the passionate kiss, and as far as I could tell, all of his snogging equipment was in fine working order. "Let's see an EMT pull that one off."

"Ya see," Gus said, "I've got the best canoodler on the planet taking care of me. That's got to beat the hell out of a bagful of electrolytes."

"Look. Get your strength back. We've got a private room. As soon as the sun sets I'm going to lock the door and . . ."

"And what?" he asked impishly.

"Let's put it this way, I'm not gonna go easy on you. I want to make sure you're roadworthy before I sign your discharge papers and take you home." I played with his freshly showered curls. "What do ya say, muscles? Wanna make out?"

"My lips are yours, gorgeous."

I heard a knock on the door followed by an exaggerated, *"A-hem."*

Commissioner Bratton stood at the door, waiting for us to acknowledge him. I did far more than that. I jumped off the bed and threw my arms around him. My emotions were still out of check. A few tears drizzled down my cheek. "Commissioner, so nice of you—"

"Call me, Joe," he said in a warm tone. He looked over at Gus. "Is this the guy causing all the fuss? He looks like he can handle himself." I released the commissioner from my grasp, and he walked over to Gus. "Joe Bratton," he announced as they shook hands. "Glad to see you're up and around, son. I heard you've been through quite an ordeal."

"Thanks for stopping by," Gus said. "Stephanie told me you were instrumental in finding me."

"Me? Instrumental? Your wife deserves all the credit. I don't think she ate, slept, or drank, the entire time you were missing. I wish I had the two of you out here in Suffolk County working for me."

"Is that a job offer?" I asked with a smile.

"Sure. But I think the NYPD commissioner might have me iced for pulling a stunt like that," he chuckled. "Look, I'm sure you want your privacy. I just stopped by to give you something." He reached into a small shopping bag and handed me a flat, gift-wrapped box."

"What's this?"

"It's an iPad and a hard drive."

Gus looked puzzled.

I was too.

"A *particular* iPad and hard drive," he said with emphasis.

"*Oh!* Got it. Thanks so much."

"My pleasure," Bratton said. "I figure we can make our case without this one specific piece of evidence, don't you?"

"Yes. I'm sure you can." I kissed Bratton on the cheek. "It's the trash heap for these."

"I figured you'd want the pleasure of destroying them yourself."

"I don't get it," Gus said. "Why do we want to trash a new iPad?

Bratton laughed. "And on that note . . ."

"I'll tell you later, babe."

"Get well soon." Bratton and Gus shook hands again, and I walked him to the door.

"How can I ever thank you for all of your help, Commissioner?"

"Help me?" He laughed. "You brought three desperate criminals to justice and solved half a dozen homicide cases. Trust me, darlin', you've thanked me plenty. Gus is safe and sound. All's well that ends well, as the saying goes." His voice turned to a whisper. "And if you ever want to leave the Big Apple . . ." He winked and gave me a Vulcan salute just like my dear departed friend, Chief of D's Sonellio, used to. "Live long and prosper."

"You too, Commissioner. Live long and all that jazz." He smiled and walked away.

I plopped back onto Gus' bed. "I guess I've got a lot to tell you."

"And I thought I had the tough part, sitting in a basement chained to a support column. So what's with the iPad?"

"Home movies."

"Of us?"

I nodded with big eyes. "U-huh."

The news seemed to shock him. He shook his head in dismay. "Unbelievable. Do we at least look good?"

"Look good? I've gotten seven-figure offers from Wicked Pictures and Naughty America. Do we look good? Does a chicken have lips?" It was almost too good to be true. Gus was only back a couple of hours, and yet here we were laughing and joking as if nothing had ever happened. I guess neither of us was ready to talk about all of the ugly details that had led to his abduction— one day soon, but not now.

You know what they say. *You don't know what you've got till it's gone.* I was just so happy to have Gus back. The idea of losing him tore me apart inside, the idea of him dying ... well, a good wife couldn't just give that one a pass. I couldn't just accept the fact that he was back without worrying what might happen the next time. Ma had always warned me about the perils of police work ... and as always, Ma was right.

Gus was dozing, and my eyes were half shut as the sun set outside the hospital window. I didn't know if either of us would have the strength to consummate an evening of wild and risky reunification sex in a hospital room, but if he was up to it ...

There were more people at the door. I turned to see the smiling faces of Ambler, Ma, Ricky, and little Max.

"What in the world?" I cried. The crew filed into the room. "*Shhh.* He's sleeping," I whispered.

"Nonsense," Ma blurted. "I didn't risk life and limb in a helicopter just to keep my mouth shut." She rushed to the bed and began slobbering kisses and tears all over Gus. She squeezed him so tightly I thought he'd have to spend the night on a ventilator.

"I love you too, Ma," Gus groaned, awakening from slumber.

I barely gave him time to open his eyes before placing his son in his arms. The little guy smiled and the big guy cried; then we all joined in the tear-fest.

"Maxwell Francis Lido, you're awfully small to go for a ride in an FBI helicopter. You must've done something seriously naughty."

"He did." Gus smiled and kissed his son on the head. "He made the Most Wanted list."

Chapter Eighty-Three

Herbert Ambler was not going to sit idly by and watch a he-man like Gus eat reconstituted hospital meatloaf for his first dinner since being rescued. He'd ordered from The Palm Restaurant. We feasted on porterhouse, creamed spinach, potatoes, and cheesecake, all within the confines of Gus' hospital room. It had been pretty late when Herb escorted everyone back to a nearby hotel to spend the night.

Several weeks had passed since Gus' rescue. I can still remember lying next to my husband in the hospital bed on that first night, thanking God for giving him back to us.

"We're all alone finally. Do you want to . . ." I asked in my most alluring voice.

"Sure," Gus said, as he started to nod out.

"Just hold me for a few minutes, okay?" Gus was out before I completed my sentence. It was satisfying enough just to hold him and know that he was safe. There'd be plenty of love making in the days ahead. *Count on it!* I got cozy next to him and watched him sleep, feeling myself drift off as well.

Somewhere in the very same hospital, Raven Gallagher was recuperating from a self-inflicted gunshot wound. She'd soon be off to prison with her brother, where they would surely spend the rest of their lives.

~~~

In the days that followed I read up on the history of these siblings so that I could try to understand the intense misery they'd endured; misery so powerful that they needed to live their lives as other people just to make it from one day to the next.

Raiden Gallagher had been living his alleged life as Jay Charnoff, a fire department investigator for the past year. My guess was that the real Charnoff was dead, murdered and disposed of in similar fashion to Bill Alden and Joshua Dane. Who had Raiden impersonated before becoming Charnoff? How many others had there been? He had survived childbirth only to be placed in an orphanage for children with special needs. Alden couldn't care for his healthy daughter let alone a mentally impaired son, and so he lied and said that his son had died. His wife was dead. Who would be the wiser? It was an easy story to peddle. My guess was that Raiden had been misdiagnosed at birth as developmentally challenged. Somehow over the years, he caught up intellectually. In fact, he was far more than average. He was bright—bright enough to learn the circumstances under which he and his sister were born and what had become of her. He was bright enough to impersonate a fire inspector and convince Richard Tate, the Montauk fire chief, that a homicide was no more than an accidental fire.

Raven had learned to live like a hermit crab because her own life was a living hell. It began the day Margo Atwater left her at the doorstep of the foster home of Celeste Thax. She could be a woman or a man, whatever she needed to be in order to survive. Just like the hermit crab, which is forced to abandon its shell when it becomes too small, Raven moved from one identity to another as needed to survive and prosper. As far as we could gather, either she or Raiden had taken the lives of Alana Moore, Sarah Fisher, Joshua Dane, and Camryn Claymore. Were there others? Raven and her brother were in custody and would be prosecuted on a multitude of felony charges. Time would reveal how many deaths they were responsible for.

They had schemed and murdered Bill Alden, the man they believed to be their father, the man who was too weak to hold onto his children. They'd intended to kill Margo Atwater for abandoning Raven and setting her upon a life journey of sorrow. Raven had no idea how hard Margo had fought for her. She only knew that Margo was the one who had dropped her off at Thax's house, and for that, Margo was going to die.

They had almost gotten away with it all when I began to poke my nose where it didn't belong. My guess was that Kaley Struthers was a sweet and caring person blinded by love. She would do anything for Camryn, even help distract a vacationing policeman while Camryn dosed him with a fast-acting tranquilizer so that they could abduct him and draw his nosy wife's attention away from her investigation. I was on a course to destroy everything Raven and Ray had worked so hard to accomplish.

Kaley had confessed to her role in Gus' abduction and swore that he was going to be let go unharmed as soon as the trio had left the country. A box of electronic igniters was found in Charnoff's gold Impala. Tate thought that a device like that could have been used to start the car fire in which Ray Claymore had allegedly burned to death. I'd never be able to prove it, but I'm sure the same fate was planned for Gus. *Let him go unharmed, my ass.* Did Kaley have any idea that the twins were murderers? I guess perhaps she didn't want to know. She swore up and down that she had not poisoned Bill Alden's cigarettes, and I believed her. She was a hapless pawn. Perhaps worse ... perhaps she was the sort of person who suspected something was wrong and looked the other way.

They had planned to run away together: Raven, Kaley, and Ray. Dubai has a no extradition treaty with the United States, so they could never have been brought back for trial. All they needed was a few more days, a few days to kill Margo Atwater and then slip silently out of the country.

I didn't hate them for taking Gus. I was over it. Gus was over it, and it was back to life as usual. I understood a small measure of what Raven and Raiden had been through, and if I ever felt that understanding slipping away, I needed to look no farther than Max's crib. My son would have every ounce of love that Gus and I had to give and then some. Growing up without parents ... Growing up without love ... I found it amazing that Raven and Ray had survived at all under such appalling circumstances. God only knew that revenge must have looked extremely tempting to them.

~~~

We went over to Ma's at the end of our shift shortly after returning to work. She was watching Max and cooking—cooking all the frustration out of her. When we arrived, the kitchen table was filled with enough food to feed a proverbial army.

I may have listened to my husband and not fed Max my sweet potato fries when I was told to, but no one and I mean *no one* was going to tell Ma how to spoil her first and only grandson. Max was in his highchair demolishing a meatball when we arrived, covered from head to toe in sauce.

I thought Gus was going to explode but he didn't. He laughed. He laughed so hard he said it made his stomach hurt. "I need another vacation," he divulged. "The last one just straight out sucked."

~~~

I hope that you enjoyed Baby Girl Doe. I always enjoy hearing your comments and questions, so please write to me at larrykelter@aol.com. For more information, please visit my website: lawrencekelter.com.

Full Length Stephanie Chalice Mysteries

Don't Close Your Eyes

Ransom Beach

The Brain Vault

Our Honored Dead

Baby Girl Doe

About the author

A resident New Yorker, Kelter often uses Manhattan and Long Island as backdrops for his stories. He is the author of the Stephanie Chalice Mystery Series and other works of fiction.

Early in his writing career, he received support from best-selling novelist, Nelson DeMille, who reviewed his work and actually put pencil to paper to assist in the editing of the first novel. When completed, DeMille said, "Lawrence Kelter is an exciting new novelist, who reminds me of an early Robert Ludlum."

His novels are quickly paced and feature twist endings.